The Dove
in the Belly

The
Dove
in the
Belly

Jim Grimsley

LQ

LEVINE QUERIDO

Montclair | Amsterdam | Hoboken

For Lynna Williams

This is an Arthur A. Levine book
Published by Levine Querido

www.levinequerido.com • info@levinequerido.com
Levine Querido is distributed by Chronicle Books, LLC
Text copyright © 2022 by Jim Grimsley
Library of Congress Cataloging-in-Publication data is available
ISBN: 978-1-64614-131-9
Printed and bound in China

MIX
Paper from
responsible sources
FSC™ C144853

Published May 2022
First Printing

The whole of appearance is a toy. For this,
The dove in the belly builds his nest and coos . . .

—Wallace Stevens

Homeless

OUT OF THE BLUE SHE CALLED. He had learned to dread news from his mother. There was always a crisis, a change, a sorrow, a complaint, a plea. The sound of her voice could bring an ache to his insides. He held the phone and watched the frame of the window, light and moody clouds, a few people hanging out on the long balconies of each floor of the dorm. They were watching the baseball game, the white-uniformed players on the green turf of the stadium just beyond the parking lot. He heard the snap of a bat as if it were next to his ear, a collective sound of consternation from the stands at commotion in the outfield. Caught. Out. He took a deep breath.

His mother's voice had that edge of brightness that he knew to be brittle and feigned. She was as happy as a woman could be, she said. He could picture her sitting on the edge of the colonial rocking chair that she had bought from Furniture Fair in Goldsboro, where she lived now. The cushions were covered in a beige cloth printed with butter churns, milking stools, and washtubs. The chair made a creaking sound, its

1

springs expanding and contracting as she moved restlessly back and forth; he could hear it, a sort of undertone to her words. She told him, in a rush, she was moving to Nevada next week and marrying a new husband.

"Oh, lord, it was like a miracle. I met him at the One Stop, you know, when I was working at the cash register—he was buying a pack of Pall Malls, my favorite cigarette. And I tell you what, a thrill ran through me like a bolt from heaven, it had to be a sign of true love. A person knows what true love feels like." The wedding would be at a casino in Las Vegas in one of those fast-turnaround chapels, Ronny didn't need to worry about being there.

All this spoken in a raspy monotone with pause for breath. This would be her fourth husband, not counting the fact that she had married one of them twice.

At first Ronny felt only the sinking sensation with which his body greeted all of her life changes. He kicked at a pizza box on the floor. "This is kind of sudden," he said.

She made a sound of irritation, a cough; she was probably smoking a Pall Mall herself. "Don't be like that, honey, just be happy for me, can't you?"

"I just mean you haven't known him that long, Mama, that's all. And you're going to move with him to Las Vegas."

"That's not where we're going to live, it's too trashy. We're going to live in Reno."

"Well," Ronny said, and a deep sadness swept through.

"I can't help it," she said. "He blows my mind. Isn't that what you say these days?"

"That sounds right. That's great, Mom, I guess. Who is he?"

"I thought I already told you about him. Maybe not. After I met him at the One Stop he took me to the fair where I was showing my flowers. You know how I do with putting up my plants at the fair. The judges give me three red ribbons and a white one and he come up to me and said, don't be blue. Because of I didn't get a blue ribbon. Don't you think that's cute?"

"How long have you known him?"

"Four and a half weeks. His name is Rayford Placid. My new name is going to be Thelma Placid. I think that's nice. Can't you be happy for your mom?"

Her new name was going to be Thelma Eurene Johnson Mallory Verner Hansome Placid. She had as many surnames as a soap opera heroine. Ronny, who had only one, Mallory, said, "Sure. I guess."

"I really think this is the one, Ronny."

"That's great." He was being very quiet, not that she would notice.

"Hell, I'm going to be forty next year, I deserve to be happy." She paused to take a sip from her cup of coffee; the swallow was audible, and Ronny pictured her standing there with her cup in one hand and her makeup mirror in the other, the phone somehow juggled between, cigarette burning in the ashtray on the table beside her. In the tiny trailer kitchenette with her pots of snake plant and lamb's ears on the windowsill. "Is everything okay, son? Is school going okay?"

He laughed quietly. "Well, no, Mom." He was feeling a kind of choking in his midsection and had a hard time getting his breath. "I mean, school is fine. Classes are almost over. But now all of a sudden I have to find a place to live and get a job for the summer. This is kind of sudden, that's all. I was expecting to come home."

"Honey, you don't want to live in this trailer one more summer, do you? I already filled up your bedroom with my shoe boxes anyway."

3

"Well, I knew you put a lot of shoes in there but I figured I could make enough room to sleep."

"Well," she said, "I'm sorry, son. But it's 1977 and I've wasted too much time. I have to move on."

Her life, as far as Ronny could remember, had consisted of little beyond her need to move on, which she announced every so often in much these terms, usually including the year, as if he did not know it. He felt an echo inside himself, as if he were hollow. But he spoke calmly. "I know you do, Mom. It's fine. I'll be all right."

Now her voice took on an anxious edge, and he would have to console her. "So you can find a place to stay for the summer, can't you?"

"I'm sure I can. Kids stay here all the time. I'll get a job, everything will be great."

"You can come out and see me when I get settled."

"But I'll have to pay for the plane ticket."

She chortled, as if this was a foregone conclusion. "Well, you know you will. I don't have any money."

"Neither do I, Mom. Scholarships don't cover plane tickets to Nevada."

Another crack of the bat from the baseball stadium, sharp as a bullet. A wave of crowd noise, drunken. He was looking at the pile of dirty laundry in his roommate's closet. He could smell sour beer and twice-worn socks. Opening a window, he studied the parking lot, the baseball stadium, and the diminutive players on the field, the regular bricks of Teague dorm behind a row of oaks and elms in the distance.

Mom was losing patience with the conversation—he could hear the change. She said she loved him, she said goodbye, and he sat on the bed with the spring breeze blowing through the window, the bright day mocking him. Perfectly motionless, hating the clutter of the room suddenly, he stood and gathered the pizza boxes in a stack.

So now he had no home left. Up until today he had still possessed the tiniest scrap of one, as long as he could keep up with his mother's latest address. But now she would be in Nevada and that would be that. He dreaded the thought of finding some place to stay, given that he had almost no money, this being the end of the semester.

He cleaned the dorm room to give himself something to do, but after a while he realized that what he was really doing was waiting for Ben to call, and the thought peeved him and so he decided to walk to North Campus. Outside there was still the crowd watching the baseball game along the iron railing of the balconies; the dorm was shaped like a cross, and two of the sides faced each other, with the balconies running along the sides, giving access to the lines of suite doors, plain and geometric. Balmy in the afternoon sun. He took the elevator to the ground floor, then headed out of the lobby into the spring warmth, past people sunbathing on the lawn in front of the dorm, waving at Sheria with someone he didn't recognize. Sheria was seated on a blanket holding a book in her lap, eating something in a plastic wrapper, frizzy hair blowing this way and that in the breeze. He had met her at Governor's School, a summer program for gifted high school students. She hollered something at him and he cupped his hand to his ear; she shook her head and said, "Come see me later," and he heard that, and signaled that he would. Scanning the bare bodies on their towels, the girls in their bathing suits, the boys in their jeans, he refused to search for Ben, who was too cool for suntan lotion and too restless for sun worship. Ronny took the path that led past the regular row of brick dormitories, counting the fans in the open windows, more sunbathers on the narrow patches of grass, a plump girl in a purple romper riding a blue bicycle slowly. The scent of pot from someone's room wafted past, and a bedraggled cat hid behind the struggling shrubbery along the front of Teague. Threads of Heart and Springsteen mingled with the fading cheers from the baseball game. The campus was all trees and brick, pine needles and shade. Near the end of semester, everybody was wearing shorts, open shirts, midriff-baring blouses, ambling with books in their arms, hoping to find a pretty spot to study for exams but distracted by the beautiful day.

He found the usual collection of creative writing students on the steps in front of Pine Hall, including Lily, her long, thick hair wrapped over one shoulder. "So it's Mr. Mallory, how lovely."

"Not feeling very lovely at the moment," he said, and sat next to her, irritating her friend, a poet, who was bending toward her with the earnest look of someone about to burst into free verse.

So he told her what had happened and she commiserated. "Well, there ought to be lots of apartments open for the summer, I guess. Your poor mom."

"Why is she the one who gets the sympathy?"

"Nevada," she said.

After a moment he laughed. "I suppose. And at least I don't have to go back to Goldsboro this year. If I can figure out what to do."

Her friend the poet had drawn away, and Lily and Ronny sat in comfortable silence for a moment. The others on the steps were beginning a conversation about their grades for the semester, what Max Steele, the creative writing director, had told them during office hours, and snipes about other students in the workshops. Ronny had taken one class in fiction writing before he realized it was not for him; now he was studying English literature and journalism.

Lily took a pen and notepad out of her purse, tapped it on her thigh. "So, seriously, what will you do?"

"I don't know. I'm almost broke, it's the end of the semester."

"Can't your mom help you?"

"Not really. I have to figure this out myself."

"At least you'll be here this summer. We can hang out."

"That will be nice." He picked oak tassels out of his hair, finding them by touch. The world felt wild with pollen and other forms of plant copulation. "You can show me more of your poems."

She appeared inordinately pleased to be asked and handed him a new poem out of her folder of work, something called "Seven Long Phrases," with a nice line at the end, "and has the last word under water." He told her he liked the syntax, not sure whether he was using the word in the right context, but he must have gotten it right because she just blushed a bit. He did like the poem, too. She said, "I just went by the newspaper office, nobody is there." They both worked for *The Daily Tar Heel*, the student newspaper. "Strange to see all those desks empty, nobody typing."

"I guess it's just the business people in there now."

Pleasant to sit there watching the traffic in and out of the bookstore and the student union. Flyers flapped on the Cube when a wind came up. The folks on the steps spent the sunset talking about the books of Virginia Woolf, the shape of the moral universe, and why a cow in a field might have an independent reality even if no human ever saw the cow; he figured they had all read *Jacob's Room*. They talked about what kind of art was the best art and why a student who majored in business administration was missing out on the roots of things. Lily's poet friend said, "I think it would kill my soul to do anything but art."

"What will kill your soul is starvation for not getting paid for doing art," said Charlotte, a Durham housewife who was taking poetry workshops; she'd made a lot of friends among the students. "Take it from an old lady."

"Then I die for art," the poet said, and everyone agreed he was brave and noble.

"What a way to go," said Charlotte, and puffed her French cigarette.

After sunset, he said goodbye to Lily, watching her walk away with her manuscripts and books in her arms, long hair swinging side to side. He walked back to his dorm, finding his roommate, Kelly, already passed out, another stack of pizza boxes in the middle of the room—really, it was as if they bred and reproduced; one person could not eat that much pizza, could he?

Ronny was sober; he was almost always sober, though sometimes he felt like the only person who did not like liquor in the whole world. He listened to the heavy breathing, almost snoring, of Kelly in the other bed. The dorm lay mostly quiet and dark and he stared out the window. The lighted rectangles of other windows glowed a dull yellow, and low lights set into the bricks spilled illumination onto the bare concrete of the balconies. The night softened the sharp lines of the building and gave it a milder contour as it looked over the dark gulf of the parking lot, the roofs of the parked cars, and the patches of trees. On the side of the dorm where the football players lived, shadows were passing back and forth in front of the suites. Seated on his bed in the dark, Ronny watched

Ben's window across the way, one floor down, the light still burning. The sight of the blank doorway, the fact that he was obsessed with watching it, made him ache. Something was going wrong now and he didn't know how to stop it.

Near midnight, though, there was a quiet knock on the door. Ronny was still sitting in the dark, fully dressed. When he answered the knock there was Ben slumped against the opposite wall, tugging at his ear, smelling of beer and smoke. Ronny closed the door softly and they walked onto the balcony. Ben was steady on his feet, blinking slowly, wearing an old flannel shirt with the sleeves rolled to his elbows. "What you up to?" he asked, awkward, leaning on the iron railing, looking down into the gulf of night.

"Nothing, hanging out here all right," Ronny said.

"Went down to He's Not Here," Ben said. That was the name of a bar. "Just wanted to say good night. You hadn't called me lately."

"You haven't called me either."

They were quiet. Ben raised his head a bit, jaw set, expression hardening. "You're jealous again. You think I don't know it?"

Ronny tried to turn away, and Ben laid hands on him and pulled him back. But they were in public, they had to be careful. They stood awkward and stiff, Ronny wrapping his arms around himself as if it were cold, though the night was all balm and sweetness. Lights like stars stretched over the campus, along the paths, in the stadium and across the athletic fields, tracing the roads. Ben said, "You act like a dope sometimes."

"Say good night to Jennifer," Ronny said.

"What the fuck?"

"She's over there, right?"

9

"Okay," Ben said, angry now, looming. "I think I better go before I get pissed."

"That's fine. Good night."

He shuffled away. Shoulders broad as anything. Ronny shivered. He watched until Ben made it to his suite door, head bowed, shoulders hunched, studying his feet as if he had to be careful about every step he took.

The Boardinghouse

ON TUESDAY HE WOKE TO FIND Kelly sitting on the edge of the bed holding his head in his hands. Kelly was barrel shaped, hairy down the spine and into the cleft of his buttocks, prone to sleep naked and stay that way for a while every morning. He walked over to the pile of pizza boxes and edged it across the floor with his toe. "Lacrosse guys brought some pizza over yesterday. You should have been here."

"You passed out kind of early."

"Passed out?"

"Fell asleep, then. I didn't get back that late."

"Well, they brought some beer, too." He grabbed at his generous waist and displayed a slab of it. "You can't keep up a gut this size drinking diet soda, Ronny."

"I guess."

Kelly pulled on underwear lying at the side of the bed. "This room smells like crap."

Ronny rose off the mattress enough to open the window.

Fresh air was welcome, and a breeze set the window shade to fluttering.

Kelly hefted the boxes and took them out the door. When he came back he found a towel, sniffed it, and slung it over his shoulder, feeling around under the dirty clothes for his shaving kit. He had a stereo atop the built-in chest of drawers and put on a Led Zeppelin album, *Houses of the Holy.* "This is one of those fucking days, right? My head feels like shit and I have to study all day."

"You must have an exam tomorrow."

He played a measure or two of air guitar, his gut swaying; he was big and solid, his skin so pale you could see the blue veins running under. "The Song Remains the Same" was starting to play. "Lucinda's coming over later," he said, opening the small refrigerator at the foot of his bed, taking out a beer. He popped it open and took a long draw from it. "You going to let us have some privacy, right?"

"Sure. I'll be out all day."

"Leave the door open if you go." Kelly's feet slapped on the floor as he headed to the bathroom.

The fact that Kelly had warned him about the girlfriend—rather than throwing him out of the room without notice—was the closest to friendship they had ever come. Ronny dressed quickly, decided to head to the student union. Soon he was alive in the clear morning, hesitating on the balcony in case Ben should appear across the way, then ambling along the brick pathways and through the pines near the football stadium. Clear, cool, dry, the air was scented of tree-flower smells, hollies in bloom, jasmine, pinesap.

At the student union he bought a copy of *The Chapel Hill Newspaper* and found a stack of apartment-finder magazines near the door to the snack bar, where a few listless

Servomation employees in ill-fitting uniforms were idly cleaning counters. He sat in one of the booths near the window and read the papers, despairing at once at the amount of the rent he would have to pay, phrases like "one month's deposit," "lease term of one year," nothing that he could rent for a summer. No time to arrange for a roommate to share expenses. Wondering idly whether he could sleep on Lily's floor—though her sister already lived with her, and the stone house they leased was tiny. A tiny gall of panic fluttered in his midsection.

He took the apartment finder to the *Daily Tar Heel* office, where there were phones he could use for free. The student union was a modern building, all glass and terrazzo, a bank of pay phones along one wall, an information desk in the central lobby, steel-framed stairs leading up and down to offices of student government above and below. The newspaper offices were an afterthought, tacked onto the corner of the building in what had been intended as a large lounge with seating, glass outer walls, gallery space for art and photographs; the space had been halfheartedly partitioned off from the outer lounge and stuffed with desks, chairs, typewriters, two news teletype units silent at the moment, and a pair of offices for the business manager and the advertising staff. Haphazard, chaotic, full of noise during the semester, haunted by the memory of all that activity now. He found a telephone and sat down, kicking at an empty metal waste can.

Managing the courage to dial a listing about a room for rent, he found less gumption when the first speaker told him that she had nothing available for just three months and was otherwise full unless somebody moved out of her building. When he rang the second listing, he got a gruff voice saying the house manager was out for the morning and all the rooms were occupied. There was no third listing to try, nothing else except apartments he could never afford. He sat numbly in the swivel chair behind the news desk, looking out the broad windows.

He wanted to call Ben and started to and then shut down the thought, a knot of hurt in his throat. Anyway, he'd barely be awake this time of day, and likely had his girlfriend wrapped around him if he was. Or at least that was the image that Ronny used to torment himself.

Finally it was time for his last class, a makeup session for a seminar about French women writers, where, while waiting for the professor to show up—everybody complaining mildly that there wasn't supposed to be a makeup class on reading day—he blurted out his situation to the other students, looking for sympathy. It was all he could do to ease his anxiety. Some of them groaned on his behalf, others ignored him, but, seated across from him at the seminar table, the fellow named Jamal said, "A guy in my boardinghouse needs somebody to take his room over the summer. You could try that."

Jamal was gangly, tall, hair intensely curly, a scrap of beard on his chin. He was the friendly sort who liked to talk to strangers, though after a semester discussing George Sand and Marguerite Duras, they were hardly strangers anymore. They had sometimes chatted a bit—about family and friends, politics and music, before and after class—and once walked to the snack bar for a cup of watery coffee. When Jamal spoke about the room for rent, Ronny felt a trace of hope and his stomach unknotted a bit. "You're kidding. Are you sure?"

He had a booming, heavy voice. "This nice old lady owns the house. I've lived there for a while."

"You think she'd let me have the room?"

He snort-laughed, an odd sound. "Why wouldn't she? She's in a bind unless she finds somebody to rent it, and it's hard to keep people for the summer. You want to come meet her after class?"

Of course he did. Already he was feeling lighter. But it would probably cost too much, wouldn't it? Or would it? Maybe not if it was only a room. Then in walked Professor Mtumbe and they began their discussion of *The Second Sex*.

After class they walked to the house, only a few blocks away on Cameron Avenue, and Jamal talked a bit about himself, about his opinion of Simone de Beauvoir and the fact that she was less appreciated than her boyfriend, Jean-Paul Sartre. "Women get the worst of the crap, don't you think? I worry about my sisters."

"How many do you have?"

"Three. I'm the only boy. My mother says I'm a better man because of all the female attention. She likes that I took this class." His jeans were baggy, not flared like Ronny's, and he walked with his books tucked under his arm and his hands shoved into his pockets, head down, purposeful, the wind in his hair.

"My mom's just glad I decided to go to college at all."

"She's unique, your mother? The way she leaves you to take care of yourself like this?"

"She's always done that. And I had to take care of her a lot, too. She doesn't like to cook and she doesn't like to clean so I had to learn how as soon as I was old enough." It felt odd to talk in this way about his mother, but the conversation had started about her, about the fact that she'd suddenly decided to marry somebody she barely knew and to move to Nevada, a place she'd never even visited. "Because naturally she likes a tidy house even if she doesn't like to do anything about it herself. My grandmother used to come over and cook for us sometimes, and Ma liked that, too."

"Mrs. Delacy will like you if you're neat like you say. Some of the guys are real slobs."

"Are you?"

Big, warm grin on his face. "Sometimes. But then I hear my sisters in my head fussing about my socks all over the place and et cetera."

"You sound like you know the landlady pretty well."

"We're friendly. She's really old, she needs help sometimes. Her husband died and left her the house and she's had a tough time taking care of everything."

They chatted a little longer about the ways that women often got left in the lurch. Fresh from the seminar, their heads were buzzing with ideas that made them feel good about themselves. Jamal had a stolid quality, as though he was older than his years. The house was across from the university-owned hotel, the Carolina Inn, all brick and old-style window pediments, sitting very close to the street. There was the traffic of the university and the cars headed to Franklin Street farther up, and then the sudden quiet of what might have been a residential street in earlier days. Now it was a mix of houses and fraternities. The boarding-house sat within a fenced yard, tall trees at the back. Ronny and Jamal stood in front of the house, a two-story clap-board, square and neat, with a porch along the front, shaded by a sturdy young oak about the height of the roof. Jamal led Ronny into the living room through a little entryway, paint faded, everything a bit tattered, and there they were, stand-ing in the midst of dark wood and the gleam of old glass, Jamal's voice booming. "Hey, Mrs. Delacy! I solved our problem."

She walked into the room, wavering in the light, as if she were not quite present, in a plain dress of pale blue, an apron at her waist, the pockets bulging with papers that she touched, once, to make sure they were in place. She had startling eyes, magnified by her glasses; the eyes appeared too close together for their size, as though she had two faces superimposed one on the other. Ronny was uncertain she actually saw him.

Jamal bent to kiss her cheek as though she were his grandmother, and she waved at him with her hand. She stood in the room so naturally it was clear she belonged to the place, and it to her. Groups of worn chairs filled the space, arms draped with doilies and lace; there was one sofa near the window and many chairs with small tables in front of them or beside them, more like a club lounge than a parlor. A sense of too much furniture, as though the room would like to breathe. On the wall above the wainscoting hung dingy, flowered wallpaper, a cream background with a foreground of streamers of yellow roses. A copy of the Venus de Milo, oddly large, stood atop a wardrobe in the far corner. The statue appeared to preside over the room, as though her arms would have been making a blessing of grace if they had been present.

"What problem are you talking about? Who is this, is this Jamal?" Mrs. Delacy was looking around, trying to get Jamal's face in her field of vision. She had a way of moving that exaggerated her poor eyesight. Her eyes shone dimly, a runny, watery blue.

"The problem with the room upstairs, Miss Dee."

Mrs. Delacy had found Ronny in front of her and was looking at him as if trying to bring him into focus. "Who's this one?"

Ronny offered his hand and touched hers for a moment, a motionless handshake. Her skin felt soft and warm, the bones tiny. "I'm a friend of Jamal's from class," he said, and gave his name.

She was beginning to understand. "Pleased to meet you."

"Ronny wants the room upstairs for the summer, Miss Dee."

"You mean the one next to you. Oh yes. That boy can't take it till the fall."

"But Ronny can take it till then."

Mrs. Delacy looked at Ronny again. "You want to rent that room, do you?"

"Yes, ma'am. I want to see it. But I'm pretty sure I'll take it."

"For the summer only, you know. You have to leave in September because I already rented it to the other boy. I forget his name, I wrote it down in my book."

"I only want it for the summer."

"Well, praise the lord." She threw up her hands and looked in the direction of the statue. "Come on and let me open it up for you."

"I'll go up first," Jamal said, and trundled up the stairs, pulling up his pants at the back as he climbed. "To make sure everybody's decent."

"You better do that. I don't need to see anybody's butt end. I don't want any shocks, old as I am." Mrs. Delacy led Ronny to the steps and he walked behind her as she climbed them one at a time. She moved lightly but deliberately, careful to touch the nearest wall or the stair banister, whatever might be closest, as though to reassure herself of something solid on which to lean. "I have all boys here, you know. I don't like young girls in the house, they make too many changes. But I like boys. I liked you right away even though I just now met you. You'll be good in this room." She stopped to get her breath. "I go pretty slow."

"I don't mind that," Ronny said. "We've got plenty of time."

Most of downstairs had been converted to bedrooms except the kitchen and the parlor; even the old back porch had been enclosed at some point, when a bathroom was added to the house. The changes were obvious to anybody who had lived in old places like this one, and Ronny had seen his share of those. Upstairs was very plain, all the walls stripped of wallpaper and painted the same shade of white. Several doors were visible from the top of the stairs, most of them closed. At one of the doors Mrs. Delacy held a key and fitted it by touch into the lock.

The room she showed him was small, high ceilinged, with a narrow bed across the end. This had probably been a storage room or a large closet at one time, or maybe it had been an open alcove at the top of the stair landing, a place where a decorative table had sat, under a window that looked out over the street. The window was still there over the bed, a small table that could serve as a desk against one wall, and a wooden chair that sat beside a chest of drawers. A part of the space had been curtained off to make a closet. The walls were a dark blue up to the wainscot, white above that; a fine soft afternoon light shone through the window onto the bed.

"Do you have a car to park?" Mrs. Delacy asked. "Because I don't have any parking."

"No, ma'am, I don't have a car."

She appeared pleased at that, and reached for her skirt, making a motion as if she meant to fluff it or rearrange it. "The rent is seventy-five dollars a month, and you can move in any time."

"Any time?"

19

"Well, once you pay me. And I will take a check as long as it doesn't bounce but if it does I want to know why and after that I want to get my money in cash."

"I'll take it." Ronny had his checkbook with him in the backpack and paid the rent on the spot, writing on the desk, thinking that it was his desk now. He had a place. The fact left him content, at least until the thought came that he only had a place provided he could find a job. Paying the rent left him about twenty dollars in the bank. He had another paycheck coming from the school newspaper but after that he was broke. "I don't know when I'll move in but I'll let you know."

She folded the check in half, by touch, matching the ends with her fingers and pressing neatly to make the fold, then slipping it into the pocket of her apron with the other papers.

Jamal appeared at the door. He was pulling another shirt over his head and adjusted it at his solid waist. "I can help you move tomorrow. I have my car."

"I don't have much stuff, just what's in my dorm room," Ronny said. "I only need to make one trip."

"You're going to take the room here, then?"

"He already paid the rent," Mrs. Delacy said, patting her pocket as she walked with those tiny steps out the door. "I'm not giving it back to him either. This is going right to the bank."

Ehringhaus

THROUGH THE CAMPUS UNDER THE GREEN canopy of poplars and oaks he walked, along the brick sidewalks past the bell tower, the football stadium, through the pine grove that led to the dorm. Barefoot, carrying his shoes in his hand, the brick path cool to the soles of his feet. Evening took shape, streetlights turning on one by one, lights in the windows in the dorms along the way, drifts of music, voices on the baseball field beside the last stretch of the path, not a game but a practice, though the stadium lights were burning up high on their poles.

The sight of it up the rise of green—Ehringhaus, a dormitory named for a former North Carolina governor—there had always been something about this walk that reminded him of his luck in coming here. He was in college, on his own, it belonged to him, he had a place he could call home that he could control, and this gave him a coming-home feeling, a sense that this was right. Fragments of thoughts led, if he allowed, backward to the years of high school, tumultuous in so many ways, the desegregation of public schools where he had lived, the sudden coming together of white people and black people, their confronting of one another, the denial he had felt in himself and in his family at the onset of integration. This had touched the streak of difference he felt in himself, the fact that he had no interest in girls when he was supposed to be obsessed with them; what this told him about his nature he had only understood once he was here. In high school he had held himself in check out of caution, but now he had begun to break open, to allow the world to carry him on its wave. This was the subtext of much of his life, the upheaval he could feel in these days of the middle 1970s, the breaking of old patterns, the sudden freedom to act in different ways from the past, so that his mother for instance, far from being trapped in a marriage to his father, could divorce him and marry again. He could follow her example in his own way.

In the dorm, he went by Ben's room to tell him about the boardinghouse, about Mom and her marriage, about Ronny moving out of the dorm. Ben's room was on the floor below Ronny's in a suite at the end of the wing. There was never any telling how Ben would behave or what mood he would be in, indifferent, friendly, surly, drunk; especially true after they had quarreled the night before. The door to his room stood open and music spilled out. His bed and desk were empty. On the second of the narrow iron beds in the room lay Tate, wearing nothing but gym shorts, one of his girlfriends draped over him, her hair spread across his skin. Ronny was careful not to look at Tate too long. He was supposed to have broken a beer bottle in a bar and swallowed glass about a month ago. "Hey, Brainhead," he called. "What the fuck do you want?"

"What do you think? Where's Ben?"

"You tutoring him tonight?" Tate sipped from a beer and ran a hand into the back of the girl's jeans. He had long, strawberry hair that looked a little dirty and uncombed, and his forehead was decorated with pink pimples clustered in a small, tight constellation. The girl was no one Ronny recognized, pretty and dark haired, her rump plush and round. She gave him an idle look, smoothed back her hair, and rested her head against Tate again. She said hey.

"No, just looking for him. Hey."

"He's out somewhere, I don't know where the fuck he went. You want to write me a paper?"

"What? No, Tate. I quit that stuff."

"Why not? It's about fucking Claudius something. One of those Roman guys."

"It's a little late for a paper to be due. Exams are about to start."

Tate gave Ronny a wide grin. His neck was the size of a small tree. "Paper was due a long time ago. It's for a fucking incomplete."

"I don't have time," Ronny said.

"You sure? I bet you know all about that Claudius motherfucker."

"No, sorry. I have my only exam tomorrow and the rest of the week I have to look for a job."

That went right over Tate's head. The girl had turned over and was looking at Ronny again and then at Tate; she was stoned, Ronny thought, and she wanted him to go. She had fingernails polished to perfection and painted a soft pink; the color was striking in the dull cinder-block room. She wore a peasant blouse, gathered along the neck and embroidered there with flowers, little ruffles on the short sleeves, the waist pulled up to leave her midriff bare. She was pudgy at the

23

midsection, her navel rising softly over her belt. She said, "This room is a pure mess. That pack of Nabs been laying there three weeks. Don't you ever clean up?"

Tate smacked her stomach, playful. "Shut up, Carla."

"Tell Ben I came by," Ronny said.

Tate rolled on top of the girl. "Take your faggot ass out of here then, if you won't help a guy who needs it."

The word "faggot" stung but Ronny ignored it. If he said anything out of line he could get his face knocked in pretty quick around Ben's friends. Ben was a redshirt defensive player for the football team and this wing of Ehringhaus was all football players, a number of whom were insane, as far as Ronny could tell. This year they had already thrown a vending machine off the balcony of the sixth floor, destroyed several refrigerators, and fouled the elevator on the weekends with excretions of one kind or another. Best to leave them alone. A word was just a word, after all. He had heard it before.

There had been a moment when Ben had called him faggot, tentatively, as if testing his reaction, the day of a beer party on the lawn out front. At twilight with the party nearly over, Ronny had been lying under a tree God knows how long, buzzed from beer, one of the few times he had tried it, such a bitter taste. He'd stood, felt dizzy, steadied himself by putting a hand on the tree trunk. Most everyone had left the party by then. But there was one figure sitting in the dark nearby. He stood while Ronny watched. Strutted toward the light of the front doors, passing close enough that he became visible, and turned to Ronny, such a striking face. Ben. They had met when Ronny was studying with Otis, one of the other football players. "Good night, faggot," Ben said, neither harshly nor angrily. He waited a beat too long to see what Ronny would do; Ronny, drunk and flippant, without thinking blew him a kiss, clearly visible under one of the lights along the brick path. Stopped Ben in his tracks. He might have responded in so many ways. But he started to laugh, walked away, shaking his head, and Ronny leaned against the tree and breathed until the bit of nausea went away and he could follow.

Later he remembered the sequence of events: he had stood, the name-calling, the kiss, the laughter. The figure on the lawn. He had stood, Ben had done the same. As if he had been there, watching in the dark, all that time. As if he had been waiting.

Boxes

THE NEXT MORNING RONNY TOOK HIS exam for England from the Late Norman Era Through the Plantagenets, his head crammed with reign dates, Edwards, Henrys, the Richards, feudalism, land surveys, tax burdens, fealty, a bit of a pageant. Sitting in the classroom with his blue book and pen, he examined cracks in the plaster walls of Hanes Hall, looked up at the open transom over the frame, paint cracked and peeling, no air-conditioning, the place as open to the day as it could be to keep cool. He had liked the class, liked history in general. The trick with an essay exam was to start writing as soon as the professor said, "Begin." He rarely worried. The only problem he had at the moment was keeping daydreams away. There were so many things he would prefer to think about than the death of Henry VI.

After two hours of penwork he went by the newspaper office to find out whether paychecks had been cut. The student union was still busy, people hanging about the lounges with rings of books round their chairs; studying for exams in public always had a hormonal edge to it, people cruising one another between the tedium of rereading notes and shuffling index cards. He might have hung out at *The Daily Tar Heel* but nobody was in the office except Phrena, the new business manager, walking stiff-legged down the row of desks, her polyester pantsuit making a rasping noise with each step. She gave him his check in a white envelope and petted him on the arm. She asked if he was sticking around to work on the summer paper. Maybe, he said. She was older, had hair like a spray-on helmet. A dachshund slept under her desk. The office smelled like old dog.

In the dorm room, Kelly was passed out from a party the night before. He or the bed smelled of old beer. The room was still a mess but the contents were different: beer cans nested among the dirty clothes, a few Chinese food containers huddled near Kelly's bed. An open biology textbook and notebooks stuffed with comics lay next to the bed; Kelly took the comic books to class to read them during lectures. He was lying facedown, drooling a thread of stuff onto the pillow, but his lips were cracked as if he had just marched through the desert without water. No need to wake him for a fond goodbye. Ronny's boxes were stacked in the corner. He had packed in the morning before his exam, using boxes from the basement of the dorm. Pathetic how little he had. Jamal was on his way to help with the move. Ronny sat at his desk reading *The Brothers Karamazov* while he waited. After a while the reading made him restless, though, so he laid the book on his desk and stretched.

On the balcony two lacrosse players were hurling water balloons at each other, and sometimes at people who passed by on the ground five floors below. They hooted and hollered when they hit somebody or when the splash was particularly big. Ronny listened. He avoided the water bombardiers by heading in the opposite direction along the balcony while they were filling more balloons. He found Sheria in her room on the women's side of the building. She was perched on her bed, her head wrapped in a bright African print; while she listened to jazz she painted her nails.

She said, "You ignored me when I was sunbathing the other day. People are not allowed to ignore me. Weren't you proud of me that I was outside? You know I don't like the outdoors."

"Well, I was shocked, I admit. You are absolutely glowing with vitamin D, by the way."

"Oh, I know." She threw back her head and laughed again, eyes glittering in a way that looked either happy or manic. Early in the year he had caught her with shallow cuts on her wrist. She had refused to admit she had them but the fact that he tried to talk to her that day had deepened their friendship. Today she was all right, as far as he could tell. Her friend Sara stuck her head in the door and said hello.

"When are you out of here?" Sara asked.

"I'm leaving the dorm today. Not leaving town, though." He told the story quickly, and they were appropriately commiserative, especially Sheria, who had heard stories about his mother before. "So I found a room in a house on Cameron. It's barely the size of a telephone booth but I rented it anyway."

"Oh, lord," said Sheria. "That's not very smart."

"Beggars and choosers, you know."

Sara said, "You'll miss the last party."

"There's a party?"

"I'm sure there is."

Sheria said, "There's always a party. But we'll be sure to tell you about it in the fall."

Sara disappeared into her room and Ronny leaned against the door frame. Sheria sat with her air of feverish stillness, one leg crossed under her, dipping the brush into the nail polish. He felt a rush of something, a feeling he could not quite name. "So, you're going home to Raleigh this summer, I guess."

"Oh, yes. To my own dear mother." She allowed her smile to fade and said, "Look, Ronny. It's all going to be fine. You know? We're both going to be all right."

"Why do you say that?"

"Because you look like you need me to say something and that's the best I can come up with."

He hugged her awkwardly, feeling the heat off her skin, the light layer of sweat.

"Keep it real, okay? Like I do." She laughed again, without the honk sound, but with such delight. As if the moment of sober assurance had not happened.

"I'll see you this fall," he said. Walking away, out the door and past her open window, watching the print of her blouse through the screen, Sara already in the room with her again, the two of them chattering and laughing.

He felt the tug of it, leaving Sheria, more than he would have expected. He had only meant to say goodbye in a friendly way; he stood at the junction of the wings of the women's side of the building and listened to the wind pulse along the exterior, watched it carry a fold of newspaper high in the air toward the pines beyond. Sheria was special, he felt her emotion as if it matched his own, and it surprised him. She was a person who felt too much. The dorm had become even more of a home than he knew if he was so sorry to leave it.

Otis was out of his room, the door closed, the shade pulled. Ben's room was open and Heart pounded a bass line on the stereo, *Dreamboat Annie,* "Crazy on You." Tate was spitting blood into a bowl and looked like he'd been in a fight the night before. Some bruising over his eye gave him the aura of a movie thug. He had a pint of brown liquor in his hand and took a hit from it.

"What happened to you?"

"Wrecked my car. Drunk. I knocked a tooth out."

"Sorry. At least it was just your head."

"Funny fucker."

"Bad wreck? What happened?"

"Ask your buddy Ben. We were trying to swap drivers while we were on the road. We had the top down, thought it would be a kick."

"What? You guys are nuts."

"It was his idea. And there's not a scratch on him. Crazy-ass idiot. Showing off to Jenny. Owes me for a fender."

It sounded to Ronny like both of the guys were idiots, as far as that went. Made him think again, what was it in Ben that made him do those things? "Where is he?"

"In the dorm some fucking where. Shit, I don't know." Tate wasn't in the mood for any talk, glaring at his TV, watching a Road Runner cartoon. Angry about the wreck or maybe sore because Ronny wouldn't help him with the paper.

So he might not see Ben again till fall, having missed him now. The thought was sobering. Walking back up the stairs, to his suite door, he focused on the heat of the concrete, warmth on his bare feet. Two of the custodians were having an easy morning out by the parking lot, sitting on the ground, sipping cold drinks—people here at school called them sodas or pop but he couldn't get used to that. He remembered what Tate had said, they'd been switching drivers in a moving car. Showing off for his girlfriend. Ronny stopped thinking after that, standing in the suite door, listening to the rooms. A slight smell of dirty socks, stale sweat, from the open doors.

He waited at his desk, turning on the light, picking up his book. Kelly had made an effort to clean the room again, the trash can fragrant of egg rolls and fried cabbage. Promptly on schedule, Jamal knocked on Ronny's door.

Relieved, Ronny picked up one of the boxes. "You're really a good guy for offering to help with this."

"No problemo." Bad Spanish was part of Jamal's style.

"I could have gotten a friend to do it but that would have taken longer. It's nice to get out of here."

"You done with exams now?"

"Yep. I only had one, the rest were all final papers. Semester's over."

They finished packing Jamal's beat-up Pinto in a couple of trips. Ronny wrote his address on a piece of notebook paper and left it for Kelly, in case he needed money for the phone bill. Though knowing Kelly he'd forget about the bill or lose the note. On the way out of the dorm Ronny fell behind Jamal, lingering to look at everything: the encroaching pines, the distant campus, the sky that remained blue and vast, empty of clouds. There were some people on the balcony, nobody Ronny recognized, and he wasn't much thinking about good-byes. While Jamal waited for the elevator, Ronny had a feeling he had left something behind and ran back to the room to check it one last time. All that was left in the room was dust mice, soda cans, and Kelly's heap of garbage.

On the balcony he looked across to the other wing and saw Ben glowering, foot on the lower rung of the balcony railing in front of his suite. Ben was a big guy, solid and dense in his clothes; his dark hair looked like he'd been sleeping on it. He had black, bold eyebrows and sharp, clear facial bones.

Jennifer was with him, slender and straight haired, a sorority girl, prim and upright, planted firmly at Ben's side.

As Ronny walked down the balcony, Ben kissed her cheek, pointed a finger at Ronny, and headed toward the stairs.

He came pounding up them in a couple of steps as Ronny waited. Ben swaggered to the balcony railing. "Who's that guy you're with?" His voice was low, his blue eyes glittering. He was grinding his jaw.

"The guy with the boxes? A friend from a class."

"He's helping you move somewhere?"

"I have to get out of the dorm for the summer. I told Tate to tell you I came by."

"Why didn't you ask me to help you?"

"Jamal offered. And I couldn't find you."

He frowned, took a deep breath, scratched a pimple on his nose. Ronny told him about the news from his mom and the boardinghouse. He was having a hard time getting his breath; he could feel how agitated Ben was. Ben frowned. "That's great. You're leaving and you weren't even going to let me know."

"I came by last night two or three times. You told me not to leave you any notes. I just found a place to stay yesterday."

He had to struggle to keep his voice down; his neck was flushed. "You don't fucking have to move out of the dorm today."

Ronny's heart was beating faster. When Ben was mad it was hard to look him in the eye. "I want to."

He glared at Ronny, who took a couple of steps away, conscious that Jamal was waiting. But Ronny was angry, too, at the unfairness of this, at the way Ben was acting.

"Say hello to Jennifer," Ronny said. "I have to go."

Ben looked as if he were going to slap Ronny for a second. "Why the fuck did you bring her up?"

"All you want is to tease me like you always do," Ronny said. "If you want to study, we can meet at the library to do that."

"You knew damn well I'd have helped you move whenever you wanted. I've got a car."

"Please, Ben."

"Are you coming back to the dorm at all?"

"Yes. This fall."

Ben was wearing an old baseball jersey stretched over his broad shoulders. His neck was brightening more; he was making a fist and relaxing it over and over.

The door to the elevator lobby opened and Jamal stuck his head out. Seeing Ben, he stayed at the door and said, "The car's loaded."

"All right." Ronny took a step toward the lobby. He could still feel how angry Ben was. Ronny felt tired and wanted to leave, to let it all go. "I'll call you. Ben?" No answer. "Okay. See you when I see you, I guess." He walked past the guy and stepped into the elevator with Jamal.

"Sorry to keep you waiting," he said. His heart was sinking now. He felt a little sick to his stomach.

After Dark

MRS. DELACY STOOD ON THE PORCH with such an air of calm she might have been there for hours, smiling as Jamal and Ronny hauled boxes up the steps. Frail as she appeared, she stood steady and held the door open. The twilight was still, bats in the air, darting from treetop to treetop, sounds of loud music drifting down the street from the Chi Psi house. Spring lent everything a fresh richness, along with the glee of the end of semester; he felt it in spite of the scene with Ben. Somehow Mrs. Delacy formed part of his sense of possibility, and in the late light she had a more vital look than earlier. She waited until the boys were making their last trip. "So is that all of it?" she asked.

"Sí, Miss Dee," said Jamal. "That didn't take long, did it?"

"No."

"I told you I didn't have much stuff," Ronny said, waiting at the bottom of the steps.

"Well, that's fine, it's not but a little room anyway."

Ronny looked up at the house, the rectangular plainness of it, tidy and solid. Such a good feeling that he had a place now, though it was not so much of a change, a room in a house instead of a room in a dorm. But it made a difference for some reason. He had paid the rent, it was his own. "A little room will suit me just fine."

"Welcome," she said, speaking deliberately, her voice lilting. She handed him keys tied to a scrap of black thread. "This is your key to the front door and this is your key to the room. We keep that front door locked at night. If you lose the key you have to buy another one from me and I'll overcharge you for it something awful. I don't share the kitchen and you can't use my telephone. Other than that you are welcome to sit out there in the parlor or on the porch and come and go at all hours like you boys do. Now you be right at home and let me know if you need anything." She appeared relieved and blinked when she finished her speech, smiled at him mildly, walked deeper into the shadowed house, passed through an archway, and disappeared.

The room did feel small, the blue walls giving the light a submarine look. There was a Tar Heel basketball picture calendar on the wall, showing a shot of Walter Davis rising above Phil Ford and some Duke player; Davis hung in the middle of the air with ease, as if he were floating, about to release the basketball. A couple of *Doonesbury* cartoons torn out of the *DTH* shook in the breeze from the open window, beside an exam schedule with a couple of dates circled. He unpacked his boxes and soon the room looked as much his own as it ever would, certainly as much as the dorm ever had. Setting his electric typewriter, bought with scholarship money, onto the worktable, he felt at home here. He placed his hardback copy of *The Lord of the Rings* beside it. He sat on the edge of the bed.

The empty boxes he broke down and took to the back of the house, putting them beside the garbage. None of the downstairs tenants was home, and Mrs. Delacy's bedroom door was closed. Quiet sound from a radio threaded through the stillness. He walked around the house and took a good look at it, poking his head into the kitchen, sitting awhile in the living room, smelling someone's barbecue at a neighboring house, hearing the blare of horns at the nearby intersection.

He breathed fresh air on the porch and walked around the yard. Grass and clover needed mowing, and little veins of green cracked through the walkway. Along the faded fence grew rosebushes that had a plump, healthy sheen, pink blossoms fallen from the blooms and littering the ground. Mrs. Delacy must like roses, he thought. Cars parked on the street had yellowed from the fall of pollen. A dog was sniffing the tires, going from one to the other, walking with a limp and a wagging tail. Maybe lost. Ronny tried to call the dog but it only stared at him for a moment, not quite hopeful, then went on with its nose-work.

He went back upstairs and read. The quiet was eerie. He would have no phone while he lived here, which was all right with him; he could get along without it for three months. No TV either, not that he ever had one in the dorm. But he was five minutes' walk from campus and equally close to downtown, so he should be able to find things to do. It was late in the semester, of course, but Lily would still be in town, and maybe Charlotte, the two of them sitting by the brick plaza called the Pit. There would be a summer weekly newspaper if he wanted to work on it.

He walked downtown and got dinner at Hector's. There were help wanted signs in a couple of the windows of the restaurants, and the sight of them cheered him a bit. He could apply for jobs tomorrow, maybe. Waiting tables in a restaurant would be all right for a summer. Or working the cash register in the bookstore or the record store. He put his hands in his pockets and walked along the street, past the Zoom Zoom toward the Little Professor Bookstore, where he waved at Hoagie the clerk through the plate window. The movie playing at the Carolina Theater had drawn a bit of a line and he studied the poster: *That Obscure Object of Desire*, in French, with subtitles, by Buñuel, whom the students in the de Beauvoir class had talked about. But he had better not pay for a movie tonight. Save his few dollars.

After dark he returned to the boardinghouse. He brushed his teeth and settled down for the evening with his book. The conversation with Ben replayed itself in his head, Ben saying this, Ben saying that, the intensity of the feeling, the wish for something he, Ronny, was too cautious to name.

About ten o'clock he heard a pounding on the door downstairs and he felt a sinking in himself, a fear. When the knocking sounded again, he went to the banister. Mrs. Delacy was peering out her door. "I thought I heard something. Did you?"

"It's somebody at the door," Ronny said.

She was tugging at the collar of her housecoat, hair done up in small rollers, peering up at him in some measure of appeal. "I don't think anybody else is home right now, and I can't go to the door."

"I'll find out who it is, Mrs. Delacy."

"Who would be coming here making such a racket so late?" Squinting toward the front of the house, soft upper arms deeply creased with wrinkles, the flesh so light.

Ronny thought he knew who it was, or who it might be, but that was only a hope, wasn't it? He hurried down the stairs with that feeling of sinking and rising and expanding in his middle, too many feelings all at once, his heart making a little thunder. At the front door stood Ben.

"It's all right," Ronny said, turning to her. "He's a friend of mine."

But Mrs. Delacy had already gone into her room and closed her door again, as though she had forgotten the commotion.

Ronny walked through the parlor wanting to stick his hands in his pockets or smooth down his hair or straighten his collar. It was as if he might suddenly fly away unless he carried himself just so. He was watching the carpet at first, then made himself look up. Ben scowled through the glass, brows furrowed together. "Open the door," he said.

Heart Line

AUGUST

How it had all happened: August of his junior year he had
moved into the dorm on a steamy afternoon, his mother pulling into the parking lot at the back of the ground floor, sitting
there with the engine running while he unloaded his bags
and typewriter and carried them up to the room, two trips,
while she listened to country music on the radio. She appeared
a bit nervous at the sight of the six floors of Ehringhaus looming over her, tapping a finger on the steering wheel, pulling
out a Barbara Cartland paperback to read while she waited,
glancing at him when he trundled to the car in the wet. "You
don't want to come inside for a minute?" he asked.

"Do you need me to?"

"I just thought you might want a pee break or something."

"Don't use that word to your mother, it's not nice. Say 'use
the bathroom.'"

"It's what you call it."

"I'm an adult, I can talk like I want. It's not respectful when you do it." Her voice was raspy, her face looked washed out—she had not put on makeup, not even lipstick. No need to waste makeup on an occasion when she would barely step out of the car. "No, I don't want to go in there. I don't want to use a boys' bathroom, they're always dirty."

She had agreed to drive him to school instead of sending him on the bus because of his suitcases and his one box of books and supplies, but she had only helped him carry his luggage to the dorm room once, on his first trip, when she had been dramatically teary eyed and hugged him every few minutes, smoothing his hair with her hands and calling him her baby. Today they were both perfunctory and economical in farewell. She did try for a burst of feeling at the end. "I've got so I enjoy having you around, Ronny."

"Me too, Ma."

"You're not such a know-it-all turd like you used to be in high school."

He'd always had to translate her bluntness into something livable. "Thanks, I guess."

She handed him a folded ten-dollar bill and kissed his forehead, standing there a moment, thin and brown, dressed in a one-piece shorts jumper and white sandals, her toenails painted and her hair brushed out. She was barely twenty years older than he. "Take care, son. Be good. Study hard."

She would want him to stand there while she drove away so he did, while a couple of other new arrivals walked past him, one with a desk lamp trailing an electrical cord, the other with a folded chair and a set of pillows, stopping a couple of times to hitch the pillows higher.

*

SEPTEMBER

One day he had been standing at the balcony railing out of the heat of his room, tee shirt and jeans, hair blowing a bit, an afternoon storm rolling in. While the football players were drifting over from the field house, he kept watch across the green of the rugby field. Ben was climbing the stairs at the end of the wing. He stopped on the landing and looked up. After a moment he waved. Trudged into his room without looking again. Classes had started. Ronny was being patient.

Otis stopped by before dinner at the training table, where the whole team ate; he asked whether Ronny could proofread for him later in the week. Just proofread, give him some feedback, as if they were colleagues. "Sure thing," Ronny said.

Brows furrowed, Otis blew out a breath; he was standing in the door frame, filling it. "I got pretty good at my deadlines in summer school," he said.

"You still planning on journalism? Maybe next spring you could write some for *The Tar Heel*."

"You think I could?"

"We always need people. Cover women's swimming or something."

He grinned, scratching at a mole high up on his skull; his hair was cropped so short you could see the scalp. "Maybe. I got a lot of work to do this year. Coach is busting us pretty good." He was wearing a gold cross at his neck. Ronny remembered the Bible beside his bed. "I'm not rooming with Ben this year, he'll probably be bugging you soon. I know he was talking about it. You're his pet tutor, he says." Made a chuckle-sound, as if it were a funny joke, then spit in the trash can. "Yeah. Anyway." Ducking his head, he backed away. "Later."

Kelly had a new girlfriend, Muriel, and brought her to the room to study but mostly to make out with her, and he was giving Ronny the look that meant he wanted privacy. Ronny took his sociology text and notebook to the first-floor study lounge in the early evening and found a couch at the back of the room where he could sit in peace. A dozen other people there. He was reading about statistical methods in sociology research, repeating every paragraph, trying to follow the near impenetrable prose. Someone turned on a radio very low; someone else asked her to turn it off or use headphones. One of the fencers cruised through in his fencing jacket and knickers, long socks grimy at the bottom, no shoes, shaking out his hair like a movie star. People switched on lamps as the windows grew darker. Ronny was making notes about the chapter, intent, when he felt a weight on the couch and saw Ben settling there. He gave Ronny a grimace, opened a thick American history text. "Brainhead," said Ben, after a while. "You mind?"

"Plenty of room," Ronny said.

Later, in the whispery tone of the room, "You study down here a lot?"

"Yes," Ronny said. "Kelly needs the room for his extracurricular stuff."

"What?"

Ronny made the finger-in-the-hole sign for sex. Ben laughed and people frowned at him and he tried to become smaller and quieter. "Going to need your help," Ben said. "They're on my back about grades."

"Yeah?"

"You willing?"

"Sure. I work at *The Tar Heel* three nights a week, though."

"Well, fuck."

"There's still weekends and such."

"You can study on the weekend?" Ben asked. He grinned, liking how funny he was. "I've got games, but maybe."

"I thought you were a redshirt."

"Don't fucking remind me. Still have to practice and go to games."

"Sorry."

"My fault. If I kept up my grades I wouldn't be in this mess." Shrugged, though, pretense of indifference. "So you're my personal educational assistant. Got it?"

Ronny chuckled, shook his head, and Ben thumped his arm. "Don't do me like that."

"Oh, I'm willing."

After a while a girl named Tamara showed up and Ben introduced her, closing his books for the night. Left with her, swaggering, looking back once. Ronny tried to sit still, managed to read for an hour or so. The girl with the radio made an attempt to turn it on again. Somebody else shut her down. She sighed and made a show of slamming her books together and walked to the lounge door in a huff. "I can't concentrate without some music," she said, and tried to slam the door but the hydraulics caught it. Everybody still in the room giggled a bit and looked at one another.

OCTOBER

In October, he was leaving the *Tar Heel* office one night after the nine o'clock deadline when he met Kathy Moore near the information desk. It had been months since she'd broken up with Ben. Ronny had forgotten how tall she was. She gave him such a smile when he spoke. He had never seen red hair so bright. "Oh, it's good to see you!" she said. "I don't get down to Ehringhaus much anymore."

"It's still the same," he said.

They did the quick catch-up. Still at *The Tar Heel* (him). Still majoring in biology (her) and doing pre-med (her). Still friends with Ben (him), still thinking about English but maybe enough journalism to get a job on a newspaper (him). "I'm living off campus now," she said. "Couple of other girls. I like it."

"You were thinking about a sorority way back when."

"Nope. Decided not to waste the money. I went to one pledge party and that was all it took."

"Crazy year," he said, after a lull.

"Can you believe we have a Baptist running for president, or whatever? Doesn't even drink."

"It's all nuts. He's probably going to win, though."

She was chewing her underlip, considering. "So you might as well tell me. How's Ben doing? Is he ever going to grow up?"

"He's fine, I guess. Not happy about being a redshirt, wants to play. He's around here somewhere. I'm going with him to the library."

"Are you serious?"

"Yes."

"Still doing his homework?"

"Helping. That's all I do." Said it simply. He had always been a good liar.

She made a sniffing sound, folded her arms. She changed the subject quickly, asked about movies. He wanted to see *The Seven-Per-Cent Solution*, yes. "I've seen it three times," she said. "It's creepy."

"Really?"

"Am I ridiculous? If I like a movie I see it a lot."

"No, that makes sense. I must have seen *The Three Musketeers* a half dozen times."

There was Ben across the lobby near the snack bar entrance. Frowning, stormy. Like most of the time these days. Recognized Kathy, turned his back, took a few steps in the other direction.

"Need to go," Ronny said.

She was picking at her nail polish. "Sure. We should get together sometime."

"Yeah." He was grinning. "We can see a movie."

"Give my love to you know who." Spoken with a sardonic lift of the eyebrow. She was about to turn away but stopped. "How's Tate, by the way?"

"Same as always. Lives like one of the great apes."

"Tell him hello for me. I liked him."

She waved goodbye, something graceful in the gesture, and headed away.

He found Ben, and they walked to the undergraduate library just across the Pit, next to the student bookstore. Pole lights burned along the brick steps of the Pit, in front of and between buildings, small moons framed against brick walls, against the tall shrubs of the library. People gathered everywhere, in and out of shadow and light, some walking bicycles, a stout boy with a dog, a girl walking two steps behind him looking anxious, counting on her fingers. "You recognize the person I was talking to?" Ronny asked.

"Oh, sure." Ben was in a sweater, tight across his shoulders, his jeans sagging and showing a bit of lean waist, walking in bedroom shoes, oddly enough. He saw Ronny watching. "I couldn't find my real shoes," he said.

"You mean your flip-flops."

"Right." Hanging his head, pausing at the stone canopy leading into the library. That burn rose inside him, visible, the sense that he was about to break something, or punch somebody. But it was in check at the moment. He said, "We don't need to go in there."

"Yes, we do."

"No we don't." He showed his notebook, waved the pages at Ronny. "I already did the crap. Three sources, all that stuff." Gritting his teeth, working his jaw, gripping his books like he wanted to hurl them into the shrubbery. Ronny looked Ben in the eye.

"Then what's going on? You look like you want to choke somebody."

Shrugged, rubbed the toe of his shoes on the bricks. "Just practice today. Sick of working like this knowing I'll be on the sidelines."

Nothing to say about that. "You're getting your grades up. That's something."

"Yeah. My ma is loving it."

"Is she?"

"You want to walk somewhere, sit for a while?"

They ambled away toward Carroll Hall, fewer people out that way. Near the old Playmaker's Theater they headed onto the lawns, found a bench near there, and sat. "Kathy have anything to say?"

"Not much. She likes *The Seven-Per-Cent Solution*."

"Maybe we could go see it. Maybe Sunday."

"You'll have a new girl by Sunday," Ronny said.

"Shithead."

"Well, you will. Probably."

"Okay. Be a shit."

"If you don't get lucky by then I'll be glad to go with you."

The bench was near a streetlight, and wide enough that they kept apart. Ben spread his legs as if he meant to take up the maximum room possible, leaned back his head, closed his eyes. "You won't believe what the guys did for the State game." N.C. State was a rivalry that everybody talked about, Carolina played them on Saturday. "Shaved their heads. They look like idiots."

"What? Why? What does that have to do with anything?"

"Getting psyched," he said. "Guess they figure they need it."

"What about you?"

"I don't need that kind of shit. And I can't play anyway." Sullen again. "My ma is glad about it, that's what gets me. She never wanted me to do football in college anyway. My dad is pouting because she won't come to any games."

"They getting along all right?"

"Sounds like it. Won't be coming here this weekend, though. So we can see that movie."

"Yeah, well. Did Tate shave his head?"

"Oh you know it. Looks like an egg. He kept that stupid little mustache, though."

"You really did your research already, you're not kidding."

Ben passed Ronny the notebook, showed him the notes and the sources. "Somebody told you I don't have a brain but she was wrong."

"What do you mean?"

"Never mind."

"Kathy never said anything like that."

"Well, she thought it. Come on." He stood, shook out his hair, chuckled as he ran his hands through it. Just like that his mood had brightened. "I still got my curls."

"So you miss Kathy, do you?"

"What? No, not a bit. Come on. We can get a hot dog at Hector's and look over this crap for the essay."

"Jesus, you sound just like a student. A regular, diligent Carolina gentleman."

Spreading his hands, walking backward along the grass. "Hey, what can I say. I'm a fucking intellectual."

NOVEMBER

He felt a fear at times, at night when he was trying to sleep, but at other times as well: when he was walking down the long balcony at the front of the suites and people were watching him; when Tate was making fun of him for being thin or smart or for helping Ben or even for helping Tate when he wrote a paper for him; in class sometimes, for no reason he could think of. Less rarely at the newspaper, where he had a function, but still it happened sometimes that he wondered what people thought of him, whether they had any idea how many secrets he kept. It was a fear old and new, familiar from the days after his father left home, when he was trying to understand what it meant that his mother called his father a queer; but it was new because at school, and especially in the presence of Ben, the fear took on so many other shapes. There was Ben himself, who was intimidating when he wanted to be, and turbulent whether he wanted to be or not—unless Ronny managed to relax him, which happened at times when they were talking, especially when they were alone. There were Ronny's feelings for Ben, which had moved beyond friendship into something that felt at times quite sinister—for Ben would never return those feelings, would he? Friendship maybe. Ben had never had a friend quite like Ronny before, he had said so. Ben was not used to talking, enjoyed it when it happened, even told his mother about it, according to his own testimony. A simple thing like talking made him happy.

Things would be different if he knew what Ronny was really wanting. But he did know, didn't he? At times when he was drinking he would lean close to Ronny, or throw an arm around him, or put a hand in his hair, teasing, deliberate. This was part of the wheel on which Ronny went round and round, the fact of himself and all that he concealed and the truth of the world in which he was, for the first time, becoming happy in spite of everything. It was a feeling you could lose so easily; once you understood it was there, very likely it was about to fade. His grandmother had told him to forget about happiness, there was nothing but misery in the world, from family, from husbands, from friends, even from grandchildren, she would say, and had shaken her finger at him. But then he would watch her while she picked her butter beans, watered her tomatoes, smelled her roses, trimmed her jasmine and trained it to grow along a trellis; at times like that there was not only happiness but joy in her expression. So she was lying to herself and to him. While her body told the truth with its radiance of bliss among the plants of the garden. The body was an entity that could not lie.

He visited Sheria a week before Thanksgiving and found her brightly happy, watching her small color television, sitting against the wall of her bed, propped against pillows. That was the time he saw that there were cuts on her wrist—not very deep, not enough to penetrate the layer of fat there. But the straight lines of the cuts were distinct, across both wrists, very neat and precise, reminding him of the frog he had dissected in high school. There was no sign of bleeding; the flesh had started to heal. "What are you looking at?" she asked. She had been talking about Pat, the RA for the boys' floor on the other side of the dorm, who was, she said, a cutie and a friend of hers.

"What's going on, Sheria?" he asked.

"Ronny, I don't know what you're talking about." The smile remained but there was a feverish cast to her expression. Sheria was like a human furnace, she exuded heat; but this was different.

He pointed. "You have cuts."

The smile scarcely changed. "No I don't. I wouldn't do anything like that."

There passed an extended moment in which they simply sat together, and he could feel it then, her fear. It had always been there but he had never noticed it before. There might be a thousand reasons for it. She had been one of the only black students at Governor's School. She was heavy. She kept to herself. There were the problems with her mother. These were just the things Ronny knew about her. After a moment he said, "I know you wouldn't."

"Do you want to sit down? You can sit on the other bed. I don't have a roommate." She was the RA for the girls' side of this floor so she had a room to herself. He started to sit on the bed and then slid to the floor beside it instead. He wasn't sure why but he was afraid, something about the moment made him so. She said, "I have been a little blue lately."

"Me, too," he said.

"I guessed you were. That's why I said something. Your mom is okay?"

"She's fine. I haven't heard from her since her boyfriend moved out."

"The one with the bad teeth?"

"Yes. Dennis. His dentures kept falling out."

She giggled, the bed shook as the laugh grew, and she waved her hand and said, "I'm picturing inappropriate moments at which that would happen."

"Oh. I know. But I think he takes them out when they have . . . you know."

"Oh, oh." She was waving an old church fan at her face. She kept the fan on the table beside her. "You are bad."

"It's true."

"I would never ever discuss my mother having sex with anyone."

"Does she?"

"Stop. Please. Of course she doesn't. She wouldn't be so visceral." That stopped her, the manic quality of the laughter dissolving. "She said the most terrible thing to me the other day on the phone. 'At least you're not wasting your time dating anybody.' Can you imagine? 'You're good at friendship but I don't think anybody will ever love you.'" She blinked at him, let the words hang there. She was no longer smiling.

He had heard other stories like this one from her. His own mother was blunt but stopped short of meanness. "Why would she say something like that? Everybody loves you, Sheria."

"You know what I mean."

"Well, that's not true either. It's not like she can see the future."

"Do you ever worry about that?" she asked. "Whether anybody will love you?"

She knew he was single, never dated; she probably suspected the truth. He said, "Yes. I do."

Having exacted the confession, she could relax. There was an *I Love Lucy* rerun on her television, the volume very low, Lucy rushing around the apartment trying to hide packages she had bought before Ricky came home. He had seen the episode before, more than once. He and Sheria were sitting together peacefully. The anxiety was subsiding. They talked about schoolwork, his job at the student newspaper. "I'm still thinking I'll go to law school," she said.

"That would be good. Your mother will pay attention to that."

She rolled her eyes and blew out her breath. Then she laughed, loud and full. "She will, won't she?"

Pretty soon after that he could feel that she was tiring of company, fixing her gaze on the television and pretending to enjoy Lucy. He stood and said good night. "Don't be a stranger," she said. She had laid her wrists flat on her thighs to conceal the cuts. It was curious that he felt she was in no danger. But the wounds on her wrist were not new. He had known that she veered from depression, from her own fear, into the brightness and gaiety she presented as herself. He had felt kin to her for it.

As it happened, Ben was moody that day following afternoon practice, when he had thrown up in his helmet and had to smell his own vomit for the last hour. You had to put up with that stuff sometimes, he said. "So how was your friend?"

"Fine. Maybe. I don't know." He told what had happened. They were sitting in Ben's old car in the parking lot, Ben eating a hamburger, the night mild, amid shouting from the dorm across the way, people watching *Monday Night Football* in their rooms. A clatter of leaves across the parking lot, a whole wave of them falling at once, spreading out in the air like a veil.

"Tough to have a mom like that. You really think she hurt herself?"

"Probably. Some people do that."

Ben balled up the food wrapper, sat back against the seat. He kept his car clean even if it was a bit of a clunker; the wrapper went back into the bag, and he would carry the bag into the dorm and trash it. "So what are you going to do?"

"Just visit her again, I guess. I think she's always up and down like this."

Ben was the same in a lot of ways. Now was a good moment. Earlier he had been tense. He shook his head, sniffed, spit onto the pavement. "Sounds like she's got friends."

"She does."

"What about you?" Ben asked. "Are you up and down?"

"You think I am?"

He shrugged. He had brought a can of beer and sipped it, then handed it back to Ronny. It was still football season and he wasn't supposed to drink, so he kept an eye on the cars. So it was Ronny's beer, officially. Every time they passed it back and forth their fingers touched. Ben said, "Doesn't really matter to me. You got my back, I got yours."

It was a strange statement, not quite like anything else he had ever said. Ronny let the words hang, gathered them one by one. Ben handed him the beer again, the brief contact of hands, and they were watching each other this time. "What's Thanksgiving like at your house?" Ronny asked.

"Same as anybody, I guess. Mom cooks, my sister comes home, we watch football, me and my dad."

"You have a big family?"

"No. My mom and her folks don't get along. My dad's folks are gone. What about you?"

"There was my grandma. She died last summer."

"Was she the grandmother who bakes cookies type? Mine sure wasn't."

"No. She was tough. They fought a lot. Mom has a sister somewhere but we never hear from her."

"I'd just as soon stay in town and take you out for Mexican some place," Ben said.

"Sounds good to me."

"I can still smell that vomit. Jesus. I need some of that VapoRub stuff."

"I can't believe you have to go through that crap."

Ben tugged at his jacket, spat on the asphalt again, ran hands through his hair. "And I still don't get to play. That's what gripes my ass. But next year I will show these sons of bitches something." He ground his jaw, stared up at the dorm; far overhead were the blinking lights of a passenger jet. "You know what a big help you been to me, don't you?"

Ronny hardly knew what to say. Ben was giving him this fierce look. "You still have a paper to write tonight," Ronny said.

"Yeah. Give me that beer." Instead of taking the beer, though, Ben laid his hand heavy on the back of Ronny's neck, squeezed him there. After a moment he broke off the touch, but it felt charged, the hand hot, Ben taut with the energy of it, the two of them like a circuit, suddenly alight.

After a while, shutting the car door, climbing the rise to the service road at the back of the dorm, Ronny said, almost hoarse, "You've been a big help to me, too."

"I know." Their shoulders bumping, jamming their hands in their pockets. "All right," Ben said. "I'll go write some. But you have to help when I get stuck."

"I have to read Suetonius, too."

"You just like to say that sucker's name. I don't think he's real."

"I'll show you the book, shithead."

"Oh, don't try to cuss. You just sound stupid."

DECEMBER

A keg party in December, people he knew from the newspaper, the editor, the associate editor, the news editor, the features editor, the sports editor, the managing editor, the copy editors, the reporters, some of whom he had classes with, some whose stories he copy-edited, some he barely knew. Lily was there, too, flirting with the fellow she had brought, very tall and angular, another poetry student with whom all the young women were in love. David something. The news editor had been standing over the keg, trying to persuade Ronny to write for the paper; Ronny was sipping the beer from time to time in order to project conviviality. "I like correcting copy, not writing it," he said.

"Oh, bullshit. I was in class with you, I read your long-form stuff."

"You're so full of it. You're just short-handed."

The news editor, whom everybody called by his last name, Roberts, shook his thick hair and took a look around the cramped apartment. One of the ad staff had given the party, insisted everybody come, and was walking around now making sure one of the assistant editors (everybody had a title, part of resumé building) was drinking heavily; she probably wanted to take him to bed later. The stereo was loud, the Who earlier, *Who's Next*; Pink Floyd at the moment, *Ummagumma*, and the sound was big enough to shake the walls of the boxy apartment; this was one of the complexes that had sprung up near

University Mall, low ceilings, bland carpet, lots of tape on the walls, as if the occupant was constantly changing her mind about where to hang her posters. There were a couple of Diane Arbus prints in frames, stark black and white. The smell of pot and burnt hot dogs. The hostess had made pigs in a blanket.

Ronny was seeing his life as separate spaces, perhaps too completely walled off from one another: the dorm, the newspaper, people he knew from class, and the folk of Goldsboro, into whose bosom he would return for the holidays. He had a feeling that he often read about in literature class, a sense of alienation, of being here in the room and being distant from it at the same time, though that could just be the pot fumes, it was hard to tell. The associate editor was a well known pothead and the sports editor had intimated that one of the reporters brought some Thai stick to the party. A group of people were clustered around the dining table, laying it all out to smoke.

Lily had been dancing a bit near to her poet friend, but he was looking bored against a wall now and flirting with someone else; Lily sipped her scotch and talked to Ronny, giving him a sleepy look. "He's a complete bastard, that guy. But he writes really well."

"That's the way it's supposed to work, isn't it? Great writers are great jerks."

She laughed, shook her hair forward to the music, then flung it back again, trying to make a bit of a show. Art, one of the news writers, was hovering at her elbow, fascinated. Knowing Art, he would stand there for an hour and never say a word, but if he sat at a typewriter he could record their dialogue with substantial accuracy. A good skill for a reporter but a bit creepy at a party. Lily said, "The thing about journalists is they only want to talk to each other."

"Are they ignoring you?"

"They think of me as the business office. You know. Not quite the newspaper."

Ronny said, "It's still a pretty good party."

She was sniffing her scotch, blinking deliberately, slowly, luxuriating in it. She took a long look at him and lowered her voice. "You're faking it with that drink, aren't you? You're sober."

"Don't tell."

"My father says these are the days we'll remember later on. Do you think it's true?"

"Maybe not this party."

She laughed. One of the reporters was dancing a bit too intensely. A couple of the sportswriters were leading him to the bathroom, planning to hose him down in the shower. There was a shouting match that followed. It was getting close to time to leave. The hostess turned out a lamp here, an overhead there. People were sprawling on the floor.

"I can give you a ride home if you're ready to go," Lily said.

"Are you sober enough to drive?"

"Absolutely." This took some time, however. She had to collect David, who was deep in conversation with the editor's girlfriend. The editor was asleep on the couch, mouth open, arms loose at either side. Someone was about to try the trick on him in which you dunk a person's hand into warm water to make him pee. The girlfriend rushed in to rescue him, so they would never know whether this method of humiliation would have worked. This freed up David, and so the three of them slipped out of the apartment and Lily drove Ronny to campus, letting him out at the cemetery while she and David were insulting each other's favorite poets; Lily favored Wallace Stevens, whom David called a watery-thin jumped-up insurance broker; and David favored T. S. Eliot, whom Lily claimed would have been better off if he'd continued to wander in the wasteland a while longer. A poet of spoons, she said. Drunken foreplay of a sadly desperate kind, Ronny thought.

He found his way to the dorm by a route he had not often walked, near the track field and the practice field for the football team, past tennis courts and along the darkened, tarp-covered baseball field. Cold air stirred him. Walking from one world to another, he thought. Ehringhaus rose over everything else, balcony lights blazing, some traffic visible from suite to suite. Not quite midnight.

It had been a few days since he talked to Ben, and he had a bleak sense that their odd friendship was waning. Ben had met somebody, more than likely. Maybe she was helping him keep up with his schoolwork, too. Ronny felt the gloom of it, told himself how stupid it was. There was nothing but a fantasy relationship between them, there was nothing to hope for, and there were plenty of actual gay people on campus that he could meet whenever he wanted. It was a thought that felt new, to use the word "gay" in his head in that easy way. It's what I am, he thought. As for what Ben was—no matter what Ronny wished—well, that was none of his business, was it?

He went to sleep with the certainty of all this, the feeling that he should stop insinuating himself into Ben's life, that he should give up on friendship; and yet the thought of that made him unhappy, because Ben's friendship felt real. Light from the balcony seeped through the shade, yellow and warm, and he stared at the strip of light that fell across his middle, the shadow beyond, for an hour or more, until he felt himself drifting.

*

JANUARY

The first Sunday in the semester, when the phone rang early, Ronny stumbled over his shoes trying to answer it, groggy and cotton-headed, and nearly knocked his head on the closet. Kelly was snoring in his bed, his girlfriend wrapped around him—Lucinda, a woman from Puerto Rico who cursed at Kelly in Spanish when he made her angry, which happened frequently. They were sound asleep, the wastebasket stacked with beer cans. Surprising they weren't scattered all over the room, along with sticky beer stains; Lucy must be a good influence.

"I wake you up?" Ben asked. Low and heartfelt, the tone.

It had been weeks. Ronny had given up, turned to stone. He thought so, anyway. But the sound of Ben's voice. "You there? Is this Ronny?"

"Yep. It's me." Speaking quietly as Lucy peered at him over Kelly's hairy shoulder.

"Need to talk."

"It's been a while."

"I know. Can you come over? Tate's out." He sounded flat, almost lifeless.

"Sure thing," Ronny said. Feeling a quickening in himself.

When he hung up and grabbed his coat, Lucy was rearranging herself with her back to Kelly, who grunted but never opened his eyes. She was watching, eyes barely open. Ronny waved to her as he was going out. Closing the door quietly, the hall cold, the balcony colder, January and icy. He rushed along the balcony to the stairs, the iron rail numbing to his hand.

Ben's door was open. He was standing there in boxers, nothing else, a sight that caught at Ronny, made his heartbeat change, the smooth skin, the shapes, the face, Ben's hair a mess. He closed the door behind Ronny and locked it, leapt into his bed, and pulled the covers over his shoulders, lying there grave and still. Ronny hovered, sat on the edge of Tate's bed, unmade and littered with socks, mail, papers, a wrapper from a PayDay candy bar.

Ben patted space on his own bed, said, "Come over here. I won't bother you."

He was staring into the gap between the window and the blind. Ronny did as he was asked, sat down gingerly, Ben's big thighs wrapped against him. Ben said, "I just need you right now, Ronny. Okay?"

"What's wrong?"

"It was a shit Christmas. Mom's sick." There was a break in his voice at the end, and he clamped his lips shut, taking one breath after another. Ronny lay his arm along Ben's side, leaned back against his belly, the thick blanket and sheets between them.

"Bad sick?"

"Yeah." He released a long, heavy sigh. "I can't talk about it much."

"That's okay."

They listened to the alarm clock ticking on Tate's desk; soft music drifted in from the back of the suite, sounded like gospel.

"I brought this girl Britt back with me last night and then I didn't want her here. I'm such a shit sometimes."

Maybe it was a warning not to presume too much. But it was too late for that anyway; the contact with Ben's mass, the physical closeness, had broken apart Ronny's shell, taken him back into the feelings he had tried to lose, wrecked his calm. Ronny said, "I wish I knew what to say."

"Guess you gave up on me, right? I haven't talked to you in so long."

"Didn't know what was going on."

"Lost it a little bit," he said.

"When did you get the news?"

"Right after Thanksgiving she went to a doctor. Got worried after that. You won't believe the mess I'm in. Barely got through exams. Three incompletes."

So it was help with schoolwork Ben needed. That was the first thought, the bitter one. But the feeling was different from that. He wanted it to be different. Ben laid his hand on Ronny's arm for a moment. "I'm fucking up again," he said.

"It's fine. Don't worry about it."

"I just want somebody to talk to. I know I can talk to you."

"You don't want to tell me what's wrong with your mom though?"

"I will. What about you? You doing okay?"

"Sure. Glad to be back at school."

He closed his eyes, the lashes looked wet, and Ronny felt so much of it, the hurt and pain flowing through Ben's body, a trembling vibration running through him, as if all that was holding him still was the weight of grief. "For some reason you settle me down a little. You know it?"

"No. But I'm glad if it's true."

After a while Ben said, tone slightly altered, "I know what you want, Ronny. But I just don't know what to do about it."

"Jesus, Ben." Running a hand through his own hair.

"Don't try to talk to me about it, okay? I just wanted to say."

Thumping, thumping in Ronny's chest. "Okay."

"My mom has cancer in the gallbladder thing," he said.

"Does she? Crap. Crap."

"I know."

"Is it? Crap. I'll just shut up."

"She's not bad sick yet. They're figuring out how to treat her. She had an appointment Friday for some kind of test, over at Duke. Finds out more Monday."

"What are they going to do?"

"Radiation, like. And then the chemotherapy stuff. We don't know how long yet."

Speaking the words aloud released Ben, and he changed position, put an arm over his head. Ronny shifted a bit, reduced the contact between them, took a deep breath. Turmoil inside him, same as inside Ben, he supposed, but for different reasons. He felt raw, as if he were gaping open, exposed. It should have been fearful but it was something else.

"Okay. Well, you said it."

Ben watched him for a fair while. A tentative moment, but neither of them turned away. They sat still together. In a shaft of light over Tate's desk dust motes were swimming, diving, spinning, as if there were a kind of life in them, in the air everywhere, that you could only see from certain angles. Ronny was agitated but held still, knowing how rare it was to be so close to Ben like this, certain it would not last.

FEBRUARY

Distance was a variable. Ben worked on finishing his incompletes from the semester before and tried to keep up with his current coursework, too; that meant a lot of time with Ronny during the week, working together in the study lounge or in the library. About eight p.m. or so Ronny went to do his duties as night editor for *The Tar Heel* and sometimes they met up again afterward, at eleven, when the newspaper was picked up by the printer. Ronny could feel their closeness during the week. On weekends there was another feeling. Ben moved steadily from girl to girl. Sometimes Ronny met them and sometimes he didn't. It was easy to think Ben was trying to prove something, but that was what Ronny wanted to think, wasn't it? So there was predictable, increased space between them, especially on Saturdays, when Ben and his friends spent the evening at He's Not Here.

If this was uncomfortable or maddening it was Ronny's fault and he told himself so; he had a choice, he could go places on his own. All over campus were flyers about the Carolina Gay Association and its coffeehouses, its meetings; there was a gay disco outside of town and a gay bar in Durham. There were boys in Ronny's classes he suspected were the same as he. But he liked the feeling he had already claimed. Maybe that was sad, but it was enough for the moment.

He went to a dorm party a couple of weeks before spring break and drank something called PJ that contained grain alcohol. Never had he been so drunk before, and he lay down under a bulletin board in the elevator lobby to keep from falling over. A tinny stereo was booming in the TV room, where the alcohol was. There were a lot of people in the lobby. People there stopped to check on Ronny and chatted with him. Sheria came to gape at him and thought he was hilarious. She sat on the floor and talked to him. "Are you seeing double?"

"Nothing holds still long enough for me to count."

"I need to find Sara, she has to see this." Sheria was sipping her own glass of PJ. "Did you really not know how strong this stuff is?"

"No. It tasted like Hawaiian Punch."

"That's what they mix the Everclear with."

"I just kept drinking it."

"Poor baby. Did you have anything to eat?"

"Yes. Part of a pizza."

"Oh, you're probably going to lose that."

A big moony head leaned over Sheria, and a voice said, "Hey there, Brainhead."

"You know this guy?" Sheria asked.

"That's my pet faggot," said Tate.

"Well, that's not very nice."

"You're drunk, Ronny," said Tate.

"I know."

"Well, shit. I never saw you drunk before."

"You want me to chase this guy away?" Sheria asked. Sara had come up beside her. Tate was looking Sara over. She was very pretty. But she ignored him, hand on Sheria's shoulder. "Look at you!" Sara said. "Sloshed!"

"I found him first," Tate said to her. "Hello. My name is Tate."

"I found him first," said Sheria.

"How long do you plan on laying down there?" Sara asked.

"Well, it depends on when I can feel my legs," Ronny said, and he could hear the slurring in his voice. He was looking straight up at the bulletin board, a flyer for the Dialectic and Philanthropic Societies. The tile walls had thin lines of stain on them. Up above was acoustic tile showing evidence of a leak. Another face swam into view, the snack bar cashier who sold him chili-dusted potato chips. Sheria was laughing and said, "He is so hilarious. Do you think he knows where he is?"

"I'm not sure," said Sara.

"What's going on? Oh, crap." That was Ben. He was leaning over, looking Ronny in the eye, shaking his head. "How long have you been down there, buddy?"

"I don't know."

"You know who I am?"

"Sure."

"All right. Wow. Who got him drunk like this? Was it you, Tate?"

"We just found him here," said Sara.

"I think he did the drunk part all by himself," said Tate. "I hope he hadn't lost too many brain cells. We need those."

There was Ben hovering over him again, face closer. "You think you ought to go on lying here?"

"I don't know what else to do," said Ronny.

"Can you stand up?"

"Oh, no way. That's how I ended up down here. I just kind of didn't have any legs anymore but there was this nice wall right here." He reached out to pat it fondly. The concrete block was rough and cool to the touch.

Sheria was laughing, Sara was laughing, Tate was shaking his head.

"Tell you what, Ronny. Let me get you to your room, okay?"

"Do you even know this guy?" Sheria asked.

"Sure I do."

"I don't want him to end up naked in the elevator or anything," said Sara, trying to look serious. "You know you guys do that sometimes."

"I wouldn't do anything like that," said Tate, but he appeared to be considering something along those lines.

"Somebody will mess with him sure as shit if we leave him here," said Ben.

"He looks so cute," said Sheria. "I never saw him drunk before."

"Nobody ever saw him drunk before," said Sara.

"I did, once," said Ben. "Hey, Ron. Don't you want to go to your room?"

"I don't know where it is," said Ronny.

"Well, I do."

Ronny blew out breath, closed his eyes. He was feeling rumbly in the midsection and he wanted to sleep. "Okay," he said.

"You know who I am, right? Say my name."

"You're Ben."

"And it's okay for me to help you up, right?" Ben asked. He was speaking low in Ronny's ear.

"Sure, Ben. Just go slow, though. I had pizza before."

"Feeling kind of queasy?"

"Probably. I'm not sure."

"Well, up you go." Only took a second and he was standing, his arm around Ben's neck. That part was nice. They were walking through the crowd. There was Sheria leading the way, shaking her head, saying to someone, "Oh, he's fine, he's just going home before he gets alcohol poisoning."

"Is your room open," Ben asked. "Do you have your key?"

"I never even had a key," Ronny said. "Oh, crap."

"Here we go. It's already open. No Kelly. Right on the bed."

"You better pull that trash can over near him," said Sheria. "I think he's about to blow."

Things got quieter then. He had his eyes closed. They were talking in the room but he could barely hear the words. Tate's voice and Sara's voice. Once when he opened his eyes Sheria was sitting on the bed. He felt as if he drifted, then it was Ben sitting there and the room was dark. Events had happened and he had a fuzzy memory of them. "You threw up," Ben said. "You should feel better. Want some water?"

"I don't remember it."

"Well, you did. Bet you can taste it."

"Shit. Yes." He drank from a glass of water. "Where's everybody?"

"Back at the party probably. Tate's trying to get something going with that Sara girl. She's cool."

"Yeah. She is. That water is nice."

"I bet. Listen. How much did you drink?"

"Just two glasses. Maybe just three."

"You're sure?"

"Yep."

"Okay, runt. You sure picked a great night to practice drinking."

"Oh, I got drunk once before. Right?"

"Yeah. I know. I was there, remember?"

"Oh, yeah."

They sat quiet. A feeling—hazy, beyond the veil of the liquor—that he was cared for, that someone was there. Ben said, "Go to sleep if you want. I'm going to wait here till Kelly gets home."

"I'm all right."

"Yeah? Well, relax then. Just pass out. Let it happen."

So he did, peaceful and drifting quietly into the night, floating through the window over the parking lot, and he thought he was happy, that everything was fine. Someone was touching his hair, pushing it out of his eyes, behind his ears, nice and easy.

*

MARCH AND APRIL

March brought the bluster of wind, spring, storm, three weeks of football practice, midterms, Ben's mother's chemotherapy, Ben's anger. A feeling of chaos overtook the quiet space in which they had spent time together. There was a feeling of union that turned into colliding, careening apart. Early one morning, wee hours, he read Ben's palm. They were in the study lounge, everybody else had gone to bed, all the other lamps were dark, and they were tucked in the back corner on a couch. Reading palms was something Ronny had done in high school and now and then still practiced at parties, a way to talk to strangers. With Ben it was an excuse to touch his hands, callused and hard, to caress his fingers, to trace his life line, his head line, his heart line, to press the mounts of Jupiter, Saturn, Apollo, Mercury; a way to talk to Ben about himself. To calm him down. Ben had come to study a little drunk, which he was not supposed to do because he was in the middle of spring practice; he had ignored curfew to stay in the study lounge. He was hard to contain, had fought with somebody at the end of practice, a late hit, he said, but wouldn't give any more details; he'd had a call from his sister about his mom, but didn't want to talk about it; he gripped his books as if he wanted to crush them; he mainly wanted to sit and pretend to study, to hear Ronny read aloud some of the education textbook, to close his eyes and breathe. They were sitting close on the couch so Ben could look at the book while Ronny read; at times their shoulders touched, at times Ben touched Ronny's hand on the textbook, tracing a line. As the night went on he started to calm a bit. "You're going to get in trouble about curfew, Ben."

"Nah. They don't really care about spring." The slight smell of beer on his breath.

So Ronny took his hands and held them and told him about himself. "This is bullshit," Ben said, but left his hands in place.

"It's just fun," Ronny said.

"Yeah. I guess."

He had clear, definite lines on his palms; his fingers were thick, with knobby joints, rounded tips; his mount of the moon was high and dense; the flesh below his fingers was thick skinned. They were leaning closer and closer, Ben's breath on Ronny's collarbone. Ronny had stopped talking and they went on sitting there like that, the books on the floor, the room dark, the building quiet. He found he could not move away. He kissed Ben lightly on the lips.

Ben shoved him back, wiped his mouth, frowned, sat with his hands in his hair, and for the first time in a while Ronny felt the terror inside himself, stood up, backed away into the dark. Ben followed, shoved him again, not hard, but enough that Ronny knelt and picked up his own books, gathering them in a stack. He could hear Ben breathing. He stood and started to walk away. "I'm sorry," he said, very quiet, a few feet away, and he heard Ben move forward, lunge at him, pull him around, knock the books out of his hand.

They kissed furiously, Ben trembling. Then he stopped and stood there, a low sound in his throat. What showed was not anger but anguish, all the trouble heaped on him, this was just one thing too many. Ronny flushed with shame. "You better go," Ben said, and he did.

The next day Ronny skipped class, stayed in his room, lay facing the wall while Lucy and Kelly moved about, Lucy asking him whether he felt all right, whether he needed anything; when they were gone the room was quiet and dim, the shade pulled, the lights out. A cloudy day, promising rain that began to fall at midmorning. He had ruined everything of course. There could be no doubt of it. Except that Ben knocked on the door about lunchtime, came inside, said, "Look. I got a B on my education midterm." Just as if nothing had happened.

When spring practice was over, there was a public scrimmage, the Blue-White game, and Ronny went to watch Ben play. Ben's family had come up as well. There was never much of a crowd for the spring game, and the players lingered among their friends and the members of their families, helmets in hand. Ben introduced Ronny to his parents. "This is the guy who keeps me on track," he said, telling his mother about his grades, standing beside her with his arm around her. Mrs. Nickelsen was tall and thin, a bit stooped, holding her purse in both hands. You could see she was struggling to stand at moments, and her husband had hold of her arm.

She said, "I'm so glad to meet you, son. I never would have believed anybody could have got Ben to settle down to his schoolwork so regular."

"He's really doing it himself, ma'am."

"I know that's not so because he tells me."

Mr. Nickelsen pulled off his felt hat and scratched at his ears. His nose was red and he smelled of beer, just a bit, and appeared content to stand next to his wife and say nothing other than the occasional monosyllable. He was mostly watching her, as if she were dissolving.

There was a girl standing near Ben, Jennifer somebody, pretty and graceful, and he introduced her to his mother, too. His girlfriend. They had just met. She was composed and tall and wore a modest skirt and carried a clutch. She smiled at

Ben's mom and they chatted. Ronny let go inside, just a bit, and said how nice it was to meet everybody, and Mrs. Nickelsen said something to him, but he didn't hear it. Walking away toward Ehringhaus.

Almost April by then. You could not be an English major without hearing, every year, that April was the cruelest month.

Jennifer was something different. She was disciplined, demanding, someone Ronny could have liked, in other circumstances. She brought her books to Ben's room and studied with him herself. In the study lounge, she took up the space between Ben and Ronny on the couch. They took many meals together, Ben and she. They walked hand in hand along the balcony toward his room. He was on good behavior with her, at first. The other side also came out to play. Ben was one of the people who threw the vending machine off the sixth floor; he set fire to his own shirt in the parking lot of a bar, came home with it scorched at the hem; he went to a frat party and helped move a Beetle out of the parking lot into a rose bed. He ate glass and threw up blood. Ronny heard the stories from Otis and Tate. A variant of spring fever, maybe.

Yet Ben still called Ronny in the afternoon or in the late evening to tell the news of the day. Asked for advice about his assignments. Complained about Tate's farts, his mess. Sometimes teased Ronny for his jealousy; on being the subject of this kind of joking Ronny felt the beginning of despair.

Ronny focused on the work he did for the newspaper, on Sheria, Lily, Charlotte and the poets, on his own work, on another project with Otis, a longer version of a Title IX story they'd written together. Now and then he made himself too busy to sit with Ben and read to him out of a textbook, to type his papers, to worry about his grades. One day he refused to answer the phone in the afternoon, just lay there on his bed reading. Somebody was riding his bicycle along the balcony, no hands, playing a harmonica very badly, back and forth in front of the window, enjoying the warm day.

The door opened and Ben stood there in jean shorts, his shirt open. "You little shit," he said, closing the door, glowering, hands on his hips. "You can't ditch me."

"What?"

"You're supposed to answer the phone when I call you. You think I don't know when you're in here?"

Ronny closed the book, sat up on the bed, Ben sat next to him and they stared at each other. The idiot on the bicycle rode past again, the window open, the reedy sound awful. "What the fuck is he doing?" Ben asked.

"I don't know. Practicing to be a circus clown maybe."

He reached across Ronny and pulled down the shade. Pitching his voice low, he said, "You know you've been acting like a dumbass lately."

"I don't know what you're talking about."

"Fuck you, I'm not stupid."

They were close to each other, there was the heat of their skins, Ronny with no shirt at all, Ben with his vast body; their faces engulfed in one another, the same feeling as before. The same result, but it was Ben who moved toward Ronny this time.

Afterward, Ben said, "Satisfied?"

Ronny failed to make a sound, nodded his head.

"I'd ask you what's going on but I already fucking know," Ben said. He left it at that. They sat awhile, and after a spell of quiet they started to talk, not about Jennifer but about ordinary things: *The Tar Heel*, the last weeks of class, the spring scrimmage, Ben's mother. There was a commotion on the balcony, some shouting, a last screech of the harmonica, the sound of the bicycle crashing over the balcony rail.

"That's enough of that shit," said a booming voice, and Ben laughed. Ronny wanted to lean against him, just barely managed to stop himself. But he had gotten the message.

The despair came back when Ben was gone. After all, he had refused to explain anything. Ronny went on as before. One night, restless, he headed onto the balcony, prowled out there, down to the lawn. Looking up at the dark sky, the glare of the pole lamps, only a week of classes left, the summer yawning. He would go home to Goldsboro, he would have that summer, a repeat of last year. Three months without. Ben found him wandering in front of the dorm. He was lit, home from the bar. Ben touched his shoulder to Ronny's as they drifted on the grass. "Let's go for a ride," Ben said. "I'm by myself for a change."

Immediately there came a flush of wakefulness, a deep breath of clean air, a feeling of relief. "Sure thing." You had to feel so stupid to let this happen, didn't you? Over and over. He took his place in the car, leaning on the open window, the fresh night. Ben was unbuttoning his shirt, looking at Ronny. There was the teasing. "You're drunk."

"So? You like me drunk, don't you?" The voice was slurred, distant.

"Not really."

He snorted, shook his head. Turned onto a street in Carrboro, heavy trees overhead, and they parked in the shadow, streetlight trapped in the low-hanging branches. He faced Ronny. He was more drunk than Ronny had seen him, the heaviness of it in his expression, the laxness of his movements. A point of pain glimmered in all that sedation, and Ronny figured he knew where that came from. They sat there.

"What would you do right now if I said you could?" Ben asked, sounding as if his mouth were dry.

"Nothing."

"Bullshit."

"Nope." His heart was pounding. He had a certainty in him that there was something wrong with this moment. "I won't do anything."

Ben pulled him close, tried to take Ronny's hand, to put it somewhere. When Ronny resisted, Ben watched him with a blankness, as if he were trying to grasp what was happening— and Ronny pulled away. "You're too drunk, Ben. No."

Ben looked at the roof of the car, stretched his arms out. He blinked heavily and shook his head back and forth, trying to become sober, eyes wide, hands in his hair tugging at the scalp. "Then shit. We'll just sit here."

"That's fine. We can sit here." Ronny was gritting his teeth, made himself relax. Was he being a fool? It wasn't a choice, though, it was a reaction; his body had rebelled, refused to be handled that way. They watched each other. Ben fell asleep briefly. That was fine. It was calming to sit here, to watch him. Easier to ease away the anger, the confusion.

When Ben woke up, he sniffed and straightened, blinked, found a piece of gum, offered half of it to Ronny. He reached a hand for Ronny. He had sobered some, had become recognizable. He pulled Ronny to him, said, "Just touch me. That's all."

It was almost too much, the smooth skin, the tough terrain of the body, breath so close. He bent his head to Ben's shoulder, heard his breathing change. He held still. Ben's expression had frozen. They were together; there was the sense that they were both staring into the same deep; then Ben started the car and drove back to the dorm. They walked from the parking lot to the elevators without saying much.

Inside, waiting for the elevator, Ben said, "I'll see you, okay? Later." He trotted to the stairs and disappeared.

Maybe it scared him a little, what he had done. For a week or so neither called the other. Then came the last day of class, the call from Ronny's mother, the marriage in Nevada, and the boardinghouse.

First Night

AT THE FRONT DOOR OF THE boardinghouse, Ronny turned the doorknob and Ben pushed the frame hard and burst in. Churning, jaw grinding, as if he were about to burst. Ronny touched his arm and he grew still, his body nearly shaking. Anger? Or what?

"Be quiet down here," Ronny said. "That poor old lady will be scared of you."

It was the physicality of him, the crispness, his body made of force, his breathing rapid, nostrils flared, dark brows folded together. But he glanced at Mrs. Delacy's door and changed stance, jaw set, lips in a line. Had he been drinking? Maybe. Ben took a deep breath and blew it out. When he spoke his voice was intense, restrained in volume only. "Fine. What do you want to do?"

"We can go up to my room or we can take a walk somewhere."

"Let's go to your room."

Ronny had learned better than to show any fear. "Come on," he said, and they went upstairs. Ben crowded behind him, looming over him, as if he wanted his body to force Ronny up the steps.

Ben stopped on the stair landing to look at the doors with a scowl. In Ronny's room he glanced from wall to wall briefly and touched the books on the desk. He paced up and down the room, hardly four steps in any direction, but he had to move. When he spoke some of his strain had eased. "You don't have much more room here than you did in the dorm."

"I don't need that much. I'm just here for the summer. How did you find out where I am?"

"I got the address from Kelly." He looked at Ronny, then plopped down on his bed. He said, "You pissed me off."

Ronny sat in the desk chair. "Yeah?"

"I am not teasing you about anything. I'm not." This was what had stung him, that Ronny had accused him of that. Once he said the words, his level of upset diminished visibly. "You need to fucking take that back."

"All right. I take it back."

He glared at Ronny, still breathing hard. "You should have given me some warning. You knew damn well I'd want to see you before I went home."

It made him flush, thrilled him really, that Ben would say so, intently, speaking as if with his whole body. "I tried to find you. I would have kept trying," Ronny said.

"You tried. How? You came to my room a couple of times."

"What was I supposed to do?"

"I don't know. You could have stayed in the dorm till you could talk to me about it." Ben was looking at Ronny, waiting for Ronny to look at him. The feeling was the same as always, wondering which way Ben would go. "You picked a pretty good place, though."

"Why do I need to talk to you about moving?"

Ben had relaxed now, grinned from the bed, and folded his arms behind his head—but there was something wounded in his bravado. "You know why. Because you're my pet faggot."

Ronny blushed. The words made him stubborn. "Why aren't you with Jennifer tonight?"

Ben shrugged, jaw set, looking at the ceiling. He leaned up, stripped the shirt over his head. He looked at Ronny and waited. Ronny moved to the edge of the bed, put his hands on Ben's chest and lay across him. Ben folded his arms over Ronny and sighed.

Ronny breathed against the center of Ben's chest. He could feel the furthering of ease in Ben, his breath slowing, his heartbeat steady.

"You know I was supposed to be living in Granville Towers this summer," Ben said. "Were you thinking about that when you got this room?"

"No, I didn't know where you'd be. That part was just luck."

Ben raised him up and looked him in the eye. He was smirking. "Yeah. Sure."

"You think I'm crazy about you or something."

"Anyway, I'm not going to be over there. I'm not coming to summer school."

Ronny shrugged. But he sank a little to hear it.

Ben's heart was a steady pulse. When he moved his arms he showed a glint of satisfaction; it appeared he liked the way Ronny reacted when his body shifted, the way Ronny's eyes followed the changes in the shapes and contours. He liked having his physicality appreciated, which his girlfriends did in one way and which Ronny, apparently, did in another. Sometimes Ronny felt he knew Ben so well he could tell what he was thinking from one moment to the next. After a while Ben said, "Sure I think you're crazy about me. What do you think you are?"

"About you?"

Ben's breathing was deep and even. He lowered one arm around Ronny's back.

"I'd have to be crazy to be crazy about you," Ronny said. "I'd sure be crazy to tell you."

Ben grinned and there was a feeling in Ronny that a sun had touched him, and sun-stuff showered through him, lit him golden. "You're right about that."

They watched each other for a moment, while the wind-up alarm clock ticked and ticked on the desk. Ronny said, "I don't know what you want me around for."

Ben looked out the window, a hand over his eyes. "Stuff."

"Yeah?"

Ben brushed hair out of his eyes, mood shifting, becoming somber. He was wearing a watch, took it off, leaned over to put it on Ronny's desk. "Why are you pushing me like this?"

"I don't mean to be."

"Yes you do. That's why you left the dorm today."

Ronny moved closer to Ben's face. Sometimes he felt unsafe there, in the space right in front of Ben. As if he might come to pieces from the intensity, as if Ben might push him away. Other times, like tonight, he felt invited. "Maybe there's not that much time," Ronny said, rubbing against Ben's stubbled cheek.

"What do you mean?"

"You're going to marry some girl like Jennifer. You're going to have kids and do all that stuff."

"So? That never bothered you before."

"Whatever we're going to do, whatever you and me are going to do, has to be now. See? That's what I mean. We're going to graduate in a year."

Ben stirred, pulled his face next to Ronny's, cheek to cheek, their bodies twined along the bed. Ben's skin was warm and his body solid, strong, almost trembling. "What do you want? You already had your hands all over me when I was drunk last time."

"I know."

"You took advantage of my boyish nature." He was still trying to make it all a joke.

"Please stop saying it that way. You were after me half that night."

Something flickered over Ben's face. The true wavelength of his longing. "Why did I have to work so hard at it if you like me so much?" He looked at Ronny, flushed, then looked away.

"I thought you were making fun of me when you told me what you wanted. I thought you'd tell your friends and stuff and I'd be the Ehringhaus faggot."

Ben grinned. "You're already the Ehringhaus faggot."

"Yeah, but nobody's got the goods on me." Ronny kissed Ben's cheek as tenderly as he knew how, and Ben made a low sound that meant he liked it. "Except you. I didn't trust you wanting me to do that stuff with you when you were so drunk."

Ben ran his hand through his hair, scratched his chin. "I could still say this is your fault and I don't know what I'm doing."

"I know."

"You don't care?"

"I care. But I can't do anything about it."

Ronny settled against Ben again and a moment later felt Ben's lips on his forehead for a moment. They stayed in that position, quiet.

"This thing with you having a room to yourself could be all right," Ben said. "Shift over this way, okay? I still want you on me."

"How long you going to be here?"

Ben shrugged. "Just be still. Okay?" His voice was deeply quiet, resounding from some depth, an exhalation. "This feels good," he said. "Lying here like this."

"I could do this for a long time." Ronny's voice felt hushed. Ben still had one arm around Ronny and tightened it.

"So what if I ask you now?" Ben was talking into Ronny's curls.

Ronny raised up on an arm, feeling Ben's heart beat under the thickness of his chest.

"You know. Ask you to do stuff."

Ronny closed his eyes, taking a long breath.

"Or what if I just start?" Ben drew Ronny's face to his. They kissed with their lips just open, sharing their breath. Ronny felt shivers along his skin and tasted Ben's chewing gum. Ben's breath caught and he turned his face away for a moment and Ronny rested his cheek against him.

"You don't have to do anything you don't want to, Ben. I don't try to make you do anything."

Ben swallowed and reddened, striking his flat palm on the mattress. Maybe he wanted to feel as if he were being coerced. Ronny lay against him, face near his neck, feeling the blood course under the skin. Ronny put his mouth on the place where a vein was pulsing, gently and lightly. Ben was waiting for something. He sighed, stirred, and it seemed okay to do more, so Ronny kissed all along his chin, kissed every part of his face he could reach. Ben's arm was tight against Ronny's back, and for a while it was hard to breathe. Ronny kissed Ben's lips and Ben made a sound and Ronny kissed his ear and touched his tongue to it.

So finally they were here and had to figure out what to do. Ben stretched like a cat, stood up uncertainly, looking at himself in the mirror on the wall by the closet. Ronny watched his expressions, wondering whether he would stay, or pull on his shirt and walk out the door, angry for a week, or a month, or forever. It was now or never, maybe. Ronny kept his mouth shut. Ben was grinding his jaw. "Touch me," he said. "Don't just leave me here."

Ronny stood beside him, touched his shoulders, his face, and leaned against him. Ben swallowed and stepped out of his jeans and laid them over the back of the desk chair. There was so much of him, his skin shining in the dark. Ronny felt the strangeness, the changing moment, a rising and sinking, same as before. He kept one breath and let it out and took in another and let it out but nothing changed, he was throbbing through and through.

"You get undressed, too," Ben said, and Ronny did, fumbling with zipper and jeans and socks and then bare, shivering in the warm air.

They stood close, pressed against each other. The fact that this aroused them was plain as night. Ronny thought he had better not try too much kissing but after a few moments Ben started it. Ronny let him lead, followed with enough hesitation that he did not seem too eager.

"You ever do this before?" Ben asked.

"No."

Voice quiet, gruff. "You're shitting me."

"No." Which was true. It was as if he'd been frozen in place, all through high school.

"Jesus."

"It's all right," Ronny said.

"What if I'm messing you up, letting you do this?"

"You're not. I know what I want."

In the dark room streetlight fell on them like gauze. The hardness in Ben's eyes was riddled now with something else, some point of vulnerability that a person could reach. Finally in that moment Ronny trusted he would stay.

Ben was easy to please and had no problem saying what he liked. They managed well enough at first and very well after that. Ronny had studied some pictures at Mac's porn shop on Franklin Street, and had watched some of the quarter movies when he had the change to spare. How hard could it be when he already knew how a penis worked? He tried to do the same things with his mouth and tongue and hands that he had seen in the movies, that he would have enjoyed if someone were doing them to him. His natural sense took over, and he could feel Ben's body respond when something felt right. Slow down, go easy, be smooth, oh, yes, that. When Ben's breath started to change, to shake him, Ronny felt warm, as if he was accomplishing something vital. Ben took over and put his hand in Ronny's hair and after that Ronny only had to try to keep up. Most of the time that was pretty easy. They felt like one thing, one flesh, same as the Bible called it, though maybe it was an odd time to think of that. But they were moving together, breathing together, feeling each other.

Ben shook and made a strangling sound, and a smell came off him, not like anything else, musky, visceral; and stuff spilled onto Ronny's hands and face. Ben was sweaty and leaned over Ronny, running his hands down Ronny's bare back. They had moved across the room and Ben had Ronny backed against a wall on his knees.

The plaster walls rang with sounds of traffic, a party at the frat house across the street. Slowly they pulled apart, Ronny getting his breath. He used a cloth to clean himself. Ben got in the bed and Ronny lay along him by the wall. The sweat was drying on Ben's skin and his nipples were starting to soften, their tips loosening. Ben's voice was so deep. He had a little smirk. "That was your first time sucking cock?"

"Yep."

"You like it?"

Ronny grinned, looked down at the tangled sheets, and nodded his head.

"You little cocksucker." Ben put his arms behind his head. "You did a pretty good job."

"Well, I guess coming from the big jock blowjob expert I should take that as a compliment."

"You should. I think you can be encouraged about your prospects." He was likely imitating one of his coaches. "With my tutelage and a little guts, son, I think maybe I can make a man out of you."

"Really, coach. You'll teach me how to suck cock at the pro level?"

Ben laughed, shoved Ronny's face hard into the pillow, twisted his arm, and held it there. Ronny gasped and tried to ease the pressure on his arm. He knew better than to complain. This was about being a boy, this kind of crap. Some of it was fun. A loud car passed, engine pulsing and heavy; a door closed downstairs; through the walls came muffled, distant voices. Ben let him go after a while. "That piss you off?"

"No. I'm used to you by now."

Ben shoved his face into the pillow again and got on top of him from the back, letting his whole weight hold Ronny down. "If you're used to it then maybe I need to turn up the knob some."

"Whatever."

He snorted. "You're no fun. You don't even squeal no more." He eased off Ronny to lie on his side and Ronny looked at him.

"I like it," Ronny says. "Besides, you're not going to mess up my night. Now I'm not a virgin anymore."

"Halfway not, anyway."

"What do you mean?"

"I got to pop you twice, once at each end." Ben was looking at Ronny intently. He was being funny but he meant it.

"Have you done this before with a guy?"

"Shut your fucking mouth before I punch you." He pressed against Ronny, shoved him roughly, scowling.

"Sorry."

Ben was breathing hard, then slowed down, trying to get himself under control. "I don't ask you about girls," he said.

Ronny said, in his ear, "That's because you know I don't have any."

"You little shit."

"You also asked me about guys before tonight, you know. You askcd me if I ever did anything with guys one of those nights we talked. Down in the study room."

"Who the fuck remembers back that far?"

"I do. I told you no, but I wanted to. I was reading your psychology paper. Or some paper. After everybody else went to bed."

Ben licked his lips, reaching for his watch, and checked the time. "Oh yeah. I remember now."

"See."

Ronny said, "You never answered my question."

"And I ain't going to answer your question. You pissed me off asking that. You got a smart mouth, you know. You're going to say something like that one of these days and I'm not going to stop long enough to think about it before I smack you."

"I'll try to watch out for that."

"You're a guy, there's no rule I can't hit you."

"You mean other than just plain ordinary civilization and all."

"Fuck you. You know what I mean."

Ronny leaned his head back under Ben's chin, and Ben pressed down and caught him there. For a long time they listened to each other, breath and heartbeat. Tuning out all the rest. Fine, dark beard on Ben's jaw, heavy. A curly hair in his nostril. Fine, tiny pores in his skin.

"What?" Ben asked, after the quiet.

"No, I don't know what you mean."

Looking at Ronny and then away, out the window. Sounds of beach music drifted from outside. "I mean, I don't want to hit you or anything but you get to me."

"Okay."

"That can be a good thing and that can be a bad thing. I mean, I like you get to me like this," bumping his partly erect self against Ronny's thigh, holding it there. "But you say this stuff that makes me nuts and I never know how I'm going to react."

Their skins grew moist all along their plane of contact. Ronny let him have the last word and lay there feeling their heartbeats, out of synch. Ben started to move again, sliding one arm around Ronny, reaching for Ronny's erection, the touch running through him like lightning.

"Get on the floor," Ben said, "on your hands and knees. Will you do that for me, baby?" His voice hung at the edge of Ronny's ear, hushed, but still commanding. "Do you have any baby oil around?"

"Man," Ronny said, shaking his head, feeling threads of electricity through him head to toe.

"You ready?"

"I think so."

"You asked for it."

"I know. Oh, man. I want to say stupid stuff to you. But I better shut my mouth."

"You say stupid stuff to me all the time. What's the problem?"

"Never mind. Yes, I have oil. You want to get off me so I can get out of bed?"

"In a minute. Now that we know what I'm going to do let's just think about it awhile." They lay there quietly. Ronny had one hand behind him on Ben's bare backside. Ben put his hand around Ronny and pulled on him again, rough skin on the palms, Ronny's breath changing. "You're as bad off as I am. You're not as big as I am but you're as bad off." He snickered.

"Vain."

"Did I ever tell you I saw Wee Neideroff tie his dick in a knot?"

"What?"

"No shit. This was all Tate's idea. He's a fucking criminal monster. The guys were giving shit to the freshmen. Anyway, Tate called the boys into the locker room and said he wanted to show them something. And the guys sat down and Neideroff comes right up butt naked and they're sitting on a bench, these kids, and Neideroff comes up and stands there and takes that big old dick of his and ties it in a knot. I'm not lying. Not a tight knot, you understand. Just kind of loops it. And one kid runs out of there as fast as he can and Neideroff walks around with his dick looped up, like he kind of enjoys it."

"You guys are insane."

"So what. We have to be insane." He rolled off the bed with a heavy thud. "All right. It's time for you to give it up. Come on."

Ben was gentle at first, rough pretty quickly after. He wanted another blowjob first, and then when he was ready he put himself into Ronny and they were together moving awhile. Ronny was so lost in being with Ben like this that the fact of what was happening, that this thing was entering him, was simple at first. Then he felt himself opened up, the pain of it, the pressure, and then the sudden pleasure; some part of his mind changed, he passed into a room of himself in which he was stripped of husk after husk of longing, the ache and hollow and echo and pulse of it was everything, the whole universe alive between the two of them. He found himself panting and making noises until Ben put a hand over his mouth. After that he kept the noise down mostly out of terror of Mrs. Delacy coming up the stairs on her blue-veined feet. He tried so hard in fact that Ben burst out laughing at him in the middle of sex and collapsed on top of him on the floor, still moving inside him. "You're too much."

"I don't want to get thrown out my first night."

"Then you shouldn't have picked tonight to lose your cherry."

"Oh, man," Ronny said. "This is amazing."

"I thought you'd like it."

88

Ben made him bark again and laughed. "This is what God made you for, little bitch."

"God help me," Ronny said.

Afterward the house was quiet. Ronny felt emptied, as if his self had poured all over the floor. Mrs. Delacy never came out of her room if she heard anything at all, and there was nothing but a sound of very quiet music from one of the other bedrooms. It was a weeknight but even so the noise from nearby parties was picking up, as was the sound of traffic on Cameron Avenue. Sneaking into the hallway, they saw all the other doors closed. Ben had grabbed one of Ronny's towels and they walked to the bathroom together, watching each other, their faces still and somber. They showered together in the cramped steel stall, dried off, and came back to bed. By then it was after midnight and Ronny was wondering how much longer he could keep Ben with him. The worst thing to do would be to ask again, so they lay down together side by side. "So, Brainhead," Ben said, "what's coming up for you?"

"I look for a job."

"I thought you had some job on the newspaper."

"I did, but, it's over. I'll probably get something making hamburgers or waiting tables."

He laughed into the back of Ronny's head. "Waiting tables? Don't you think you're a little too much of a dork?"

"Hey, I can do it. I may not be a high-powered college athlete like yourself but I can carry plates."

"You fall down a lot."

"I do not."

"You do. You fell on your ass in your room. You fell in front of the dorm at that beer party."

"I was drunk. I didn't fall so much as I slid down ungracefully from the vertical."

"You should try to find an office job. One where you can use your brain."

"Thanks."

"Just some friendly advice from your local high-powered college athlete."

"Wow. He even takes time for the little people."

Ben felt easy and light at Ronny's back; bright in spirit, at least; his body was comfortable and calm. He picked at something on his nose and wiped it on Ronny's neck. "Gross," Ronny said.

"You've had it easy, you don't even know what gross is."

"Yeah?"

"Gross is puking on yourself because you can't stop the drill to bend over or you'll catch shit from the fucking coach. And then having to smell it on yourself for the rest of practice."

"Okay. I know where this is going. I give."

"Gross is getting tackled and landing in the one fucking spot on the practice field where somebody walked their fucking dog and having your face guard shoved into dog shit."

"Ew. All right, that's pretty bad."

"You had enough?"

"Of the gross? Yes."

Ben's lips were close to Ronny's ears. "You think you're going to like this place?"

"For the summer, sure."

"You're back in the dorm next year?"

"Yes." Ronny turned around, facing the big boy, rearranging his legs.

"Okay, easy with that knee there, I hope to have children one day."

"Sorry."

"Settle it in there. That's right." Ben pulled the covers down and eased his head over Ronny's. He sighed. "Man. I'm tired. I'm not even partying. I'll get shit for this."

"The guys are out at the bar tonight?"

"What do you think? That's where we always are."

"You'll miss it if Tate eats glass again. I hear the two of you wrecked his car."

"I know. We were idiots."

Ronny kissed the inside of Ben's arm, which was traced with veins, hard. At one point during spring practice it had been covered with bruises; after that the bruises just went away and he could hit bricks with it if he wanted to, or so he said. Ronny asked, "Does he really need that paper?"

"The one for his grade? Shit, yeah. He was pissed about you. I think he was counting on it."

"Tell him I'll call him to find out what he needs. If it's not too long I can knock it out pretty quick."

"I wasn't going to ask."

"I know. He's a good guy in his own sick way."

"It could be worse. Some of the guys are out of control. Maybe all of us are sometimes. Chug-a-lug broke a hole in his wall at the beginning of the semester. Busted it through to the next suite. He's in a lot of shit about that. Another one of the defensive backs just shoved his hand through a glass door, did it yesterday. Cut his hand up bad. He said he just needed to hit something and he hit that door before and everything was fine."

"Shit."

"You said you heard from your mom?"

"She's moving to Nevada and getting married. That's why I had to get this place, I can't go to Goldsboro this summer because she won't be there."

91

"This place is a room."

"All right. This room."

"You talk about it like it's an apartment."

"I only had it one night," Ronny said. "I hardly talked about it at all."

The tension had left Ben completely; he gave Ronny an easy smirk, and tugged at his hair, a tiny, dull pain that flared and subsided. "That's what happens when they move out of the dorm. They get proud. Scoot over. I have to piss."

Ronny held his breath while the door was open. When Ben was done he closed the door, came back to bed, and crawled in again. "Somebody else is home."

"Is it late?"

"No."

"What about you?" Ronny asked. "What's up with you till summer school?"

"I told you, I'm not going to summer school. I go home. I take a trip to the beach. If I come back here it'll be to see you."

The trip to the beach would be with Jennifer, Ronny thought. But he decided not to ask.

"Jen's not coming to summer session either," Ben said, exactly as if Ronny had asked about her. "She's got an internship." Speaking as if it were normal, to have a girlfriend, to talk about her after sex with someone else.

"Yeah?"

"But I am taking her to the beach. I know you were wanting to ask." He yawned. "You mind if we get quiet and sleep a little bit? Then maybe you can do me down there again."

"Maybe I should put my back against you," Ronny said. "To keep from getting distracted."

Ben laughed. "You won't be any safer that way, boy. I can get you from either end now."

Five seconds of quiet and Ben was asleep, breathing peacefully, then snoring lightly against Ronny's shoulder. Ronny was ringing inside, a peaceful open feeling, the covers torn off him, his boxes opened, his windows wide. Here was Ben, warm and bare; here was a moment that ought to linger, a feeling inside which he would float, joyous, the rest of time, so why would he want to sleep? The fact of Ben inside him. Light on the wall rose and fell as breezes arced through branches. But he was tired, too, and drowsed some, drifted to sleep in spite of himself, and opened his eyes to find Ben watching him.

Ben had a teasing, playful look. "You woke up."

"Hey."

"Be still. Nothing's happening. I was just laying here."

Ronny put his head against Ben's shoulder and Ben held him there. Pretty soon Ben rolled onto his back and pulled Ronny on top of him. "You awake?"

"Yes. What time is it?"

"Three thirty."

Ronny pulled himself up level to Ben's face, his cheek against Ben's. "You want me to do something?"

"Not right now. Pretty soon." Ben murmured the words against his face, lips touching the skin. "I slept good."

"I did, too. I didn't think I would."

"I need to go pretty soon. I won't get so many questions as long as I get in the room tonight."

"What are you going to tell them?"

"I went to Greensboro to see my sister. Same thing I told Jennifer I had to do."

"That's Nina, right? Your sister?"

"Yeah. She's not out of school yet, either. Helps that she doesn't have a phone so Jen can't call over there."

"Not that I need to know what your cover story is."

"I wish I was coming to summer school now. It would be easier to see you."

"I can wait."

"What if I don't want to wait?"

Ronny kissed Ben's mouth, kissed it again. He had never really expected this from Ben, it was almost the best part. Ben closed his eyes and reached for Ronny's hair.

"How's your mom?" Ronny asked.

A heaviness came into Ben's voice. "She's starting her treatments. She says they're pretty horrible."

"I'm sorry. She's a nice lady."

"She still likes I'm hanging out with somebody who studies. She never liked me playing." He was about to say "football." Something shut him down at that point and he stopped talking and they lay there together. A wind was blowing the tree limb that hung over the roof of the porch, faster now. "Thanks for asking."

"You scared? For her?"

"I'm more scared for me. I should be scared for her." Ben rubbed his heavy hand in Ronny's hair, roughed it. When he talked about his mom, his voice had a calmer quality, and he shed the need for sarcasm. "The doctor says she's got a good chance. She's a tough lady."

"She's seeing the doctors at Duke, right? They're supposed to be really good."

"She had it diagnosed there but she's getting chemotherapy closer to home. She's got this really good Korean doctor. She says she can't understand much of what he says but he's got good nurses and they help her understand what's going on."

"Tell her I said hello."

"I will. I'm not leaving for another couple of days. I got an exam tomorrow and my last one the next day."

"You're kidding. Jesus, why didn't you say so?"

"It's Portuguese. All I have to do is show up." He was stroking Ronny's hair. A rare kind of peace in Ben's body. "How come you can ask me stuff like this and I know how to answer?"

"You mean about what exam you're having?"

"Don't be a shit. About my mom. She's been on my mind."

"I figured."

"Sometimes it's like you read my mind and shit. You say stuff I'm thinking."

Ronny wanted to say Ben did the same thing sometimes but held his tongue at the last second.

"Do I ever do that for you?"

"You did it a couple of times tonight."

"When?"

"When you knew I wanted to ask about Jennifer."

"Oh." He grimaced. "That one was easy to figure out. It was all over you."

"I try not to let it show. Except I can't help myself."

Ben gave him a look, a frown, and some of the peace ebbed out of the moment.

"I'll shut up."

"You were doing so great and then you had to start up about my girl."

As if that made sense. As if Ronny ought not to be bothered by the fact of Ben's girlfriend.

They were both awake by then, a little sweaty from contact. Even Ben was trying to keep quiet; the house was very still. They had been moving against each other, and after a moment or so the thought of Jennifer passed out of the room.

Near five in the morning Ben dressed and stood by the bed. "If we go downstairs I bet that old lady's already up."

The house was still now, except for the creaking of the old wood as the wind shifted it. "We'll just have to be quiet."

But Ben was opening the window over the bed. "I can climb out on the roof," he said. "She'll never see."

"You sure?"

"I can be real quiet when I want to."

Ronny stood beside him and put his hand on Ben's neck. Touching Ben had become easy when it had seemed so difficult before. An exit through the window did look like an easier way to avoid Mrs. Delacy, and she struck Ronny, too, as an early riser.

"I didn't break any rules though," Ronny said. "We're only not allowed to have girls in the rooms."

Ben gave him that look again, totally deadpan. Ronny ran his hand under Ben's shirt at the back.

"Okay," Ben said. "You'll get me started again."

"That's not much of a threat if you're trying to stop me."

"I do have to go."

"I know."

Ben rubbed his cheek against Ronny's, and they pressed together for a second. "Great night. You learned a lot."

"Asshole."

"You did."

Some kind of bird was singing in one of the trees outside, one of those pre-dawn calls that unfurled and extended impossibly far and high, a banner of sound. Ronny felt as if he might remember it all his life, a dawn calling, a morning bird, a sunrise soon to follow.

"I'm reading your mind again, I think." Ben kissed Ronny quietly, mouths mostly closed, Ronny's hand warm on Ben's shoulders. Ben sighed.

Ronny said, "I'm glad you came."

"Don't say bullshit stuff like that."

"Okay. Then fuck you, I hope you break your leg on the way down the porch."

"That's better." He stood there another moment, solid as the rising light. The sarcasm softened out of his face as he stood there. Anybody could see he wanted to stay. He said, "You got your wish though. Tonight. Right?" He chuckled, and slid out the window, needing no answer at all. Ronny watched as he crept down the roof and over the edge. Streetlight caught him at the curb, turning back, hands shoved in his pockets. He looked back, stood there a moment. Then he started a dogtrot down the street, stride after stride, so easy, the way he ran, as if he could go forever.

Odd Job

WHEN HE FELL NEARLY TO SLEEP a part of him would think, but Ben was here, but Ben was on top of me, surrounding me, and he said this, and this, and this. Ronny lingered over each word, each tone of voice, each change of expression. There was too much intoxication in the room for rest. So he lay there with his eyes open and his brain in a long monologue of memory, one image of Ben followed by another, one ache of longing and desire followed by another, as the morning came and the day brightened. As if he had to catalogue each moment, sort it all, to make sure he remembered.

There was a vibration inside him, a warmth, like a throb or a cooing, as though a peaceful bird had nested there, and it occurred to him how close this feeling was to the fear he felt at times that also settled in his belly and hung there, palpable. The same bird, only anxious and fluttery.

He dozed even so, off and on, until near noon he realized he had things to do and should stop pretending to rest. Behind all the happiness a part of him was fretted with his situation, the fact that he had twenty-odd dollars in the bank and needed to look for a job. He had promised to call Tate about the paper but no longer had a telephone. Mrs. Delacy had made it clear that she did not allow the boys to use her phone. So he rolled into his jeans and sweatshirt, bought cheap coffee at a convenience store near the stone church with its neat hedges on Franklin Street. He was headed across campus to the student union to use the phones in the *Daily Tar Heel* office; the walk through North Campus struck him fiercely, as if he were seeing it new. This was the oldest part of the university, scattered with trees, neatly mowed grass, haphazard plantings, buildings of different styles, ages, shapes, grouped roughly around McCorkle Place, where stood the Davie Poplar, a hoary bole said to hold the fate of the campus in its roots. Sacred space to alumni, the Old Well, subject of postcards and Polaroids, sat in its circle of shrubbery and bricks. People fought to live in the dorms on either side because they were among the oldest buildings on campus. Chapel Hill was like that—puffed up about its age, self-important as a city of bankers—but it was a lovable place. That morning it all struck him as fresh and clean and unfathomably wonderful.

The outer suite door to the newspaper office was locked so he used his keys. He had worked for the paper a year and a half and had been night editor this semester. It had amazed him, at first, that he could be part of the making of the student paper that he read every morning, that he could be good at it and then be put in charge of part of it. His job had been to oversee the graphic production of the paper in the evening. He had done a lot of different jobs for the newspaper and when that thought occurred to him as he walked into the suite, it gave him a notion for where to look for a job for the summer. But that would be later. Right now he made his phone call.

After a couple of rings Ben answered, with a lot of noise in the background, people yelling, bottles clinking. "Hey," Ben said. "It's hard to hear you. There's a baseball game over here in the stadium, we're playing Clemson and getting our asses beat."

Ronny wanted to sound casual, as if it were nothing to him to hear Ben's voice; he took a deep breath, ran a hand through his hair. "Sounds like Ehringhaus. You got some rest?"

"Didn't need it. Rested all I wanted to at your house. Laid down for a couple hours here but that was gravy."

"Man."

"What?" A note in Ben's voice, a softness that was unexpected.

"Well, I was calling for Tate. You're a nice bonus."

Hearing this quiet breathing reminded Ronny of that breath on his cheek. Ben said, "I told him you'd write it for him. He's jumping up and down. He says you're his pet faggot, too, now."

"Well, no, I'm not."

Ben's voice turned husky, the tone changed, as though he had pulled the receiver close. "That's what I want to hear. Stick with me and only me. That's the solution." Then his voice roughened again. "Fucking Tate just walked in." In his usual tone of athletic bluster.

"Okay. Well, I'll see you when I see you."

"There's no way to call you over there?"

"No. There's no phone in the room and I don't have the money to put one in, not for just three months."

"You need to make friends with that old lady. Here's Tate."

"Hey, little motherfucker," Tate said. "Listen. You do this for me and I owe you big. I'll buy you a big piece of pussy for your birthday, how's that?"

Ronny took a deep breath and put some effort into sounding blithe. He was looking down the long row of desks where the reporters sat at their typewriters and tapped out their stories. A couple of the sportswriters were sitting in their section at the far end. Ronny said, "I'm putting my moral and ethical well-being on the line for you, Tate."

"Then I hereby grant you the privilege of calling me Mule Man."

"Okay."

"Then do it."

"Okay, Mule Man."

"I like it. Say it again."

"Mule Man."

A deep chuckle, followed by a sound like he was hawking and spitting. "There. We're better buddies already."

"You're out of your mind."

"So?"

"What do you need?"

"I actually have a handout which I personally picked up from the class by attending it. You know about this Claudius motherfucker?"

"Claudius Nero Germanicus, the fourth emperor of Rome, one of the Julio-Claudians."

"Down, boy. Don't get yourself all excited. We had to read this dull-ass book about him by some writer man. Some novel shit, I mean."

"Probably *I, Claudius* by Robert Graves."

"That may indeed be the very book itself, Brainhead. So what do you need?"

101

Ronny sighed, watching the newspaper's business manager unlock the side door, dragging her heavy purse and a stack of folders. He had promised himself he wouldn't do this again, no matter how much he needed money, but here he was. "I have the book. I need the handout."

"When are you coming back to the dorm?"

"I'm not. I will not enter that stinking cesspit from hell again until the fall."

Tate snorted. "Unless Ben sends for you, and then you'll come."

"Not even for Ben."

"You're my pet faggot, too, you could suck my dick once in a while."

"Not on your life. Not even if Coach Dooley paid me. You don't wash it."

"My girls like me funky."

"You want to meet me halfway? I'm at the student union."

"Fuck, since you're writing the fucking paper, I'll come all the way up there. All you need is this shit-ass handout?"

"Why don't you bring your course syllabus if you still have it. And your copy of the book."

"Yeah, right. My course syllabus. It's so sweet you think I have one." He gave a booming laugh, and Ben said something in the background, and Ronny gripped the phone a little tighter.

Ronny said, "Okay. Well, just the handout will be all right. The library's open if I need any more books."

"You charging me for this?"

"You don't think I do it because I'm a Tar Heel born and a Tar Heel bred, do you?"

"When I bust you in the face you'll be a Tar Heel dead. You're so far piled up with shit you're going to fall off it one day. You're pretty sassy on the phone."

"That's because you're not looming over me threatening to break my face. Mule Man."

They agreed to twenty bucks, payable up front. Ronny waited for him on the steps in front of the union. Soon enough the giant came lumbering through the pine trees, swatting at something flying about his head, hair wild, catching the bright sunlight and blazing. Upright, Tate was about six four, so far past two hundred pounds you might have fashioned most of another person out of the overage. He had been a redshirt, too, a linebacker. Like Ben, he'd been frustrated to learn that he'd be held out of play this year in order to extend his eligibility. Ben had explained all this; Ronny knew less than nothing about football six months ago. None of the redshirts liked it, but the extra year made them want to play all the more. But Ben and Tate had lived through the year now and it was over. Tate crossed the street near Woollen Gym and sauntered up to Ronny with a piece of paper crumpled in one hand and a paperback book in the other. Grabbing Ronny by the back of the neck, he shoved him around the sidewalk a couple of times, like a playful bear, then let him go. "Here it is. You really think you can do this?"

Ronny blushed, a bit angry at being handled that way, but holding his temper, since this was Tate's usual way of saying hello. He scanned the paper, saw it was what he expected, mildly surprised that Tate had bothered to buy the book. Ronny took a lot of history and thought he knew the survey course that this paper was for. "Okay, sure. It looks simple. It's not even a very long paper."

"I know. I'm a lazy shit."

"I don't have to try for an A."

"Shit, no. People would know it ain't mine if it gets an A. I just want this fucking incomplete off my back."

Out of the dorm, big as Tate was, he had a more ordinary demeanor. His eye was still swollen from his car wreck, but in his jean shorts and baggy jersey he was less menacing. He still carried himself like a tank. At the moment he wasn't scowling, mostly because he needed the paper written, of course, but it was a pleasant change. There was something freakish about his bulk; he had a belly the size of a beer keg. A fly was still buzzing around his face and he slapped at it and cursed. Ronny said, "Sure. Okay. I'll get it done by tomorrow."

"You're shitting me."

"I already read that book over the summer last year. It's a good book. He's not asking you to write anything hard."

"She. This bitch is a she. Actually she's not even a bitch. I just never got the paper done."

"So."

Tate scratched his head. "You could bring it by the dorm tomorrow and see who I fuck tonight. She'll still be there."

"Hmm, no. Tempting but, no. Why don't I call you?"

"Yeah. All right."

"I can meet you here and you can take it to the history building."

"See there. That's why we call you the Brainhead." Tate thumped him hard on the back. "What's tomorrow, Friday?"

"Yes, Tate. Do you even know your exam schedule?"

"Are we having exams? Holy shit." A girl crossing to the brick sidewalk from Woollen was watching him, so he performed a rambunctious mating dance for a couple of moments and grinned at her. "Okay, Braindead, I mean, Brainhead, this is now officially exceeding my attention span."

"I need to get to work on this anyway."

A moment like a click. Tate dropped his persona for just an instant, giving Ronny a sidewise look. He had a good face just then, calm and friendly, the kind of person you might trust. "You're all right. You don't mind I give you so much shit?"

"You wouldn't give a shit if I did."

"You're probably right. But I'm in a good mood. I thought I'd ask."

"Why would I mind?" It was on the tip of his tongue to say more. He had to take a moment to stop himself. "It's all for football. I give back what I can. Minus the physical abuse."

"What physical abuse?" Tate shook him around the sidewalk by the neck some more and shoved him toward the steps, then handed him a crumpled twenty-dollar bill. "Go home. You got work to do."

"All right." Ronny felt himself bright and blushing. Relieved that he had some money in his pocket. People on the union steps were watching, maybe wondering whether he needed help. He ran hands though his hair.

Tate was grinning and pointed a finger at him. "And you don't do anything for that motherfucker Ben till you get mine done."

"Now, you know I can't promise that. I'll call tomorrow."

Tate headed back to the dorm again, all swagger and strut, and started to sing at the top of his lungs, lyrics from "Dancing Queen" by ABBA. Ronny shook his head. Somebody blared a horn at Tate from the road and he waved, disappearing into the pines.

Ambiguous

RONNY HAD NEVER INTENDED TO HELP anyone cheat and thought of himself as an honest person. In the spring of his sophomore year he had a class with Otis Pike, one of the linebackers on the football team, who sat at his desk in the basic newswriting class as if he were about to crash it to the floor, his bulk overpowering. Ronny recognized him from the dorm, lumbering along the concrete, his big hands wrapped around a tiny book or a tiny beer or carefully touching the tiny hand of a minuscule girl.

Otis looked fierce in the dorm but awkward in the class. The work was exacting, learning the principles of newswriting, the composition of a lead, the inverted pyramid of paragraphs (structuring each article so that it could be quickly cut from the end, the most important matter close to the lead), the use of sources, the number needed for veracity, the accuracy required. Ronny had already begun working on the copy desk of *The Tar Heel* a couple of evenings a week. He liked the way the reporters talked about their writing;

newswriting felt less precious than the creative writing class he had tried. So he took to it. Through the early weeks of term, the trees bare outside Howell Hall, the classroom cold, steam barely flowing in the radiators, he lost himself in study. He was accustomed to standing out in class, so it was no surprise in February, when the professor gave a team assignment, to find he had his choice of partners, Otis among them.

He agreed to work with Otis because they both lived in the same dorm, he claimed, even to himself. Otis was a good partner to a degree. A person could imagine being afraid of him on the football field, but sitting in his dorm room, talking about who to interview about the athletic department's compliance with Title IX, Otis was like any other student struggling to figure out how to do something he had never done before. He thought he might want to be a sportswriter, he said. He'd been involved in athletics all his life. It was he who suggested the topic for the article because his ex-girlfriend Amanda was on the swim team. She'd broken up with him at the beginning of term, but she'd made him think about whether the athletic department was doing everything it could to develop sports programs for women.

Otis had a slightly high-pitched voice, a way of furrowing his eyebrows when he was thinking, a nose that had been broken a couple of times, a poster of Joni Mitchell on his wall. Beside his bed on the windowsill was a worn Bible. Never crude in the show-off style of his teammates or of the other guys in the dorm, he talked haltingly, unwillingly, at first. But the two of them made a good team. Only later would Ronny find out Otis thought of him as a friend, in a way.

Otis wrote well if he had the time, but the class schedule required speed, and he had none, in terms of making sentences.

Sitting in Ronny's dorm room, cement block walls traced with shadows from the desk light, working to turn their notes into prose, Ronny witnessed the guy's struggle, earnest and even endearing. Hunched over his notes with a pen worrying at his lip, he fretted over interview questions, wondered whether his interview notes were clear enough.

The night before their story was due Otis said, "People always talk about what a lummox I am."

"Yeah, well. People are like that. People talk about what a sissy I am."

Otis grunted, nodded slowly as though his head were a great weight. "Dumb stuff." He had been scribbling on his legal pad and showed it to Ronny.

"That's a good sentence," Ronny said, looking it over.

"Maybe for the lead."

"I think so. But we've got to go faster if we're going to get this done." So Ronny took over the writing and typed the story with Otis looking over his shoulder. The two of them worked into early morning, going back and forth from notes to manuscript. Kelly had gone to his girlfriend's apartment for the night. Sirens sounded through the closed window, a typewriter banged and clattered. A blackbird hopped along the windowsill looking for food.

When it was graded, Ronny visited Otis and drank half a glass of beer. Ronny was used to excellent grades; Otis was surprised and quietly happy, holding the paper in his thick hand while Ronny looked over his shoulder. "That's something," Otis said. "Amanda would be tickled." He hoped she would come back to him, which was evident from the number of times he had mentioned her during the course of the project, as if she were keeping watch on him secretly.

"She would," Ronny said.

"Maybe you can help me out with the feature assignment. Just read it, you know. To check it."

About that time Otis's roommate came into the room. Ben Nickelsen and his girlfriend, Kathy Moore. She was a tall, pretty girl, freckled, with a sultry voice, smiling as she set her purse on Ben's desk, talking about her calculus professor, who was Eastern European, with one long eyebrow across her face, stretching almost as far as her ears, she said. Ben was sleepy and lay on the bed. Handsome, it was hard not to stare.

Kathy went on complaining about her calculus exam. "I just don't get that little 'f' thing. Do you?"

"Function? No, I never quite got it either," Ronny said. "I'm not a math person."

"What grade did you get on the paper, dude?" Ben asked Otis, leaning up on one elbow. Blue eyes pale and arresting, shaking his hair out of his eyes, perfect. Impressed when Otis showed him the grade. Ronny forced himself to look away.

After that there was a curious period of weeks until the end of exams—Ronny helping Otis with his feature story, Ben lounging on the other bed sometimes studying and sometimes pretending, Kathy with him sometimes and sometimes not. When she was there, she and Ronny kept up an easy conversation about their families, the university, the best places for omelettes, the terrible taste of beer, why Fleetwood Mac was the best band ever. When she was not, when Ben was studying and Otis was writing, Ronny helped them both, their private tutor, and in the heat of all that, feeling the draw of Ben's presence, he sometimes wrote for Ben; he also went so far as to write parts of Otis's feature for him—drawing the thoughts out of him, typing them onto the page, with Otis accepting this because he had no time, and Ronny had already finished the assignment himself.

Later, in April, Ben went out with his friends and trashed a parking lot in Carrboro, almost getting arrested. Kathy broke up with him, not because of the craziness but because there had been a girl involved and Ben had screwed her in the backseat of a car in the parking lot. Kathy had found out about it from Tate, who was also her friend—Ben never said much about the details, just sat slumped on the bed and kept his hands at his sides while Kathy berated him—which Otis told Ronny about. The whole sequence of events grew tangled to the point that it was hard for Ronny to understand—and he had become involved because he wanted to be there, close to Ben—and he knew why but he kept it out of his thinking when he was there—and Ben still had papers due and needed somebody to mind him while he studied—and there was Ronny, ready and willing, yes, to do almost anything.

One morning that May, near the end of exams, Ben appeared in the door of Ronny's room, shirt open, pretty skin showing, hair tousled from sleep, barefoot, hungover, quiet. Ronny had the room to himself by then; Kelly had packed and gone home. Ben padded to the bed and sat beside Ronny, put his hand on Ronny's shoulder, friendly, maybe a hint more. "I'm a piece of shit," he said. "You know it?"

"What's wrong?"

"I was such a shit to Kathy. She was a good kid."

"She was cool. Can't you call her or something?"

Ben made a face. Indifferent, resigned. "Nah. Might as well move on and fuck up the next one." Still the hand, heavy and tangible, rested on Ronny's shoulder, a sign of connection, but what kind? He hoped he knew better than to hope. He knew he could hardly stop himself.

But even if it was friendly and nothing else, it was there. Ronny said, "Yep, I guess you've got no choice. If your destiny is to ruin girls' young lives, you need to stay in practice."

Shaking his head, laughing, Ben said, "You fucker. That's mean. I kind of like it."

"You don't go home for a few more days, right? You still have time, you can find somebody else and probably wreck her life, too."

"Shut the fuck up." Snickering. "All right. I feel all cheerful and shit. You're a weird dude."

"I'm in good company."

"Otis thinks you're some kind of genius."

Ronny shrugged, spread his hands, looked modest, and Ben slapped his shoulder and then drew the hand away.

"You pulled my ass out of the fire anyway," Ben said. "I get to keep playing football because of you. You coming back to the dorm next year?"

"Oh, yes. I would not miss the apes of Ehringhaus for anything."

"Watch it. I might get offended."

"What, and throw me off the balcony or something?"

"No, I guess not. I need you around to keep my grades up." Scratching his head, then his elbow. "You still in town?"

"Till the dorm closes. I don't want to go home till I have to."

"I got that. Me, too. So maybe I'll bug you later." He said it as if he was about to leave but he went on sitting there, next to Ronny on Ronny's bed. There was something reassuring about the fact. A minute later he said something about his hometown, which was Turtletrack, Virginia, and Ronny chortled at the name and tried to make a joke about it. Ben slid against the wall, leaned his back there, put his feet on the edge of the bed. They talked until they were hungry, then drove to breakfast, along streets alight with new green, and talked some more.

African Violet

RONNY BOUGHT A COPY OF *THE Chapel Hill Newspaper* to look for jobs in the want ads, then headed back to Cameron Avenue, grabbed the copy of *I, Claudius*, and sat on the porch with it. A heat had settled over the house and yard in the late morning and his clothes felt heavy and sticky; soon enough the wind picked up and he wondered whether there might be rain. The porch was quiet, though he could still hear horns blaring on Columbia Street, which he could see from the porch, carrying all the traffic along the border of the university and into town, past the Carolina Inn and the row of fraternities. This was the week he would have moved back to Goldsboro if his mother had not found her current true love; there would have been no Ben to remember, no night in the boardinghouse. He wondered what that would have felt like, and how his mother was feeling now, headed so far away from North Carolina, where she had lived her whole life. The newspaper, unopened, accused him a bit from the floor of the porch. But reading the novel a second time was like visiting with an old friend. The writing was supple and evocative; he slipped into it easily and drifted there, in Rome with all the problems of an empire laid at his feet.

Mrs. Delacy was watching him. She had a very small flowerpot in her hand with one tiny African violet leaf buried in it. A few gardening tools were spread out neatly on a metal chair beside one of the porch posts. She adjusted her glasses and studied the space around Ronny, perhaps plotting her path around him. Her voice was hoarse, as though she had not spoken this morning. "Don't mind me, I just need to move this plant into the sun."

"Looks like you're rooting that."

"It's an African veye-let," she said, and the coloring of her vowels was beautiful, the elongated sounds, partly sung. The plant pot trembled in her hand. She moved with precise economy, settling the pot on the porch railing, withdrawing, leaning forward to look at it. "I love to grow them but mine never do." She pronounced that "do" with emphasis. "Well, sometimes they do all right. But I have one now that's dying so I'm fixing to root some more from the leaves. You must like plants like I do."

"Yes, ma'am. My grandmother liked to raise plants, and so does my mother."

"That's so nice. People who take care of flowers, you know. I like people like that."

Ronny laid the book in his lap a moment, watched a bird flutter into the yard, a robin grubbing for food. Remembering his grandmother's vegetable garden, her turning bean pods over on her palm, cutting okra with a sharp, quick knife, her scolding when he complained about the weeding, the bean shelling, the work. "My grandmother always had a garden when I was growing up."

"I used to have one here, back when I could keep it up. Can't no more. Sold that part of the yard a long time ago."

"You still keep up your roses."

She raised her head to study them, her fingers moving absently, long narrow bones and sharp nails, a gold ring on her finger, a small watch on the wrist. "Oh, yes, I can't let them go. They don't do so good any more. I can't prune them with my hands so weak."

He resisted an urge to offer to help her with the rose bed, or with other things, though he felt the impulse. He was always trying to endear himself to people. Desperate to be liked, said Lily, his constant critic. He said, "They look plenty healthy to me."

"They'll do. They'll do." Mrs. Delacy stood there another moment, then adjusted her glasses as if trying to bring him into focus. "Well, let me get on with what I'm doing. You go on and read, now, don't let me bother you."

He did as she said and she went into the house again, coming out after a few minutes with another flowerpot, the same size, with another tiny leaf in it, and set it beside the first. She brought out four pots in all, one at a time, and more and more he no longer noticed her frailty but instead saw the intensity, the efficiency, with which she went about her tasks; he could almost trace her thoughts. It would not do to root only one new plant because that one might not live. She should carry something in only one hand at a time so she could manage the screen door. The directest path from one point to another was rarely a straight line due to the furniture. Small steps were safer than large ones. Hurry only caused trouble.

"Do you think you're going to like your room?" she asked. "I hope so."

"It's a great room, I like it fine."

"I know it's small. It used to be part of the landing, back when we bought this house. Then we closed it in for storage."

"It suits me fine. All I need is a desk and a bed."

"Now don't like it too much because you can't keep it, you know. Even if I start to like you."

"That's all right. I'm going back to the dorm in the fall."

She was touching one of the pots along the top of the soil, pressing with her fingertip. "Lord, I hate how my hand shakes. You like living in the dorm?"

"Yes, ma'am. I figure I'll never get that experience again so I might as well know what it's like."

"What experience?"

"Living in a dorm with all those people around me."

She nodded but he was not sure she understood him, even so. After a moment she said, "Young people are all so bad these days. Noisy and all. And with the drugs. I don't like those drugs."

"I don't either, Mrs. Delacy. I don't even drink."

"Well, that's good." She was at the screen door. "You can call me Miss Dee, you know, like the boys all do. It's fine."

"Well, thank you."

I, Claudius

HE READ UNTIL HE HAD REMEMBERED enough about the book to know what to write. One part of him was already planning the paragraphs of the paper. Tate never would have read the Robert Graves book anyway, so was Ronny really depriving him of anything? Other than the failing grade he deserved, of course. But that was an excuse. The twenty dollars, though, that was an actual reason. He needed that. And this would be the last time he cheated. It would.

Upstairs, he settled at the desk with a pad. He enjoyed the work of study, reading and constructing arguments. The kind of exercise he needed to do for Tate's paper was interesting, too, because he had to write less like himself and less cleanly and correctly than was his custom. He only had to write a paper, not get a good grade on it. He had read Tate's writing before in order to correct it and knew the kind of mistakes Tate would ordinarily make. He could make Tate sound dumb, if he wanted. But he ought not go too far. It would not do, for instance, to discuss "that Claudius motherfucker," though that's what Tate would say. In a paper he actually wrote himself, assuming he had ever done such a thing, he would have distorted his voice on his own, for propriety's sake. But he would have done so awkwardly and halfheartedly. So Ronny did the same thing.

It was also interesting in the case of writing a paper for another person to think of himself as constructing an idea that this specific person might have. What kind of reaction might Tate have had if he had really read the novel? How would he have translated that into writing for a class? (Better to think like this than to wring his hands over what he had decided to do.) Ronny began to hear sentences in his head and wrote them down on the pad and pretty soon was fleshing out some of these into paragraphs, crudely drawn and partially shaped, with enough of an idea expressed, and enough strain showing in the idea, to convince the history professor that this was Tate's work.

"In Rome when Claudius lived there a lot of people were upset because of the emperor, who could not do anything about it. The emperor was a young guy named Caligula. In this book about him, Claudius, who was the uncle of Caligula, by Robert Graves, who was an English author, there are a lot of evidences of meaning, most of them coming from Claudius, who is telling his own story. His story is very revealing. Like in the first chapter." Ronny set out to write and was soon done.

He revised as he typed so the paper would look a little messy. The typewriter hummed and clacked, a thump at each carriage return. When he used Wite-Out to make a correction he drew little hills of white on the lines of type. It was like art, in a way, to produce such a fake. By the time he had done half the typing he realized he was starving, he'd eaten last when he bought the Hector's hot dogs the night before. Some of the

Graves text was sitting in his head as he walked. When he came back from grabbing a sandwich on Franklin Street, Jamal and a girl were standing in the living room of the house.

"How's it going?" Jamal waved at Ronny with a copy of *The Tar Heel* in his hand. "You feeling all at home?"

"It's quiet around here. This is going to work great."

"I know. A lot of the guys who live here don't stay in the rooms that much over the summer, but they want to keep them, so they pay the rent. That's the way it was last summer, anyway."

"You'll be around, I guess?"

He nodded. Arm around the girl, loosely, at the waist, a comfortable movement. "Ronny, this is my girlfriend, Sheila."

"Pleased to meet you," she said, and put out her hand. She had a long, sharp, bladelike nose dominating the center of her face so that she looked like a blonde crow. Her eyes were soft and luminous, green, with long, curved lashes. Her smile had a real sweetness and she spoke with a small-town drawl that made Ronny feel at home. "You guys just have the cutest house here. I love what you've done with it."

"Don't you?" Ronny agreed. "I crocheted all these doilies myself, you know. I get the good yellowy thread imported direct from Europe."

"All this hard work," Sheila said. "I so admire you."

"It's ruining my eyes but it's worth it. I want to leave a legacy."

"You guys should hush before Mrs. Delacy hears you making fun of her living room."

"She's out back in the yard, I think," Ronny said. "And I need to go anyway, I'm typing this paper for a guy."

Jamal grinned. "I thought you were writing something in there when I heard the typewriter."

119

"I hope it's not too loud."

"Oh, no. It's fine."

He found himself watching Sheila and thinking that she gave off a nice feeling; but she caught him staring and cocked her head a bit. "You're looking at my nose, aren't you?"

"No," he said quickly, and shook his head.

"It's okay, everybody does. I'm not self-conscious about it. Well, I am, but I don't care. My mom says it looks like a hatchet."

"I like it," said Jamal, and kissed her nose along the bridge.

"I really wasn't," Ronny said. "I mean, I was looking at it before, and then I thought what nice eyes you have. And then I thought you were kind of nice, or something. I get feelings about people."

"So do I." She smiled and crossed her arms over her chest. She had a small upper body and big hips; she was wearing a loose blouse, jeans, and sandals; and her fingernails and toe-nails were painted with glitter. "So what do you think my nose looks like?"

"I think it looks fine," he said, though he was tempted to tell her that he had compared her to a crow. While she was putting on a good show about it, anybody could see she was sensitive about her looks. Most people were.

They talked longer and agreed to go out to dinner together sometime over the summer. All of what they said was in the category of polite chatter, but there was something pleasant about it. He remembered Ben from last night—this morning, really—telling him not to say bullshit things. It was a nice idea for two people but tough in the everyday world. Anyway, politeness wasn't really the same as bullshit, was it?

That Obscure Object

LATER HE READ THE NEWSPAPER AGAIN and looked at the want ads, in the late of the day with shadows longer on the lawn, the house still quiet, a bit of music hanging in the air from the fraternity next door. Somebody was playing a Springsteen album over and over again. The page of job ads made him feel hopeful enough that he felt free to spend a bit of money that evening. He went to the Buñuel movie with Lily. It made him feel grown-up, sitting in an art movie house with Lily wrapped in her elegant scarves of white and gray, she enraptured by the beauty of it, the obscure object of desire, the thought of the phrase. Eating salty popcorn and watching a French film.

Afterward, in the pools of light on Franklin Street, standing across from the Intimate Bookstore, she asked, "Are you really sure you're gay? Don't get upset."

"You're not starting this again, are you? I thought you were done being angry with me."

"I am. I just wonder how you can be sure." Lily was one of those people who were born to critique the world and everything in it, but there was something warm and careful about her at the same time. She was the first person he had told he was gay. She had brought it up at odd moments ever since. Maybe something in the movie had reminded her of the conversation? It made him smile to remember what he had been doing the night before, and he almost answered her question more fully. He wanted to talk about Ben to someone. But he wanted to keep it quiet at the same time, to hold it solitary inside himself, lest he should break the spell.

"I'm sure," he said.

She gave him a moment of study, maybe hearing some new quality in his voice. Lifting an eyebrow, tilting her head. "Oh."

"What's that 'oh'?"

"Something's different." Warming, sliding her arm into his, walking toward the Carolina Coffee Shop, where they were headed for food. "Ronny, if you have a boyfriend it's a good thing. I really do mean it. I know I was weird when you told me. You know."

He put his arm across her shoulders and they walked side by side. It was a rare thing for him to touch her like this, or to touch anyone. A pigeon settled on the pavement ahead of them, took definite, considered steps toward a bit of crumb, then burst upward again, all feathers and blur.

"I'll tell you all about it when I'm ready," he said.

She appeared so very pleased with herself, it was charming to see. They went into the coffee shop and he had a long, lingering cup of coffee with a side of eggs and potatoes. She showed him her latest poem.

Later he said goodbye to her and came home, expecting to write in his journal and go to bed. Into the late evening he sat like that, in peace, reading awhile and stopping and thinking of last night, looking over the paper he had typed for Tate. His life was lost in the air, hanging out there somewhere, having become a cloud around Ben, as if that part of him were realer than this one; his physical body was sitting in a chair holding a book, his spirit was following Ben wherever he went. But after Ronny had read a few pages, the book caught him up again, and he forgot himself. He was close to the end of *The Brothers Karamazov*, in the trial section, when a knock sounded at the window, Ben's face pressed against the glass. Ben opened the sash, which had no lock, and slid over the sill onto the bed inside. He was grinning, proud of himself for climbing the roof. "Seemed simpler than knocking."

"Wow. What a nice burglar."

He clambered off the bed and pulled Ronny out of the chair. They came together easily, though Ben kept them out of sight of the window. "You have to get a fucking phone."

"I already told you I can't afford it."

"Make friends with the old lady, like I said. You can do it. She'll let me call you on her phone. I could get her to do it."

"I bet you could."

"I will, if I have to. I could have called you half a dozen times today."

Nice to hear the words, maybe too nice. A moment of happiness could feel almost like a wound. Ben was watching him; Ben was lost, too. Ronny said, "If you start calling me from your dorm room all the time Tate's going to wonder what's up."

"All I wanted was to talk to you. Tate wouldn't give a shit about that. Nobody else would either. Besides, I'm going home soon." He was tugging at Ronny's hair a little, squeezing the back of his neck, playing rough in a tiny way. They stood together like that, Ben framed by the streetlight from the window, his skin warm in lamplight. He smelled like soap and maybe a hint of earth. His jeans looked like he had worn them awhile. After a long breath he shook his head and stepped away.

"What's wrong?"

Ben shrugged, looked sullen. He walked around the room a bit, stretching. "Why do you make me be the one to kiss you all the time? Are you still scared of me?"

Obedient, Ronny put his hand in Ben's tangled hair. A hollow ache opened in him, sweet but hurtful. Ben was eager, nothing held back, reaching. They eased away from each other and opened their eyes and Ben swallowed and closed his eyes again and they came back together, the intensity startling, Ronny feeling an edge of its violence in Ben or in the air.

"The first time you did that to me I almost punched you. You ought to know I like it now."

"I was pretty stupid that night."

"It was just going to be like that the first time, that's all."

Ben was wearing a tight black tee shirt with a Harley-Davidson logo. He sat down in the chair and pulled Ronny on his lap. "You think what we're doing makes me gay?" he asked.

"You're the only one who can answer that."

"Bullshit. If I wanted to talk to fucking Buddha I'd have asked him. What do you think? I'm asking you." His face was clear. This was an important question, plainly, but he was far from being afraid of it. He took the thought like most everything else, like it was a problem he could beat down with his hands, that he could defeat with his body.

Ronny tapped on the edge of the desk, moving the pen there to another angle. "I don't think you are."

"Why am I doing this then?" He reached to touch a finger to Ronny's arm. Some curious tenderness in him. Ronny had never seen this mood before. "You know what I mean. I don't mean anything bad by asking."

"Maybe you just want to know what it's like. Maybe you've got a certain amount of this kind of stuff you need to work out."

"Stuff I need to work out?"

"Sex with me. Being with me. Maybe you just need to see what it's like for some reason."

"Maybe." He had closed his eyes and leaned his forehead against Ronny's.

"If you felt like you were gay I probably wouldn't like you anyway," Ronny said.

"That's fucked up. You don't like gay guys?"

"I know. I need to fix that. But not right now."

"Why not?"

Ronny looked at Ben. For the second night he felt this safety and steadiness between them. "Because I want to enjoy it while you're here. You won't be here long."

"You keep saying that."

"It's what I think."

He started to raise his voice and then caught himself and flushed. "Well, stop saying it to me. You're going to make it true that way." He leaned down to pull a twig out of his shoelaces and took a deep breath, followed by another.

Ronny pulled off Ben's shoes, kneeling at his feet, then guided him onto the bed and climbed onto him. As soon as he touched Ben to move him, the big boy chuckled and complied, his expression clearing. Ronny pulled at Ben's shirt and lifted it and Ben stripped the shirt over his head. "Got to have the body, huh?"

"I'm not stupid."

"Good thing I brought it." He chuckled again, giving Ronny the shirt to hang on the chair. "You're taking charge. Good boy."

They were quiet together for a second, faces side by side, touching.

"I'll stop saying that thing. You know. The one I'm not supposed to say."

"Talk to me a little bit first. I like it when you answer shit, you're so slick. Why do you think I'm not going to be around?"

At the moment Ronny felt no slickness in himself, not in thought or in speech; his heart was pounding again. He was speaking in a rush. "I don't know why you're even doing this with me. Except you're such a nasty son of a bitch, you don't care who sucks your cock."

"Hey, fucker."

"So I think you can find a woman and be with her just as well. You always have."

"Why ain't I doing that right now?"

"Because you have such miserable taste in women."

"You shit."

Ben wrestled him, rough, even play-punched him a couple of times, all contained so as not to create much racket in the room. They got into it and kept it up until Ronny was breathing hard, pinned in the corner of the room, between the bed and wall.

"You done?" Ben asked.

"Me?"

"Yes. You going to keep still now or do I need to give you some more?"

"I almost had you there."

"Uh, yeah. Dream on."

"I'm done."

"Want to know what I think?"

Ronny started to straighten out his shirt and Ben opened it for him. Unbuttoned each button, fingers large, concentrating, as if it were a difficult task. Ronny said, "Sure."

"I think what you think is full of shit."

"Yeah?"

"You're right what you say about me, mostly, you got that part. But you're crazy if you think I can feel like I do this last few days and just walk away." He was serious, staring out the window toward something in the sky. "Hell, last few weeks, really. I don't know what the fuck is going on with me. But I know I ain't going anywhere."

It was not the expected thing, had not been; Ben should have been angry, even the first time Ronny touched his shoulder, should have shoved him away, should have treated him as if he were a freak—he felt a freak—but Ben had yielded. There wasn't anything to say, though Ronny felt warm enough and happy enough at the words and wanted to believe them.

"I never meant you'd just leave me, Ben. But there might not be a choice."

"That doesn't make sense."

"What if you're all of a sudden a starting football player for Carolina, you think we'll be able to get away with this?"

The words had finally taken a shape that hit Ben without his having to think about them, words he could see, and he knew what Ronny meant. He pulled Ronny closer.

He turned over on top of Ronny and closed his eyes. "What the hell. Every good thing gets fucked up anyway." Lifting his head, he looked at Ronny, heavy and sad. "Right? We'll do the best that we can fucking do and forget about it."

"You all right?"

He sighed. "I'm fine. I was high all day from last night. I don't know what's wrong with me now."

"Did you talk to your mom?"

He was quiet for a moment. "Yeah. My old man is freaking out and taking it out on her. So she's got that to worry about on top of being sick now."

"He's not hurting her."

"Hell, no. I'd beat the shit out of him. He hit her once when I was fifteen and that was the last time he ever did." Rubbing his eyes. "No, he's just getting scared about what's going on with her. And he's fighting about stupid stuff, she says."

"It's probably all he knows to do."

"Yeah. Well, he's got to do better than this. I'm going home tomorrow after my exam." They watched each other. Ben was considering something. He said, finally, "That's why I had to say fuck it to summer school."

That brought a heaviness to the room, and Ben opened his eyes again. Ronny kissed his face quietly and they held still. Ben said, "I'm staying all night tonight. That all right?"

"Yes."

"I won't see you for a few days. It's going to drive me crazy if I can't call."

"I'll talk to Miss Dee tomorrow. I promise."

"Can't we just get you a phone? I don't have much money but I got enough for that."

Without warning, the words that Ben was saying—as if it were perfectly natural for him to want to get Ronny a phone, so simple and clear, as if they had always been close like this—pierced Ronny all the way through. The feeling came so completely and penetrated so thoroughly he could not breathe, as if he were washed in the purest joy that contained the purest pain, and neither could ever be separated from the other. Whoever wanted to feel one had to feel both. For a moment, Ronny thought he understood his mother better. Following love, as she did, from one place to another. He was quiet, and Ben leaned up to look at him. "What's the matter?"

"Nothing at all." His voice shaking. "Everything feels right, as a matter of fact."

Ben pulled him tight again, lay there beside him. "I know. Just hush. Stay still."

Ben was shaking some, and Ronny gripped him hard. "You feel it the same way I do," Ronny said. "About not having time to waste."

"What makes you think so?"

"That's why you want me to get a phone."

Ben considered the notion. "Maybe. Truth is, you little fucker, I want to be able to talk to you."

"Okay," Ronny said. "I'll do it. What the hell. I'll have a job, I'll work it out."

"I told you I'd give you the money. Don't even fucking think about getting proud with me."

"No. That's fine. I'll need help if I'm going to do it now."

"Mom wants me to bring you home for a visit."

"Yeah?"

"I keep talking about you, I guess. How you help me study. Stuff you say." They were too close now for Ronny to see his expression. "I'd like to have you there."

"Just say when."

"When are you getting a job?"

"As soon as I can."

"Well, I have to take this trip to the beach. Maybe I can come and get you after that. You should know when you're working by then." Ben sighed. "I'm taking Jennifer to the beach. I wish I had a gun to blow my brains out instead."

"Hush."

"She's better in a crowd."

"Sounds like true love is no longer running so true."

"Shut the fuck up. Don't say I told you so or I'll smack the shit out of you. Don't think I won't do it. I'm not letting you get out of hand."

"I'm not saying anything."

"How come we're not already fucking?" Ben asked.

So they did, starting then with conscious ease and running through the whole repertory from the night before, with variations. Ronny got lost in it all, the movement of his body leading him into new territory, Ben furled over him from behind, breathing against his neck, arm around Ronny's waist, the two of them blowing and making sounds, sweat running along the place where their skins came together. Such a fire, this pleasure was, coursing inside and out. They both had the feeling that this was merely the edge of the thing they could do and be. Nothing in that moment had anything temporary in it. In the midst of the thought they looked at each other and understood it and never said anything about it.

When they were done and settled in to talk again, Ronny asked, "Where does she think you are tonight?"

"Jen? We had a fight."

"Oh."

"What a piece of shit I am, telling you what a great day I've had and I just had a fight with my girlfriend before I came over here."

He was ignoring the fact that he was here in the first place, cheating on her; but that was how he was. He and Jen had only been seeing each other for a few weeks. Listening to Ben complain about his girlfriends had become part of the game. Ronny kept his face turned carefully away but Ben pulled it toward him.

"Hey," Ronny said.

"I just wanted to see the smirk."

"Is it there?"

"Shit yes. You know it is." He threw himself out of bed onto his feet, landing quiet like a cat. "Let's just don't talk about this anymore, okay? I'll be right back. Any of your roommates here?"

"I don't know." Ronny stood behind him, went to the door.

"Oh, to hell with it," Ben said, and opened the door and walked naked into the bathroom. He strutted, in fact, and pissed with the door open, and watched Ronny, and came back the same way. He closed the door and pulled Ronny against him. He said, "You read my mind again tonight in a serious way."

"When?"

Ben shook his head. "I'll tell you one of these days."

"Okay." Ronny leaned against Ben, trying to lend him some calm. He led Ben back to bed after a few more moments, and they fell into sex again immediately, the luxury of being twenty and tireless, wide open in each other's presence. That time they were both shaken and lay trembling and getting their breath, tangled on sheets on the floor, Ronny's head almost under the fabric of the closet divider.

"I don't have to hold anything back," Ben said. His upper lip was covered with sweat. "Man."

"Sure doesn't feel like you are."

"Am I too rough?"

Ronny laughed. "Oh, man. No. Not a bit."

Ben laughed, too, looking at Ronny's face. "What a shit-eating grin you've got. Did we get down here on purpose or did we fall off the bed?"

"I think it was a little of both."

"Man. Any other time that would have cracked me up." He picked up Ronny and the mess of sheets and carried him back to bed. "Even if it is May it's too fucking cold to be on the floor. You warm enough?"

"I'm fine. Oh, man."

"I guess I'm doing my job up here," Ben said, flexing his arm and grinning.

"Don't look so smug. You were there, too."

"I know." Ben chuckled. But he looked happy, and calm. "You want to change any of what you said before? About this thing we do not lasting too long?"

Ronny looked thoughtful and turned his back to Ben, pressing back against him at the same time.

"What?" Ben waited for a moment. "What?"

"Maybe you're right."

Ben rested his head, said nothing, breathed out slowly against Ronny's ear. He whispered, "So, what?"

"So we do what we want and the world finds a way to fuck us big-time."

"You're so full of it."

Ronny shrugged. "Not really. I mean, so what if it does. I can take a fuck."

Ben cracked up, had to lean off the bed for room. He laughed and reached over to turn off the lamp. They lay in darkness with only the streetlight pouring in. Ben was still chuckling. "Yes, you can," he said.

"Sweet man."

"The fuck I am." He bumped Ronny's butt with his hips, hard.

Ronny turned around and, as soon as he did, knew what would happen again. Easily and gently, rocking back and forth on the bed.

"You don't get tired," Ronny said. "You're not even out of breath."

"Conditioning. And fucking gut checks."

"The torture drill things?"

"Not torture. You got to weed out the weak little runts who can't cut it." He grinned to show he meant nothing by it.

"I know I'm a runt."

"Nice runt. Right now you're my runt."

"That sounds nasty."

"Don't it?"

Ronny mussed his hair, touched the curls. Ben pressed against the fingers. "This is sweet," Ben said. "But you can't expect this part to last. The getting lost while you're screwing because it's so good part. The fucking over and over again part. It goes away after a while. That much I do know."

"Who was your best girl?"

He studied for a moment, poked out his lips a bit. "At this point it could be you."

"I'm not a girl. Don't talk about me like that. Really, who?" By then he'd heard something about them all.

He sighed. "Kathy, probably. She was a good kid. Two months was a record for me, right? I fucked that up."

Ronny shrugged. "Maybe."

"You got a critique of her, too?"

"No, I liked Kathy. We could talk."

"I know."

"She's probably still around."

"No, I think I fucked that up too bad. What are you doing trying to marry me off, anyway?"

"I'm just talking. It doesn't make me jealous at the moment."

"That's because neither one of them is here now."

"Yeah. I know. Sorry."

Ben butted his head gently. "They'd be the ones jealous right now, you know. Little bitch boy."

"Yeah. Scoot up a minute."

"Okay. That's good." Ben settled onto him again. "Why don't you like gay guys?"

Ronny was lying on his back now, inside Ben's arm. Ben's other arm was crooked behind his head and he sprawled one heavy leg onto Ronny, who said, "I was hoping you'd forget I said that."

"I didn't. There's something really fucked up about it."

Why was it so easy to talk tonight? If he stopped to think about it he would lose the feeling, so he took a breath. "It's just something I need to work on. Like I said."

They lay there listening to the clock ticking, a car passing on the street, lights splashed against the wall. Ben said, "I had to know you were not really a sissy before I could think anything about you."

"Yeah? But I am a sissy."

"When I called you a faggot and you blew me that kiss. I don't know, maybe it was the way you did it. You cracked me up. You always crack me up." There were sounds from the house, the toilet flushing, someone's door closing. "You think your roommates will rat us out if they hear us?"

"I don't know these guys yet. Jamal won't. I don't think."

"I need to come over here and meet this Miss Dee lady, and work on her."

"You going to charm her?"

"Don't laugh. I bet she loves football players. Ask her. I'll bet you the price of the phone."

"I ought to take you up on that but I know I'd lose."

"Pussy."

"Look at you, babe. You're solid charm head to toe, when you can remember not to spit."

Ben chuckled. "My mom's going to love you, saying that kind of crap."

"I might not say it in front of her."

"Oh, please. You can't keep your mouth shut."

"I can for a while."

"Yeah. But once you get started."

"How long do her treatments last? Another month?"

"They don't even know if the tumor's going down yet. She finds that out next week. She gets a break after three more weeks from the chemo stuff but she may have to do more."

"Maybe that's when I should go, when she's on a break."

"What if she wants you to come earlier?"

"Would she?"

Ben shrugged. "I think maybe she knows something's going on. I don't know. I get the feeling."

"Us?"

He nodded. "She hasn't said anything. She asks about you but it's not like she's asking about a friend of mine. She wants me to know she thinks something different about you. At first I thought it was because I told her you were smart and I could talk to you. She's about the only other person I was ever able to talk to. But now it's like that and something else, too, and I don't know what, so don't ask."

"You could just be self-conscious and that's all it is."

"Don't be such a hardheaded dope. She's asking you to come and visit when she's sick with cancer."

"Yeah, you're right. I'll come whenever she wants me to and you want me to. I'll go tomorrow if you want. I can get a job later when I get back."

"I'll ask her. I need to get this trip with Jen out of the way but I'll ask her. You're right, why not just find out when she wants us to come."

He said "us" and "we" so easily, even more so than Ronny, who could only do that in his private thoughts. A mother would hear that.

A boy like Ben was smart enough to have one voice for his mother and one voice for his buddies in the zoo.

A boy like Ben could put a voice in his body and say with it, silently, I need you while I'm afraid like this. Please don't make me admit it.

"I'm hungry. You want to go somewhere?"

"Is there anywhere? You know."

He shrugged, blew out his lips in a fart. "I don't care if anybody sees me with you tonight. Everybody knows we're friends now. Tate's talking so much shit about you to his buddies you'd think you saved him from hellfire."

"Well, tell Tate to be quiet about this, please. I don't want to end up in front of the honors court. I'm not writing any more papers for people."

Ben was already pulling on his jeans. "Suit yourself. You're the one who started that shit. We'll go out the window. I like doing that, it makes me feel like fucking Romeo."

"Those guys in the frat house are going to see."

"That old lady in the bedroom is going to hear if we go downstairs. Besides, there's a tree between here and the frat, you can't see anything up here. Look."

"Now I'm a fucking gymnast," Ronny said.

"That's the spirit. Don't be chickenshit or you're going to fall again." Ben was opening the window. He had paused to look at himself in the mirror, running fingers through his hair.

"I'm sober now, I'm not going to fall."

"I guess we better not get drunk tonight, huh?"

"No. Not if we're coming back here up the roof."

"I'm not ready for that, anyway."

"Why?"

"I'm a nasty drunk."

It was like that, the talk too fast for pauses, for thought, so that each one ended up saying more than he planned, and the words tumbled faster. They were on the roof by then. For all his bulk Ben made very little noise, and Ronny was full of enough adrenaline that he managed all right, without help, all the way to the ground.

They drove to a place in Carrboro that was open all night, Breadmens, where the parking lot was full and a tow truck was hitching up a VW van to haul it away. Ben drove an old Impala, bottle green, the size of a small boat. It was already after five a.m. by the time they got to the diner. Siding of old metal, rusted, glass door grimy with use, in need of washing, like the worn-out mat on the tile floor inside, the feeling of grease in the air. Booths along the wall, bedraggled patrons, hippies with ripped jeans and flip-flops, staff in jeans and tee shirts, laminated menus on the Formica tabletops. Everyone looked surprised at the hour, at seeing so many people, a bubble of commotion in a sleeping town. They picked a booth at the front and sat facing the kitchen. "Where you going to look for a job?" Ben asked.

"*Chapel Hill Newspaper.* I read an ad that said they need people to do pasteup."

Ben was smirking, spooning sugar into his coffee. "You might as well go ahead and tell me what that means. I know you want to."

"That's when you put a newspaper page together. The articles come out printed on this photographic paper and you put hot wax on the back and paste them onto a big sheet. You make the whole newspaper page up like that and then they take a picture of that and print it."

"You know how to do that?"

"I did pasteup when I was night editor for *The Tar Heel* and I bet I can get a job doing that at the other place."

"When would you have to work?"

"I don't know. Depends on what they need. Days, I hope."

Ben was watching other people come into the restaurant, emerging out of the dark. The streets looked lonely now that the tow truck had pulled away, and the restaurant was quiet in an early morning way; there was a sense that this was a hidden world, maybe because of the hour. The waitress had holes in her jeans, freckles, big frizzy hair, too tired to say much, just writing down the order and bringing the food and the check.

By the time they finished eating, the sky was alight and birds were making the tops of the trees echo and ring. They took a drive along one of the farm roads, as far as Harland Creek. A low bird went swooping dark-winged along the creek as the car passed. Ben turned off the radio and they listened to the car and the rush of wind through the open windows.

On the ride back to town the talk went on; now they were open to it the words flowed back and forth. If we were driving somewhere right now. On a trip. Where would we be headed? New Orleans. Oh, that would be wild. But farther, maybe. Heading west. Grand Canyon. I'd kidnap you. You'd be all, like, I got to get a job, I got exams, I got to read a fucking book, and shit. No, I would not. We could drive to Las Vegas. Oh, sure, and I could go to my mom's wedding. And that story. And other stories about her; Ben laughing, shaking his head. You're the one who's the wild child, he said. Not me. My family is more, like, normal than that.

What do you want to do after all this? When you're not playing football anymore. Coach? I can't see that, not really. Me? I want to work on a newspaper, I guess. Or write stuff for a company. What I really want to do is read books for the rest of my life. Fuck that shit. If you're around me you're not sitting with a goddamn book in your lap the whole day. I'll get a motorcycle. We'll go places on it. Costs next to nothing. We'll just get stupid little jobs and bum around. Go up to Alaska. I think I'd like it up there? I don't know why, just like it's in my head.

Near town Ben slowed the car and went back toward the boardinghouse. He parked on campus near the formidable mass of the science buildings, some of the windows still showing light, steam rising from the air handling units. As they walked back to Cameron Avenue, they saw Mrs. Delacy sitting on the porch, which gave Ben a bit of a start. Likely he was picturing himself climbing down that porch post only to find her sitting in this wooden chair. From somewhere in the neighborhood echoed the crowing of a poor urban rooster.

When Ronny introduced them, it was clear enough that even had she been sitting there during one of his climbs, Ben would get a good shot at escaping undetected. There was no question of her hearing them on the roof or, likely, on the stairs outside her room, not if they were the least bit careful. Her world was smaller than that. But she did seem aware of Ben's charms, even though she could not see him clearly.

"You boys look like you've been out all night," she said. "You college boys burn the candle at all three ends."

Ben liked that and snorted. Ronny said, "No, ma'am, Miss Dee, we were studying. We have exams now."

"Where were you?"

"In the library."

"My lord. You must be something tired. If I read the least thing I fall asleep."

Ben laughed and bent on his knee toward her. "I do that, Miss Dee. Books put me to sleep as soon as I open them. That's nothing to worry about."

"You must have a tough time with the studying." She laughed a cautious laugh and adjusted her spectacles. "You go here to school then. What was your name?"

"Ben. Yes, ma'am, I go to school here."

"Well, where are you from?"

"Right across the line in Virginia." He sat next to her chair on the porch.

"Miss Dee," Ronny asked, "what do you think about me putting a phone up there?"

"I don't think anything at all as long as you turn the ring down and pay the bill. There's been a phone up there before, there's already a line, all you got to do is get them to turn it on."

"Yes, ma'am, I think I'll do that, then."

"Mind you pay that bill now. God don't like a deadbeat." She had an old album of photos on her lap, unopened. Had she been looking through them before? "You boys headed upstairs?"

"Yes, ma'am."

"Go right on in, we're open for business. Wake some of these lazybones up."

They slept for a while. Ben snored and drooled on Ronny's neck. Ronny drifted between sleep and drowsiness, pressed against the wall by Ben's weight or under Ben's heavy leg.

About ten Ben woke up and Ronny watched as he tried to open his eyes. He fumbled for his watch. "You awake?" he asked.

"Yes."

He lay back down, felt for Ronny, covered him again and put a leg across him. He sighed. "I have to go."

"I was about to wake you up."

"I know. Oh, man." He shook his face hard and blew out a breath.

"No more exams after today?"

"This is it. I'm headed out right after. I put some money on that desk last night for the phone. I wrote down my number at home so call me when you get it."

"I have your number at home right here." Ronny pointed at his head.

Ben grinned, looking more awake. "You're going to the phone company today, right?"

"It's Friday. They're not going to turn it on the same day I put down a deposit."

"Go right now," Ben said. "Maybe they will. You can at least try."

Ronny got out of bed, hearing the tone in Ben's voice, the strain and the thoughts of his mother. That was when Ronny reached in the closet for a shirt and spotted an old phone on the shelf. He pulled it down and showed it to Ben.

"All right. Mother fuck, would you look at that."

"Write down this number," Ronny said. "Maybe it's like the dorm phone and I just get the number turned on or something."

Ben scratched it on paper torn out of Ronny's notebook and shoved it in his back pocket. "It would shit be nice if it was that easy."

"You want to take Tate his paper?"

"You mind if I don't?"

"No."

"I don't want to tell him anything if I don't have to. He don't need to know where I been all night. I need to stay cool for my exam."

"What class?"

"Geology. That's why I made you review my rocks last night." He was awake now and enjoyed his joke. At the door he said, "The taste of my mouth sucks, you might want to stay away from me."

Ronny kissed him on the mouth and he shut up. He tasted fine. Maybe at first a little sour from overnight, but that passed. The kiss went on too long and started again and Ben said, "Maybe we shouldn't have done this," pulling Ronny against him.

They were quick, though, and quiet, and then Ben was gone.

Brainhead

HE WALKED TO THE PHONE COMPANY office on Franklin Street carrying Ben's cash in his pocket, the morning air thick with moisture, clouds overhead growing heavier, the weight of a flood on his shoulders. He sat in the hard wooden chair to which he was directed, filled out the proper forms using a pen that had an untidy tip, blotching stains of ink on the paper, and carried the result to a woman with a name tag that read Hollenholler, a thickset person with bright skin and large, mournful eyes, dressed severely in black, buttoned to the neck, two white round earbobs on her ears. She smelled of roses and lime or something like that, pleasant, and when she talked to him she had the aspect of a religious acolyte, the sister of an order of helpful nuns. She asked why he was staying in Chapel Hill for the summer and whether he had a job. He answered yes, meaning his job at *The Daily Tar Heel*, which he did have, in a technical sense. At any rate she was not very curious.

On her desk was a wallet-sized photo of a child, a girl with braided hair and ribbons, and she picked it up during the conversation, running one perfect nail over the image, then setting it down again.

She took his deposit, which turned out to be smaller than he had expected, informed him that service would be turned on no earlier than Monday, and that he would have a new phone number, which she supplied to him on a piece of notepaper from a scratch pad on her desk—not a whole piece of notepaper but rather a ribbon that she sliced precisely with scissors that she removed from her drawer and then replaced. "Everything must be done just so," she said. She handed him the new phone number with a slightly dour expression. She sounded sincerely informative and familiar, a low voice. "You can pay the bill here every month; we have a cashier window that's open six days a week. Or you can send us a check through the mail, though in my opinion that would be a waste of a stamp."

"Yes, ma'am," he said, and she nodded that he could go now, so he stood from the chair and left the building and thought, I will have a phone soon.

He walked to the *Chapel Hill Newspaper* offices and talked to the receptionist, who told him the composition shop needed a person to do pasteup three days a week, that he should fill out an application and come back on Monday. The receptionist had a thick head of silver hair put up in a chignon, looking stylish; the rest of her was dressed for comfort, a loose tee shirt and faded jeans. She said that the people in the composition department would probably be pleased that Ronny already had experience in page assembly, to make sure he wrote that down. The application was short. He wrote on the back, "I already know how to do pasteup; I worked for the *Tar Heel* and did a lot of their pages last fall."

Walking through the light rain that had begun to fall, he sat in the student union until Tate appeared to fetch the paper on *I, Claudius.* Tate called him one brainheaded useful motherfucker and gave him a swat on the shoulder that all but sprung the bone out of the socket.

By evening rain was falling steadily over the parking lot and raising a mist in the pines near the football stadium. He sat in the *DTH* office for a long time, the space unnaturally quiet, desks clean, wire printers turned off. He had been thinking of Ben through the hours, holding the thought in his head, warming himself by the memory, by the fact of what had happened over the last semester. Finally he decided to call on the newspaper's phone, even though he could get in trouble for it. He had access to the long-distance line in the morgue, the home of back issues of the newspaper, to which only editors had the key. Closing the door behind him, he felt like more of a criminal. In Sunday school—when his grandmother took him there—he had heard stories about people who took a first step on the path to sin, and then a second, lured ever forward by the promise of easy reward. Maybe he was on such a path himself, writing papers for Ben, then Tate, now stealing long-distance phone time. Having feelings for a boy was another sin. He stood among the volumes of old *Tar Heels* smelling acrid; the room held copies of the paper all the way back to the Thomas Wolfe years, but the big books were so dusty he was afraid to dial the phone until he had a good sneeze.

He called and Mr. Nickelsen answered, deep and loud. "He's around here somewheres, Ronny, I'll find him. Keep your shirt on." Coughing, fumbling with the phone, muffled sounds.

"You got it?" Ben asked, picking up the line with no warning.

"No. I mean yes, I got a phone but they don't turn on the line till Monday."

"Where are you calling from?"

"*Tar Heel.* I'm in the archive room with all the old papers. It's cool."

"So is the number the same?" Ben asked, and Ronny gave him the new one, and they sat listening to each other breathe. Ease passed into Ronny like a wave.

"I have some money back for you. It cost hardly anything except the deposit."

"Keep it till I get back. Use it if you need it." Ben was breathing like he was walking around. "I want to sit down. Can you talk?"

"Not too long. I don't want this call to stick out. But yes. Exam?"

"Went fine."

"Don't make any bad jokes about rocks, please."

"Fuck you, that was a good joke. If I can figure out how to tell it to Tate without compromising our security, I'm going to."

"You sound pretty cheerful."

"I feel better now I'm home. I just got here twenty minutes ago."

"I didn't even think about that. Seven o'clock."

"It's not that far. Right across the line. Mom's up and feeling pretty good. She's off from treatment today, we go in tomorrow."

"You holding up?"

"Sure."

"You'd tell me, right?"

"Yeah. I think so. You'd probably know anyway." He paused. "You know I don't like to say stupid stuff or fucking chitchat stuff."

"Am I doing that?"

"No. But that's why I'm not saying much. Like it's good you called. Which it is."

Ben still sounded all right, his breathing normal. "Say something," he said.

"It's all right if we just sit here," Ronny said. "You don't have to say anything. I don't want to say a bunch of chitchat stuff either."

"You'd piss me off bad."

"I know. So."

"Tomorrow's going to suck," he said. "She has to go in on a Saturday, that's fucked."

"You want me to call again?"

"Yeah. You mind?"

"Nope."

"Use that money if you have to."

The next silence was not frightening, and longer. Ronny said, "You must be feeling like you don't know where you are."

"Yep. She's lost a lot of her hair. Her skin's gray. She weighs nothing."

"I wish I was there."

"I'm all right."

This verged on stupid stuff, and chatter, and so Ronny shut up. "I guess I could talk dirty to you but I don't think I'd be very good at it."

"You can't even cuss."

"No?"

"Not worth a shit."

Ronny laughed. "I'll learn."

"You're like some fucking preacher's kid."

"The preacher's kids I know are mostly just a mess."

"See."

"I should probably get off soon."

"Yeah."

"You staying home tonight?"

"Me and Dad are making dinner. I know you got to go. Call me, okay?"

"Yeah."

"Hey. How about your job?"

"I have to go back Monday morning and talk to the shop supervisor. They need somebody for part-time. Which is probably enough for me to live on if they pay something decent."

"Oh, sure. It's Chapel Hill, remember? Who pays students decent? I work like a dick for room and board."

"Anyway, I can make it work."

"So if you hear about this job Monday, I could come get you then. And bring you back here."

"Depends on when I start work. Your mom said it's okay?"

"Yes. She will. Believe me she will, I can tell." He lowered his voice some. "Sorry, I don't want my dad to hear. He can be the biggest moron. She asked about you already, that's all."

"So?"

"So I got you reading my mind and I got her reading my mind."

Ronny laughed, had a hard time stopping.

"Laugh, you little fuck."

"I think one other reason you like me is because you don't have to watch your mouth."

"Don't get me started on that."

"What happened to the beach?"

"What? Oh, that. I'm taking Jen Sunday. That's all. I told her we can't stay. She'll just have to deal with it."

There was first the closeness, the feeling there was no distance between them, and then so casually the mention of Jen, the confusion that followed. Ronny said, "Okay. I have to go."

"What's wrong?"

"Nothing."

"You're the one who brought her up, Ronny. Jesus."

"Don't worry about it. I really can't stay on this phone for any longer."

"You all right?'

"Yes. I'll talk to you tomorrow."

But when he hung up he felt the hollowness again, and a little sick from the feeling, knowing Ben would see Jennifer, knowing they would touch each other, do other stuff. The feeling of jealousy shook through him, so that he fumbled with the door when he turned the lock, forgot about the light and had to open the door again, and felt how foolish it was, what he was doing, if you thought about it from a slightly different perspective. He turned out the light and closed the door.

Architecture

CAMPUS WAS A UNIVERSE OF TREES, poplars and oaks on McCorkle Place, on Polk Place, both squares fogged by branches and leaves; pines stood sentinel around the gray curves of the football stadium; this part of campus was a walk through a forest woven with brick paths, punctuated by people from the physical plant department who moved from place to place taking up the bricks and laying them down again. Light filtered through the leaves in a fluttering way, found wavering routes to the ground. The quiet of the place, between the end of classes and summer school, gave him an awed feeling, that he was a wanderer here, that all these buildings were vacant, a wilderness of classrooms. He glimpsed rows of old wooden desks through the windows of Bingham Hall, plaster walls all cracked, chalkboards that needed cleaning. The round dome of Wilson Library rose above the treetops and made some kind of assertion, the building itself massive, all pale stone from the rotunda to the foundation. The sharp peak of the tall, thin Morehead Bell Tower stood just behind it at the center of neatly pruned shrubbery; there was a story that the Wilsons and the Moreheads hated one another, and the bell tower aimed to put a dunce cap on the dome of the library if you viewed it from South Building, the home of the university chancellor, at the head of Polk Place. The tale was handed down from student to student, taking on the form of truth in the wake of so much repetition. Could be it really was.

For Ronny the place had become a home, the first one he could claim on his own. Especially now, when he could walk anywhere he liked, he explored one building after another, wondering how each one came to be. North Campus with its old brick classroom buildings, nothing consistent about their style; South Campus with its high-rise dormitories standing over forest that had yet to be cleared, trees receding beyond them toward the neighborhoods of Chapel Hill. Immersed in the physical history of the place, Ronny found himself set within its machinery, a tiny piece of the whole, only another of the students who had started coming to this university a long time ago, who came here still to walk among the trees and find one another and grow into the branches.

He walked for hours on Saturday morning, barefoot, bell-bottomed jeans, hems ragged, an old Sears uniform shirt with the name Leander sewn onto a patch, left in his mom's trailer in Goldsboro by a boyfriend (hers) a couple of years back. No reason for the walk except that he was restless, the feelings of the last days too big to contain. A copy of *The Daily Tar Heel* blew across the plaza between cube-shaped Greenlaw and the student bookstore; the windows of the upper level of Lenoir Hall were open and a couple of art students were painting there; in the gravel parking lot next to the student union a couple sat on the back of a pickup, the girl in the boy's lap, their long, straight hair mingling, their faces lost in the mix. Both wore blue jean shorts that barely covered their butts. Today he knew how it felt to sit like that, close to someone, an ache of feeling all through the bodies, running from one to another. A radio in the truck played the Grateful Dead. An older fellow stood near the student union watching, holding a camera but taking no pictures. No one else in sight.

Ronny walked to the outdoor theater in Battle Park and sat on the highest of the stone seats while a wind played the branches overhead, a shrieking of birds in a quarrel, one squirrel falling out of a tree in front of him, stunned for a moment, then streaking back to the tree. Occasional sirens, car horns, snatches of music. Otherwise the quiet was eerie. He sat until he was gnawed at by hunger and had to give way, spend money, buy food. He was down again to his last few dollars.

In the afternoon, he did laundry in the coin-op place in the shopping center. Waiting for his clothes to dry, he stopped in the Little Professor Bookstore where he had seen Hoagie sitting at the cashier desk when he was out walking. They had been friendly at Governor's School, the same place Ronny had met Sheria, in the summer after their junior year of high school. Hoagie was sitting with near perfect posture, long faced, big eyed, his hair a snowy blond color; he had been merry and cheerful at Governor's School, a drama student, but now his face had a sad look about it, shadows about the eyes.

Walking up to the cashier stand, Ronny said, "You're having a quiet day, looks like."

"Hey, Ronny. It's been a while, how you been?" His smile brightened as it used to, face lit with a friendly light. Had something happened? "You're still in school, I guess."

"Yes. End of junior year. Have to turn into an adult some-time next year."

"Well, it's no fun."

"What, you're not at college anymore?"

Hoagie hesitated, hand on the edge of the cashier desk, fingernails immaculately trimmed, fingers long and blunt, not the delicate hands to match his features, which were ethereal—blue eyes with long lashes, full lips, small ears. "I dropped out. I had some problems." Waving his hand a bit. "Nothing I want to talk about, parent stuff."

"Well, I know how that goes. My mom just married her fourth husband and dumped me here for the summer to move to Nevada."

He giggled, studying something on the desk for a moment. "Yeah, I remember your stories about your mom. She's a trip."

"That's all right. Better that than one of these moms who calls every day to see if I'm changing my underwear. My first roommate had one like that."

"My mom was like that, too," Hoagie said. "But not any-more." Wistful. Ronny wanted to ask. But Hoagie went back to his work, which appeared to be checking a shipment of books against an invoice.

Ronny wandered to the literature shelves, lost himself in book covers, titles, names of writers, listening to Hoagie hum "Stop! In the Name of Love," low and toneless. The store was quiet, no other customers. Ronny knew he should not buy a book and exercised his willpower fairly well until he found a copy of a Forster novel he had never read, *The Longest Journey,* cheap enough that he could manage it.

Along the front of the cashier stand, leaflets fluttered a bit as someone let a breeze into the store. A flyer for the Southeastern Gay Conference, which had been sponsored by Chapel Hill students a few weeks ago, still hung there. Hoagie had come down to the sales floor and was watching. He said, "I went to that," watching Ronny carefully, and the weariness of his expression had increased, as though the comment weighed him down.

It was a moment that clarified many things. At Governor's School Ronny had gravitated to a group of boys like him, who were called sissies by the other boys. He remembered the feeling of walking down the crumbling plaster hallway of Clewell Dorm at Salem College, where the summer program was held; there was a cluster of fellows, jocks and would-be jocks, who hung around his neighbor's room, and one of them, Johnny something, had publicly invited Ronny to suck his cock a couple of times. For some reason he bore the brunt of the teasing. Hoagie had been at the edge of that group of Ronny's friends, though he spent most of his time with the theater kids. Now, in the bookstore, Ronny understood: he and Hoagie were alike, had always been.

So there was no real need for them to come out to each other. "I was too chicken to go," Ronny said, which was true.

"Well, I was scared to death, but I wasn't going to miss it."

"What was it like?"

"I don't know. All right. Everybody was cruising each other mostly, that's what I remember. There was some good stuff. They talked about pride and all. But it was mostly cruising." He had lowered his voice and moved closer so the other customer, who was browsing the cookbooks, could not hear. "But don't think gay people are going to be the cure for your problem. A lot of them are jerks, just like everybody else."

"Is that what happened with your parents?"

"Sort of. They found out. About me. That was before the conference, though." Sighing as if he were adrift, an involuntary sound, as if he could not escape the response. "I dropped out of school this semester. I don't think I can go back."

"I'm so sorry."

"Don't be. I'm all right. I like being on my own. I like my job." He shook his hair out of his eyes and brightened a bit. "If you're in town this summer come by and talk whenever."

"Sure thing."

He paid for the Forster novel and Hoagie looked down on him from the height of the cashier perch and smiled. How odd it felt; there was no question of attraction between them, but there was a kind of relief. Ronny felt it and was sure Hoagie did, too.

He wandered farther along Franklin Street, wondering. Was he afraid to be gay, officially—wary of attending that conference, for instance, out of fear of facing himself? Or of facing the fact that he was like his own father, something that had been on his mind since the first night with Ben? Or was he afraid of being publicly known, even to the small degree of attending a meeting? He was never shy when talking to Mac at the adult bookstore about what kinds of gay magazines to buy, or when he pored through every new edition of *After Dark* as soon as he could find it. Would any of that change now, because of Ben?

There was a pay phone in front of Fowler's grocery store, but a man with a homemade sign that read "Jesus repent your sins hellfire and damnation await thou" was waiting to use it. Besides, Ronny could hardly picture himself standing there, feeling all the things he felt when he talked to

Ben while traffic passed and grocery store customers rolled their shopping carts to their cars, wheels creaking and kids shrieking.

When the time came he used a phone in the student union. The place was empty except for him and some people in the student government offices. He sat at the bank of pay phones, dialed the number, and shoved in leftover quarters from the coin-op laundry. Ben answered on the first ring. "You're two fucking minutes late, boy. Explain yourself."

"Had to stop to expectorate. Sir."

"Spit on your own fucking time."

Maybe this was what a drug was like, the feeling of Ben spreading through his body, a tension easing away. Ronny laughed. "You're a little drunk."

"Me and dad had a few when we got home. Pretty quick, one right after the other."

Ronny waited. He was hearing an edge of hurt in Ben's voice.

"You there?"

"Oh, yeah. Just listening. How's your mom doing?"

"Like shit. Like she's been wrung out." He was quiet for a minute. "They tell you right up front that to kill the cancer they have to come close to killing the patient."

"That's what they do, all right."

"It's a fucking mess to watch. It makes me fucking want to break something."

"You sure you feel like talking?"

"Hell yes. Don't get scared of me."

Silence. "I'm not. Promise."

"She just looks so wasted and keeps throwing up." Quiet after that, the sound of Ben's breathing.

"I'm still here," Ronny said. "I got plenty of quarters." Though he didn't, really. This was Ben's money he was using, left over from the deposit on the phone.

"Where are you?"

"Student union. There's nobody here. It's kind of cool."

"I settled Dad down today, I think," Ben said. "We had a talk but that didn't do any fucking good so I told him if I heard about him fighting with Mom again I would bust his face in. He knew what I meant then. He kind of cracked up and bawled all over me. I couldn't take it."

"Beer help?"

"Not a goddamn bit."

Ronny put in more money at the tone. "I could get up there on the bus."

"Thanks. I think I can hang on to Monday if you can."

"Tate brought me a case of beer to the boardinghouse. I don't have anywhere to put it."

"Put it under the bed. I'll drink it if you don't." Over the phone he sounded as if he was wired pretty tight. "Jen's here right now. I should probably get off the phone pretty soon."

"Sure."

"I said pretty soon."

Ronny laughed. "You're the boss."

"It's a good thing you know it, too." The sound changed, a television in another room, someone talking in the room with him, and then Ben's voice came through again, but different. "I'll be off in a minute," he said. "No, I can't come sit on the couch with you right now. You see I'm on the phone." A moment later, "I'm talking to Ronny, that's who. Get the fuck out of the door, Jen." He was breathing into the receiver. In the background a door closed, the sound of television diminished.

"I better get off the phone, baby, before I have to break something here."

"Sure."

"Tomorrow?"

"I'll come back here to call."

Ben sat on the line a moment longer. "Thanks for not giving me any argument. Right? You get it?"

"Yes." Ronny touched his head to the phone booth. "No argument. Okay?"

"Man."

"I just wish you were fucking me right now," Ronny said.

"Oh, you bitch. Don't even bring that shit up."

"I can't help it."

"You fucking cunt."

"Man," Ronny said.

"I would tear you up if I could get through this phone right now for bringing that shit up when I can't do anything about it."

Ronny laughed. After a minute Ben did, too. "I may need to get in a shower," Ben said.

"Okay. We have to change the subject or I have to get off the phone. I'm in public."

"Right. But nobody's there."

"The security people are."

"You got no guts."

"Like you're any different standing there with Jen waiting right outside the room."

"You hit that on the fucking head," he said. "Tomorrow. On time this time."

"But what about the beach?"

"Can't. I already told Jen. I can't leave Mom."

Petty and wrong, but satisfying, to contemplate the fact that there would be no beach trip for Jennifer. He walked home very pleased.

In the afternoon on Sunday Ronny caught Sheila upstairs standing in the door of Jamal's bedroom. When she saw him her eyes grew very wide. "Miss Dee's not here," Sheila said, quickly. "Besides, I can come upstairs, I just can't go in the room."

The lower part of Jamal's belly was drooping over his jeans and there was a dark smattering of hair along the skin. He was carrying a can of beer and half a hamburger. He smirked at Ronny and kept chewing, leaning against the door.

"You trying to pretend you haven't been in that room with that young man, miss? Do you think I was born this morning?"

Sheila hung her head and poked out her lower lip. "My mama would be so ashamed."

"You guys keep my secret and I keep yours. Deal?"

She grinned at him. Her skin had such a brightness, really beautiful, Ronny thought, like milk. Her body looked ripe and had a sheen, a softness like light, all along it. "You have a secret?"

"I thought I was hearing somebody over there," Jamal said, between bites.

Sheila hopped up and down a couple of times and made fists. "Ooh. Tell!"

"Oh, no. Why spoil the mystery?"

"That's not fair at all."

"The better part of valor, you know." When she looked puzzled, he went on. "Discretion."

She was wearing a tube top with what looked like pizza stain crusted on it near the seam. Flaking away the stain with her fingernails, not the least bit self-conscious. "You can trust us. Well, you can't really trust Jamal. But you can trust me."

The idea that he had a secret pleased Ronny no end. But at the same time he worried what he might reveal. "I've just had a friend here studying with me a couple of nights."

"Unless you were studying professional wrestling," Jamal said, "I have to cast aspersions on your veracity. That was not studying."

Ronny looked at the guy, impressed. "Nice."

"I know big words, too."

"He does," Sheila agreed. "That's the third one I've heard him use."

Jamal set down the burger, grabbed her, and pulled her into the room. He was smacking at her hand to keep her from worrying the food stain. She chuckled and slapped his shoulder. He said, "Seriously, Miss Dee goes to church and then meets with her women's circle so she's not here most of Sunday. We don't take advantage and have parties or anything but as long as nobody gets caught, it's okay."

"Has she ever caught anybody?"

Jamal giggled. "No. We just make sure nothing gets changed in the house and keep out of sight and that takes care of it. We try to take care of her."

"She's sweet."

"She's barely getting by in terms of money," Jamal added. "She almost lost this house when a fraternity rented it and messed it up."

They closed their door after a while and Ronny went into his room to listen. He couldn't hear much, but maybe they weren't very loud. He pictured them as boisterous, uncomplicated, though he knew nothing at all about them, really. They had nothing to worry about except Miss Dee, who had her prohibition about girls upstairs but had no real way to keep track of what went on. Maybe the challenge of sneaking Sheila in and out of the house gave them a feeling of delicious wickedness. Later the door opened and one of them went to the bathroom. It relaxed him to think that the walls were solid. But it was an uncomfortable thought to realize he still felt the need to hide.

Long Distance

MAYBE IT WAS BEN'S ABSENCE THAT brought all those memories hurtling back. Now in May with the first edge of summer heat in the air, after many of his doubts were resolved, it was easy for Ronny to think about that uncertainty. Later on Sunday at the appointed time he called Ben's number and Mrs. Nickelsen answered. For the first moment she sounded surprisingly strong, her voice clear, the tone of a bell in her speech. "Hello, young man. I hear you're coming to see us."

"I sure hope so."

"We'll be glad to have you here. I know Ben will be."

"I hear you're not doing so good," Ronny said.

She tried to laugh and ended up coughing a bit. She took a moment to continue, and he could hear then the labored quality of her breath. "I've been better, I know that. I know you've been mighty good to Ben through all this. He tells me." She spoke more slowly as a sentence went on, and had to stop in the middle. Now Ronny was hearing more of her weakness.

"He's a good friend."

There was still the noise of television in the background. She asked, "So when are we going to have you up our way?"

"Soon, I hope. If everything works out."

She chuckled. "Well, it better. Ben's already driving to you."

"What?"

"He told me you would call." She faded away for a moment.

"Take your time," Ronny said, when he knew she was listening again. "I'm not in any hurry."

"He just had to get out of here. Dad driving him crazy. And this morning was awful. So I sent him to you early."

"He sounded like he was feeling it yesterday."

"He'll tell you about it." She took a breath. "I can't talk much longer, it's good to hear from you though."

"I'll see you when I get there."

But there was a sound he heard, something beyond the long-distance connection. He could feel her anguish through the line and turned toward the phone, leaned into the partition there, and sadness came over him. "He really needs somebody to talk to," she said. "I'm worried about him." She made a sound like a sob, and then another. She could not stop herself. He waited. She said, "I didn't mean to do this but it's been a hard day. Let me go."

"Take care of yourself."

He put the phone receiver on the hook when it started to buzz and stood and walked around the student union lobby, went in the bathroom, and splashed his face with water.

At the boardinghouse he opened the door to his room and a shadow turned on the bed. Ben sat up, backlit by the twilight. Shorts and a tee shirt, barefoot. Not the same feeling, though; something had made him smaller, more lonely.

"I booked it," he said. "I thought I might get here before you made the call."

"I talked to your mom. She told me you were on the way."

That broken expression, anger and hurt. "She answer the phone?"

"Yes."

He made a sound of disgust, getting off the bed. "I knew she wouldn't leave it to Dad. But she had no business sitting up."

"She was pretty weak. She sounded all right at first but she loses her voice when she talks."

His lips were set in a hard line, his brow furrowed. He was trying not to feel too much. "I know. It gets better the days after treatment. But then she has to go back for another one."

They stood there looking at each other. The changes in Ronny's body were immediate, something unfolding inside him, a warmth spreading through. In spite of what they were talking about: a surge of joy at seeing Ben, at the reality he had been granted. They were watching each other eye to eye. The rest of the world receded.

"Come on," Ronny said. "Let's walk. All right?"

"You want to go out?"

"Yeah. I do."

Ben frowned and looked around, slipped on his sneakers, shouldered past Ronny, waited at the door, then came back into the room, and they held each other. He was big and warm, stilled with hurt. He rubbed his cheek onto Ronny's, slow and easy, and they breathed against each other. Desire, yes, but for something else, for this space where they stood so close, for the quiet of it. Tension flowed all through Ben, wound so tight he nearly shivered, so Ronny squeezed him hard, and Ben made a sound, pulled Ronny against him, and then released. He made a sound again. "I been waiting for this all day."

They went for a walk along Cameron Avenue, along the line of frats and family homes, shadows lengthening, heat starting to break. They moved along the street without speaking. Ben stretched his arms, touched his toes, ran his hands through his hair, blew out his breath. The awful feeling of his stillness was passing. He bumped his shoulder against Ronny's, they looked at each other sidewise. "Miss Dee let me in your room. She gave me a key, I mean. Loaned me one. I took it back to her."

"I guess you did charm her."

"Seems like it. I told you."

"You had a hard day."

He had shoved his hands in his shorts, sullen in the dusk, not sure where to look or what to do. "Did Mom tell you about it?"

"She said you would. She was saving her breath."

"She wasn't this morning. She got in a fight with Jen. She threw Jen out. I had decided to call it off with her this afternoon anyway but I had to go ahead and do it right then."

"Your mom threw her out?"

"Oh, you should have heard her. It's the quiet ones you have to watch out for." Ben laid his hand briefly on the back of Ronny's neck. "Jen was driving her crazy. She didn't mean to, I guess, but the house shocked her. She's a doctor's daughter and such shit as that. She turned her nose up. She couldn't even hide it. I shouldn't have brought her home with Ma as sick as she is. Wasn't fair."

"Wow."

"No smirk?"

"No. I'm sure that took a lot out of your mom." Ronny started to ask another question and closed his mouth.

Ben was watching. "You know you ain't getting away with that. Say it."

"I just wondered what was the fight about?"

"Jen was mad we didn't go to the beach. I don't blame her, I'd been promising. But I couldn't fucking help it. She kept trying to corner me for talks and get me alone in a room with her. It was like she was jealous or something. Mom told her flat out she didn't like it. Then she said something Ma didn't like and Ma told me I needed to take her home."

They were standing on a corner where the street ran down a hill, everything quiet. Ronny kept his mouth shut. Ben looked one way, then another. "Come on, let's go back to the room. I can't do what I want to do out here." He had already turned back, and now was waiting. "Hell. I only knew the girl a month. She's not a bad person, she just wanted the wrong thing from me. Maybe I didn't fuck her up too bad."

"I didn't really know her so I can't say."

"Well, that's the first fucking break she ever caught from you."

"Hey, I never said anything about her, nothing that bad anyway."

Ben cocked his head and snorted, then threw up his hands. "Like I couldn't tell what you were thinking. What the hell do I care now? It's done." He waited for Ronny to catch up. "You think it makes any more difference to her than it does to me?"

Ronny shrugged. "How should I know?"

Ben watched him intently. "You always know more than you should."

"Well, how much did you really like her?"

"I thought I liked her all right."

"Yeah?"

He snagged a leaf from a low hanging oak branch, shredding it piece by piece in his blunt, square fingers. "Hell, I hate talking about crap."

"I'm not making you do it."

They walked side by side under crepe myrtles showing new green leaves, almost glowing in the night. Some of the cockiness and swagger restored to Ben's posture. He said, "God help me, I was never such a son of a bitch before."

"Really?"

"I treat my girls pretty good. At least I think I do."

"Please. You've gone through women like they were standing wheat."

The moment turned, Ben holding some deep amusement close. "Whereas you . . ." He had a twisted grin, now; he had thought of something.

"Oh, I'm waiting for this."

"I mean, fuck, Ronny, how can you tell a man is a virgin any fucking way? You were probably a virgin twenty times last month."

Ronny fell speechless. He felt a flash of protest and then shook his head.

Ben chuckled, then got quiet. "I piss you off?"

"Of course not. You were always a fucking tease anyway."

"Not me. I'm very direct."

"And I never pretended to be a virgin more than five times in a month. So fuck you."

He laughed. "You're getting better at cussing, a little bit. Must be my influence."

Inside the room Ben flung Ronny onto the bed and jumped onto him. The bed swayed some but held up. "Better not do that again. You got that beer?"

"Under the bed, if you didn't just flatten it."

"You mind?"

"I hear you're a mean drunk."

He reached for the warm beer, popped it, swallowed, leaned back against the wall. Putting the can to Ronny's face, feeding Ronny beer as if he were an infant or a pet, all the while smirking. Ronny fought with the notion that he should refuse to drink, then gave in, so quickly he wondered whether there was anything he would refuse Ben. They did beer kisses and Ronny licked beer off Ben's chest. Ben poured it, careful not to make a mess. "This is not a dorm, Ben," he admonished himself, "this is that lady's house. Delancey, right?"

"Mrs. Delacy."

"That's too long. What did you call her?"

"Miss Dee."

"I like that. Miss Dee." He swallowed with intense satisfaction, drank the rest of the can, reached for another one, fed more to Ronny. "I promise I'm not going to get stupid. I just feel so goddamn much better."

They came into focus for each other, in the easy place, and the talk turned simple again. Ronny relaxed. "Do what you want, boss."

"You're being so fucking congenial I may have to slap the shit out of you." He grinned, set down the beer, and pulled Ronny against him. "That was me speaking out of my darker nature."

"I was definitely impressed."

"The queer-bashing jock side of my personality that I can barely repress."

"Eek."

Ben doubled up, spitting beer. When he got his breath he said, "You fucking shit."

"They're my sheets you sprayed beer on."

"Baby, we've got so much other shit on these sheets the beer is acting as a detergent."

"All of a sudden you are so fucking funny."

"Guess you were looking for a dumb jock, huh? Sorry, too bad. This is a life lesson for you. Ex-virgins who are putting out nonstop need more than one set of sheets."

Ronny shook his head. "Here we go. And I just washed the sheets yesterday."

"Do you really want to stop to think about that now? You might start to worry that you're having too much sex and you're going to die."

"Hmm."

"Don't even try to count it up."

"Man, you're good with this beer stuff."

"You want some more? I like to pour it in your mouth."

"I wish I had a joint now," Ronny said.

"Oh, man, don't even bring that shit up. You never smoked a joint in your life, you told me so."

"I guess you're corrupting me. We'd have to go for a walk or something. I hear it stinks."

"We have a wonderful smoking patio just through the French fucking doors." Ben pointed to the window and the porch roof.

"As I've always thought, a master criminal."

"I would bow but I'm so fucking comfortable."

Best of Times

FALLING ASLEEP TOWARD MORNING AGAIN, BEN woke up once when Ronny was drawing the shade and another time to piss, not even hesitating anymore, maybe because he was more used to the sounds of the house. Ronny's jaw was sore and he rubbed the ends of the mandibles with his fingers. Ben came back and flung himself down on Ronny and rolled him around until they were both partly drowsing and partly aroused. Ben was tired, though, and fell asleep with Ronny tangled against him.

When Ronny woke again, he got out of bed while Ben's eyes were still closed, but they opened at once, Ben reaching for Ronny's thigh. He sat on the bed next to Ben and put his hand on Ben's face. "I need to get dressed and go down to the paper."

"Hmm," Ben said. "Sit there a second."

"Sure."

"Slept so hard," Ben said. "Man."

"You must not have been resting at home."

170

"No. You want me to get up?"

"Why don't you sleep some more?"

After a moment he sagged into the pillow. Ronny went on sitting there, feeling there was something more. Ben's hand traced up and down Ronny's lower spine. "What do you do to calm me down like this?"

"I don't know. Just talk to you, I guess."

"I never felt like this, you know."

"Never?"

He shook his head. Smiling a little. "Listen to me, talking this fucking bullshit."

They watched each other, and Ben cupped Ronny's face with a hand, the calluses rough. This look of him coming into himself, a liquid light along his skin, a change in his body as though he were testing each limb. Ronny felt a catch inside himself, a moment in which something opened up, yawning and deep. Ben grinned, eyes more open now. He sat back on the pillows, pulled Ronny on top of him. "Just for a minute."

"Nice," Ronny said, and settled under the sheets.

"You still scared of me?"

"Maybe. Sometimes."

"When?"

"In the dorm sometimes. When you're with a lot of guys from the team. You guys are pretty rough."

After a moment he brushed his mouth on Ronny's ear. "Nothing I can do about that. That's the way it is to play football."

"I don't really mind."

"Don't let this soft shit fool you, that's still who I am."

"The way you change up, never a dull moment."

"Can't let things get dull, babe. I'd knock you around every day before I'd let that happen." He was grinning, but there was something harsh in the words, an edge that made Ronny wary.

"You keep me on my toes all right."

"You need to leave yet?" Low, in Ronny's ear. Pulling their bodies together, his hands on Ronny's back.

"I can always cut my shower short," he answered. "It's not like they're expecting me at any certain time. I just want to look eager."

"You look pretty eager right now," Ben said, and took him in, engulfed him, and they were tangled up again and that was the whole world.

Turtletrack

SO IT WAS LATER INSTEAD OF earlier when, in the *Chapel Hill Newspaper* office, he met Amber Twayne Gibbs, the composition shop supervisor, and within a few minutes he had the job—because he already knew how to do it—and she was showing him the setup at the worktables. A feeling of relief pervaded even as Amber told him about his duties. "Oh, man, so cool you did stuff before. Training new people is a bitch."

She was shorter than Ronny, her hair colored red from a drugstore hair dye, freckled across the nose and cheeks, earnest, dressed like an old hippie; but that didn't mean much, since there were so many hippies in Chapel Hill. Her eyes were red and he wondered whether she was stoned. Maybe she was another student who had come to the university and found the town so comfortable she never left. But she was his boss, so he decided not to ask any questions.

Typesetting computers on one wall, a headline machine, layout tables made of cheap particle board, grimy carpet patched with duct tape, reporters stepping in and out of the room—a newspaper back shop, familiar enough. The lights blared and buzzed a bit. He could get used to it.

He would work Thursday and Friday afternoons and evenings, assembling the sections of the Sunday edition that were printed ahead of time, then he would come in Saturday nights for the news and sports sections for the Sunday paper. Sometimes he might be called in to help with the weekday work. The hourly wage was all right. He could live on it.

"This Thursday?"

"Yeah. Come about one, dude. That's when we get the daily pages off and you can have the boards."

When he walked back to the boardinghouse his room was empty, a curious letdown. On the desk lay a scrawled note: "Done an gone owt for vittels. Git packt." Part of Ben's dumb jock routine. Ronny got out his suitcase and filled it with clean clothes.

When he was finished, he sat at the desk. He pulled out the journal he tried to keep intermittently and wrote: Cold hot wind blowing through me, feeling of falling any time I'm next to him, feel like I am coming apart sometimes, feel like the sun is on me even at midnight, feel like midnight even at noon, want to think about Ben's face, just think about his face, hold it in front of me. I feel so screwed up. Just here because he's hurting and I make him feel better, just scared now and needs me because he can talk to me, this can't be real, nobody could really like me this much, don't even like myself this much, have faith. Have faith. Hold on. Happy.

But there was trouble in him whatever words he wrote on the page, that he had plunged into some abyss and could not find any solid world around him, that he had risked his quiet and solitude for something that burned him and chilled him and soothed him and frightened him all at once. Away from

Ben he felt more of the fear of how open to Ben he had become, what he risked in doing that, because Ben could change his mind, after all.

Something hit the window at his back and he stood and turned. Ben stood there poised with another pecan. A flood of relief washed through Ronny at the sight, that face so open and content, that body so large and welcoming. He gestured to Ronny to come and so Ronny carried the suitcase downstairs, past Miss Dee, who was standing in her kitchen door. She appeared quite lively today and came toward him smiling, recognizing him from farther away. Beyond her, in the kitchen, sat another woman in a green coat with a hat on her head and a purse in her lap.

"Hello, son, how are you?"

"Great, Miss Dee. I found a job."

Ben came walking up to the front door, open for the breeze; he had his hands in his pockets, grinning.

"Here's your friend," she said, watching Ben. "He got a job. Did you hear?"

"I figured he would."

"Isn't that just marvelous? And on such a beautiful day."

"It's a nice day all right," Ben said, and smiled at her to show off his dimples.

"Oh, look at that!" The woman in the kitchen had turned in her seat. She was holding a little glass of clear brown liquid and her cheeks were flushed. "You are such a handsome young man!"

"Oh hush, Clara, and don't act the fool."

"Well, I'm just telling the truth."

"Don't pay any attention to her. We've just been talking and having a little glass of sherry wine and it went right straight to her head."

"Oh, Miss Dee," Ben said. "You're running wild."

Miss Dee said, "Now don't you be like that. I'm old enough for a drink when I want one."

"We may be old but we're not dead yet," said Clara, adjusting her hat. She had applied some lipstick that brightened her face but her attempt at mascara was mostly smears. "I hadn't seen you here before."

"That's because he doesn't live here," said Miss Dee. "His friend Ronny does."

Seeing her so bright, in the company of Clara, who took so much trouble to look colorful and put-together (in spite of the rather heavy coat)—and even Miss Dee wearing a crisp dress with silver buttons—he understood them, just for a moment, more exactly as they were: two flickering beings, alive as anything, moving at a distance of a different type. It was so easy to think of her, and maybe both of them, as faded and lonely. But as Miss Dee said to Clara, "Stop this flirting with the young men, Clara, it won't get you anywhere," he could see the whole woman in her expression, in her grin at her joke.

"I think it's a shame to be so old," said Clara, and laughed, and reached for the sherry bottle.

"You ladies aren't old, you're fully ripened," Ronny said. They looked at him for a moment, and so did Ben, and they burst out laughing.

"Can't get much riper," said Miss Dee. "Right about to fall off the tree."

"Well, me oh my, I am sure glad this bottle is not empty."

"If you don't take that coat off, you're going to start sweating after all this sherry."

"Oh, leave me alone, Alberta. You know I'm cold natured."

"You look like you're going on a trip," said Miss Dee to Ronny; she was seeing his bag, of course, and he fidgeted and Ben said, "Yes, ma'am, he's coming to my house for a visit. We're old friends like that."

"Did you lock your room?"

Ronny said, "Yes, ma'am."

"Well, you boys have a good time."

"And you ladies keep yourselves under control." Ben patted Clara on the back and they tittered, and as the boys walked out of the house they could hear the talking resume, the clinking of glasses in the kitchen, a burst of laughter, and outside the spring day, the smell of the jessamine along the side fence, two birds darting back and forth, chasing each other in the air.

On the way to the car, Ben walked fast, looking brighter today, as if he had a slight glow. "Did you notice I got rid of the beer cans and made that filthy bed?"

"No, I didn't even think about it. Man. You're domestic. Thank you."

Ben was grinning in that lopsided way. "Careful. You don't want me to crack you on the head."

"You might give me amnesia, you know, like on a soap opera. Then who would do your homework?"

"Fuck you."

This time Ben had parked in the driveway, the car gleaming and clean. Seeing it in daylight, anybody could see the care Ben took to maintain it, the chrome polished, the body waxed, the vinyl roof gleaming. Bags carefully packed in the boot. "You name your car?"

Ben gave him a shove, an excuse to touch. "Don't be stupid. Who names a car?"

"I would."

"Well, you're special."

In the front seat Ronny felt the density of Ben next to him, taking up width, relaxed and unself-conscious as he headed out of Chapel Hill through the traffic. He drove with one hand on the steering wheel, his thighs sprawled under it, his other arm at rest on the open window. The car stirred with the warm rush of air, rattling some scraps of paper on the seat and the floor until Ronny gathered them up and wadded them together, trash, to dispose of the next time the car stopped. Ben watched him and grinned. "You're cleaning my car."

"The sound is irritating."

Ben shrugged. "I don't mind. I'd have never thought you liked things tidy from the way you and your roommate keep your dorm room."

"That's all Kelly. I clean that room all the time but it doesn't do a bit of good."

"You complain to him?"

Ronny shrugged. "Why be a pain in the ass? It wouldn't make any difference anyway."

Quiet then, and Ronny asked about where they were headed. Ben's hometown, Turtletrack, was a spot on the map, the back end of Virginia, he said. The Nickelsens had lived there the last ten years or so, when Ben's dad got a job at a farm supply house. Ben turned into a star football player for the high school. His sister became a hippie and a feminist.

"What about your mom? Did she ever work?"

"She had a job at the post office till about a year ago. She took early retirement. My mom and dad had kids kind of late."

"You close to your sister?"

"Kind of. She might come tomorrow or the next day. She's out of classes, too. Or she may wait and come when I take you back. She hasn't decided."

That meant they had talked about Ronny's visit. He had met Ben's parents but not his sister. "She's not uncomfortable with me being around your mom?"

"Why would she be?"

"People are funny sometimes. Especially when there's sickness in the family."

"Nina's cool. She's sharp but she's kind of a space cadet. Half the time she might as well be an oyster. The other half she won't shut up."

"Yeah?"

"You'll see what I mean. It's nothing wrong, it's just how she is. She'll be fine with you."

"Sure. She sounds kind of cool, actually."

"She'll probably have some pot. She usually does."

"Nice, I guess."

"You want to try it?"

Ronny shrugged. The thought made him uneasy. He had felt guilty about drinking the beer.

"You don't have to worry about Nina, if that's what you're doing. It's not like everybody can tell you're queer just by looking at you."

Something about the statement was not quite comfortable. There was more than one way to read it. What did queer look like anyway? Ben thought of hiding Ronny, of keeping him secret; but so did Ronny, didn't he? "I was more worried about being a stranger in the house than that," Ronny said.

Ben was quiet. They were driving along the outskirts of Roanoke Rapids, the traffic heavy, and he appeared to be concentrating on that; but a moment later he said, "I always feel like I have to defend you from somebody but most of the time I'm not sure who it is."

The thought of being protected, of being necessary in that way, made Ronny almost golden in the quiet. Ben's eyes stayed fixed on the road even when he was talking, like a commitment. Ronny asked, "Defend me?"

"Like, I'm listening to Tate talk to his boys about you the day you said you'd do that paper and I'm wondering if he's going to say some crap to piss me off to the point I have to do something. He never does. So far nobody does. But it's like I'm always edgy."

"That doesn't sound so good, Ben."

"I'm making it sound like more than it is. I don't even know what one of those jerk-offs would say, really. I mean, I still call you a faggot myself. I don't mind when Tate jokes around about you sucking his cock because I know you can handle that. And he jokes like that with a lot of people, not just you."

"I don't care what he calls me. Or what you call me." Anger in the assertion, a touch of it, and Ronny sat up straight. Looking ahead at the road. "Or what anybody calls me."

Ben wet his lips and asked, "Your dad was gay? You told me that one time but we never talked about it."

"He left my mom when I was little. For some dork man he stayed with for two weeks."

Scowling, Ben said, "Sounds like an asshole."

"Why would he trick my mom like that? I never even dated a girl. What kind of crap would that be, me taking a girl out when I know I don't really want to be with her."

"You think he was confused?"

"I've never been confused." A dark anger took over, and he felt the same bitterness as whenever he talked about his dad. "Why would he have been?"

"I don't know."

"How can you be confused about what makes your dick hard?"

Ben laughed quietly, watching the road. "You got me, there. That's what clued me in."

But Ronny wasn't quite comfortable, suddenly. He had a need to put his hand on Ben's thigh for a moment, to make a connection, so it would be all right to talk like this. Ben moved it to show it was all right. The anger drained into the point of contact. They glanced at each other. They were both still there. "My dad and I get along better these days but that doesn't take much. I hear from him a couple times a year and I see him when I see him. He's with this guy that I don't like."

"Keep your hand there. Where does he live?"

A new delight: the solidity of Ben's thigh in the ragged jeans. "Richmond."

"He know you're gay?"

"No." He could feel Ben waiting. "I'll tell him when I feel like it will make any difference. I ought not to hold so much against him but I can't help it. The divorce really screwed my mom up. Well, what really screwed my mom up was knowing her husband left her for a guy. But she really loved him."

"That kind of thing would fuck a person up, all right. So you never dated any girl at all?"

"Once. Right after I got my driver's license. I mean, one time, one date. This nice girl named Phoebe. I took her to see *Carnal Knowledge*. I had no idea what it was. There was Jack Nicholson screwing Ann-Margret on screen. Phoebe and I were sitting there holding hands and I kept wanting to get kissed by Jack Nicholson. My hand was sweating. I drove her home and decided I didn't care how many people called me a sissy or a fag, I wasn't going through that."

A moment. Passing trucks on the road, the press of wind, the heavy car shifting on its shocks. "I had sex with one guy before you."

Ronny quiet, feeling the stillness around the words.

"That make you jealous?"

"Not unless you've got him in the trunk."

Ben chuckled. "It was this kid I didn't even know. This skinny kid on my street when I was in junior high. We did it in the shed in the back of my house."

"What was his name?"

Ben thought about it and laughed. "God damn, I don't remember."

"What made you do it?"

"I could just feel him wanting me so much. I didn't even know I was thinking about doing it till he touched me one day. Then I got hot, like, all at once, and I did it."

"What?"

"You know. Not the first part I like but the second. The fuck and not the blowjob. You're definitely the first guy to suck my dick."

"I'll write that down in my book of important accomplishments as soon as we get to your house."

"Dickhead."

"I sure didn't think you were going to tell me anything like that."

Ben shrugged, looking cocky. "Just thought you would want to know another interesting fact about me." He set his hand on Ronny's. "You mind the radio?"

"No."

"I know we'll probably keep talking anyway. You never shut up."

"Oh, so it's me."

"When I have somebody else in the car I don't say ten words. I don't know what you do to make me talk so much." He was smiling, though, and it appeared he liked the difference.

During the remainder of the ride, though, a long silence did come, Ronny looking out the side window while Ben kept them moving toward Turtletrack. Farm country, rolling hills, a scattering of cows in fields, dilapidated old farm buildings, neat houses set back from the road under groves of trees, followed by towns that were clusters of strip malls and vacant storefronts. The quiet contained their fullness in the presence of each other, mixed eddies of their contentment. On the surface Ronny felt peace but inside was restless, edgy, glad to be in the car alone with Ben but at the same time and without any feeling of contradiction wishing the ride were over so he could move around.

It occurred to Ronny, at some point during the quiet, that Ben had almost confessed that he was gay himself. Had almost admitted it. But not quite. It should not have been a fleeting thought but it was. He put it away.

"We're pretty close," Ben said, turning down the radio. They were listening to "Stairway to Heaven," Ben singing tunelessly to lines he knew.

"Yeah?"

"You nervous?"

Ronny shook his head. "I don't know why but I'm not."

"They should be back from the hospital by now. Dad's probably ready to freak again."

"What does he do?"

"Tells her not to throw up if she can help it. Gets grossed out when he has to deal with it. Hates having to help her on and off the toilet. That kind of stuff."

"That must make her feel great."

"I think she knows he can't help it. But it would be a lot easier for her if he would get used to some of this."

"Man, I'm starving all of a sudden."

"Did you eat anything this morning?"

Ronny had to stop to think. "No."

"Shit for brains, what's wrong with you? Don't just sit there, tell me what you want."

"We were so busy talking I just didn't think about it."

They stopped at the next place that served anything edible, a hamburger stand called Bobanne's Burger Palace, outside Pinkley. "This place is all right," Ben said. "I came here a couple of times. Just get something for the car. I'm hungry, too."

By the time they had eaten, they were nearly there. The outskirts of Turtletrack emerged out of a curve of the road and across from a broad swath of fields under cultivation, mostly soybeans and corn. Ben pointed out the fertilizer dealership and a few of the other landmarks, including the high school where he had played football. The town sprawled for a fair distance away from its main intersection, marked by neither river nor creek. Smaller than Goldsboro, and located in that part of Virginia and North Carolina that people only find if they mean to. There were pretty elms arched over Main Street—all of them dying of Dutch elm disease, according to Ben. Houses lay so scattered among treetops that they appeared to be growing under the canopy. Even at first glance the town had an appearance of quiet desperation, as though it no longer knew why it was there.

Ronny took a deep breath, feeling sudden tension in his middle, in spite of his earlier claim. A town where everybody knew everybody, like so many other places in this rural part of the world. One of these houses belonged to Ben, and his family was there. What would they think of him?

Hospital Bed

THE NICKELSEN HOUSE SAT ON A small wooded lot on what looked like a third of an acre of yard or so, in a tidy neighborhood of similar houses, on a street named Crosscreek. Brick on the first floor, siding on the second, nothing in particular to distinguish it beyond a couple of flower beds that needed weeding and a pair of pink flamingos that looked to have stood in the same spot, at the side of the front stoop, since the days of Eisenhower. The grass needed mowing but not badly and the windows needed cleaning at the front but that, too, appeared to be dirt of recent vintage. A huge old magnolia dominated the front yard. Ronny fetched his bag and Ben took it from him and walked him into the house.

Mr. Nickelsen met them at the door and scratched his hairy belly under his shirt. "Come on in, boys. We're back, we're here. You boys have a good drive?"

Ben said, "Oh, yeah, it was fine. Easy traffic."

Father and son made no move to acknowledge each other, no hug, no slap on the back, just a stunned awkwardness.

Mr. Nickelsen, bulky and balding, scratched the scalp on the top of his head. He was looking down at the bag Ben was carrying.

"Is Mom okay?" Ben asked, pushing past him, setting the suitcase down and stretching his shoulders.

Mr. Nickelsen started to nod his head, though he was still staring downward, at nothing. He slumped a bit, as if he were barely making the effort to stand, as if he might slide to the floor at any moment. Now he had stopped scratching and held one palm across his head. Maybe he had forgotten where he was, why he was waiting at the door. "Mom's fine. She's laying down in the den on the hospital bed. You hadn't seen it yet."

"You got a bed in here?"

"The people brung it yesterday. Set it up in the den right pretty, real close to the TV. She's saying it helps a lot. You all come on in here now. Leave your bag there, Ronny, Maylene wants to see you boys."

As he walked, his shirt drifted open showing the stains on his tee shirt and the grizzled white hair above its neckline. His skin was grayed and full of broken capillaries. He wore a pair of black framed glasses and walked like a farmer, straddling a row. "You need anything, Ben? Anything to drink? Ronny?"

"No, Dad, we just had something."

"I'm fine, sir," Ronny said. "Thank you for asking."

The den was a good-sized room lined with pine paneling, the bed set up along the inner wall of the house, the look of it stark and out of place. Mrs. Nickelsen was lying under a sheet and blanket, fringes of short white hair covering her skull, longer strands at her temple and along the base of her neck. Her eyes were dulled and heavy at first, brightening when she saw her son. A touch of color came back to her skin at the sight of him. Her thin arms lay on the sheet, the inner areas, near the elbow, covered with bandages and bruises, as were the backs of her hands.

"Hello, son," she said, lifting a hand. "You're back."

He bent to her, somehow softened in all his lines. Near her he appeared to move with care, touching her arm lightly. "I brought somebody to see you."

"Hey, is this Ronny? I remember you."

"Hey, Mrs. Nickelsen. It's good to see you but I don't like seeing you like this so much."

"We can't help it, can we?" she asked, smiling at him. "You boys have a good drive? Did you eat?"

"We stopped down the road and got something," Ben said. "Don't worry."

He told her the drive had been easy and the weather was nice, mostly just to ease the silence, or so it appeared. "And Ronny got a job for the summer. So that's all taken care of."

"Well, I'm glad." She hadn't the strength to say more and lay back on the pillow, taking slow breaths. She was watching nothing in particular for a moment, as if there was something going on inside her that held her attention.

"Do you need anything, Maylene?" Mr. Nickelsen asked.

She came back from her distance and said, "No, honey. You set down. You been going with me all day."

Mr. Nickelsen sighed and settled into his recliner, which faced in the direction of the bed, almost as if he were in the studio audience and she were the program. He was grateful to be told to sit. A sense, watching him, that he agreed he deserved a rest and was pleased she said so. "I could sure enough get off my feet. Lord a mercy."

"He has been so good to me today," Mrs. Nickelsen said.

"I've been a fecking angel," Mr. Nickelsen said, glancing at his son.

"Hush that language," she said.

"Fecking is not a bad word. I made it up."

"Well, it sure sounds like a bad word."

He waved his hand at her but he was chuckling, as if it tickled him to be scolded, made him feel as if he knew better who and where he was. When the laughter was done, though, he had an air of shock around him, a creature at the edge of a blast, something ripped away.

Ben leaned close, pressing his lips to his mom's forehead. "I told Ronny about our great day on Sunday."

"Wasn't that some mess?" she asked, looking at Ronny. "You would have thought I was doing something wrong wanting to sit with my son in my own house."

"Son, you can sure pick them sometimes," Mr. Nickelsen said, shaking his head, blowing his nose into a mostly clean handkerchief.

Ben gave him a sharp look and then cracked a grin. "I know it, Dad. I was just talking about that with somebody."

"We'd have horsewhooped a girl like that when my daddy was alive."

"Hush that, Harley," Mrs. Nickelsen said, but she was laughing.

"You can sure pick them," Mr. Nickelsen repeated.

"Now, I've liked some of Ben's girls all right," Mrs. Nickelsen said.

Her husband snorted.

"I have," she said, her voice thin and soft; and her husband and son laughed harder.

"Don't shake my bed, now, son."

In the midst of the laughter Mrs. Nickelsen grew pale and sat up slowly, hands on her midsection. She caught Ben's eye and gestured to him; she couldn't speak but pointed to a pan on the table by the bed. He gave it to her and stood next to her. Ronny saw the look of fear on Mr. Nickelsen and watched him turn away. Ben held the pan, helping her keep back what was left of her hair. It was hard to watch, her pained body, the racking, heaving movement, the sense that it embarrassed her. The room had gone quiet. Ronny said, "I thought it looked like rain when we were driving up."

"It's a rain coming," Mr. Nickelsen said, wandering to the window, looking out.

She lay back on the pillow. There were wet cloths by the bed. Ronny looked at Ben, who was red faced, jaw grinding. "She might like a glass of ice water, Ben," he said, and Ben looked at him, face relaxing some.

Mrs. Nickelsen nodded that she would, hand trembling on the side of the bed, reaching for one of the cloths. Ben strode into the kitchen. Ronny sat on the bed and took the cloth, wiped her mouth with it. He set the pan on the table and adjusted her blanket. She looked fixedly at the ceiling, breathing with effort at first, then more easily. He cleaned her face carefully. Mr. Nickelsen watched for a moment by the window.

Ben held the glass of water to her lips, took the cloth from Ronny, and sat on the other side of the bed. "You can rinse your mouth out and spit in the cloth," Ben said.

She nodded and did. Ben gave her more water and Mr. Nickelsen continued to hover. "Take the pan to the bathroom, Dad," Ben said, and Mr. Nickelsen sighed heavily, did as he was told, gray and frightened, wishing for his chair, most likely.

Ronny had moved away from the bed and tucked himself into the corner of a brown plaid couch, ruffled along the bottom, while Ben sat on a stool near his mother, talking to her quietly. But it made him restless to sit still, to feel useless. The room was pleasant enough, furnished with this ordinary couch and chairs, modular tables, basic clean lines. When the room was tidy it likely had a pleasant aspect, but at the moment it was littered with newspapers, paper plates, glasses partly filled with tea or soda, cups where coffee had dried on the bottom. From the couch he could see the backyard, neatly kept but also in need of mowing, like the front, hydrangeas in bloom along a fence, a brick patio extending out from the sliding doors, some yard furniture visible.

He slipped into the kitchen and found another mess in there, dishes waiting to be washed, food out of the cupboards, a floor that needed sweeping and mopping, a laundry room full of dirty clothes. The idea that he might sort this out became a relief, a way to keep out of the way, something to do. He took the clean dishes out of the dishwasher, opening cabinets and drawers until he found places for them, and started loading the dirty ones, gathering them from wherever they were. The action was a reflex with him; he had done his share of housework when he lived with his mother. He had made enough room to clean the counters, started the dishwasher, and was sweeping the floor when Ben came to the doorway.

He looked around the room. Taking a few steps in. He was maybe a little embarrassed. "I didn't bring you to do this. My dad and I should be cleaning."

Ronny shook his head, went on scrubbing the countertop, where what looked like egg had dried. "It's fine. I don't mind."

"It's not your house, Ronny."

"Just let me help, all right?" Ronny's tone was firm and he felt his expression harden, to mask the other feeling beneath, the tenderness. "I mean it. I want to."

Ben looked mournful for a moment, more vulnerable than Ronny had seen him, and he slumped a little, bewildered, unprotected. A throaty sound, then shaking his head, unafraid that Ronny was watching. "I was going to do this stuff myself yesterday. Clean up. But I just sat here."

"You were worried about your mom."

After a moment Ben nodded. He leaned against the door. "She's asking where you are."

"Does she want me to come in there?"

"It might not hurt. She looks like she wants to close her eyes."

Ronny set the broom aside. Ben stopped him in the middle of the room and Ronny, for once, was the one who could not meet his eyes. The feeling between them, the pull between their bodies, the need to close the space. A stinging in Ronny's eyes. "Don't say anything bullshit, Ben, okay? You know how I feel."

"Yeah." Such emotion in the one word, in the tone of his voice.

"We came to do this, right?"

"Right."

He walked into the den and directly up to the hospital bed. Mr. Nickelsen was standing next to it, watching his wife. "What do these boys want for dinner?" Mrs. Nickelsen asked.

"I was going to grill some more steaks."

"I know you love doing all this grilling," she said, touching his hand fondly.

Mr. Nickelsen grinned, rubbed his hand where she had touched him. He turned toward the wall for a moment. She gazed at him with such intensity. She reached for his hand again. His eyes were glistening.

Ben asked, "What about you, Mom?"

"I can't keep much down. I have these milkylike drinks with all the vitamins and all that other stuff, in them. The nutrition."

What followed was new information, this gentle person tending his mother, opening the doors for fresh air, carrying her into the sun, worrying over what she might eat. Sitting quiet with her, his body stilled, smiling like a boy; this was inside Ben, this remnant of a sprite.

As for Ronny, it eased him to work, so he ran the vacuum and emptied trash, carrying silverware and cups to the sink, tidying. Mr. Nickelsen puttered about, too, gathering dirty dishes from the den, gradually making his own stack next to the sink. He decided he would make a run to the grocery store. He said, "I'm glad you boys are helping out like this. It was too much for me. I ain't cut out for taking care of sick people."

Ronny rearranged her bed and organized some of the stuff she needed, like tissues, her pills, wipe cloths, and water, on a higher table that she could reach more easily. He found an arrangement of dried flowers on one of the displaced pieces of furniture and put it on the lower table, adjusting it to sit where she could see. When Ben brought her inside again, the room was tidy. "Well, I declare, I can see my house," she said.

Ben was embracing her, holding her up.

"I don't like where they put that bed, it's too close to the TV," she said, and they talked about it, and Ben unlocked the casters and moved it along the wall so she could see out the window if she was propped on the pillows. They moved the recliner so that

Mr. Nickelsen could sit more beside his wife, like before, to keep him from staring at her, she said. Ben carried some of the displaced furniture into the other rooms and the place looked less cluttered.

"You changed these sheets," she said, sliding onto the bed, breathing heavily, suddenly tired. "I'm surprised you could find anything clean to put on it. Good gracious. Look at everything."

She was pleased that the house was cleaner, and told Ronny she did not like mess and she was embarrassed that he had to see the house dirty as it was. She got sick again pretty soon after that, and Ben tended her. This time she seemed less reluctant to ask for help and called for the pan when she first felt the nausea start. Ben was ready beside her when she needed someone to hold the pan and her hair, to wipe her mouth and ease her to the pillow. Exhausted when it was done. Ronny carried the pan away and left Ben to stay with her. He sat calmly at the bedside, hand on her thin shoulder. As far as Ronny could tell, Ben was all right, no sign of more turmoil than a person would expect.

Wife and Husband

THE LATE AFTERNOON SETTLED INTO A heavy kind of peace, the house empty except for Ronny and his tidying, the drift of voices from the backyard, Mrs. Nickelsen laughing in bell tones, a deeper undercurrent of Ben, sun breaking through the clouds, birdcalls. They had gone outside again to sit. She was fussing because the yard needed mowing, and Ben said he would take care of it tomorrow. Ronny relaxed, strain subsiding; strangers made him nervous, especially strangers like Ben's parents, whom he wanted to know better and yet feared to face. He focused on the tasks he was doing, the scrubbing of a pot in which someone had burned soup, the folding of dry towels and the search for the linen closet to which they should be carried.

Mr. Nickelsen opened the back door, puffing out breath as if he had exerted himself greatly, carrying brown bags of groceries from the car. He waved off Ronny's offer to help and told him to keep doing whatever it was he was doing—so he went back to putting laundry away. Mr. Nickelsen made one

more trip to his truck and returned with a bouquet of flowers. "I need to set these in some water," he said, and poked
through cabinets until he found a vase.

"Those are pretty. You got those at the grocery store?"

"Oh, yeah. They sell near about everything down there
these days. She likes these flowerdy things, you know. So I
thought I would bring her some." He was blushing, a bit embarrassed, but still pleased by his gesture.

"Here," Ronny said, and trimmed the ends from the stems
while Mr. Nickelsen filled the vase. When they were done and
the vase was ready to present, Mr. Nickelsen squared his
shoulders and marched to the hospital bed. By then she had
come inside again, to rest out of the sun. He stood at her
side with the determined posture of a soldier, presenting the
vase with a grim look, as if he expected wind to knock him
down. Mrs. Nickelsen cried out in shock and reached up to
him. He blushed deeply red. The moment felt raw and naked
in some way. Ronny returned quickly to the kitchen, feeling
as if he should not watch.

While the dishwasher was running Ronny made chicken
broth, thinking Mrs. Nickelsen might be able to drink it. Ben
cleaned the adjacent half-bathroom, which smelled of vomit
and needed a round of bleach before the odor went away.
Outside Mr. Nickelsen was starting the charcoal for grilling.
They were quiet, working near one another, the sound of the
television news providing an easy background. Something
funny about Jimmy Carter's mother, Miss Lillian. When it
was ready, Ronny took a cup of the soup to Mrs. Nickelsen to
taste. She sipped it and made a face. "Well, it's pretty good
I guess. I guess you can cook."

She had a slightly petulant expression, and he wondered
whether she wished he would leave her alone, or whether she

might be in pain. After a moment she took another sip and said, with more of a smile, "I think I really might be able to eat that if you put a little rice in it."

"I'm glad."

"I ought to drink a can of that milky mess, too, to make the doctors happy."

"You do whatever you want to," said Ben, standing close again, so that Ronny felt his nearness.

"Thank you, son. I believe I will."

"When do you need to take these pills?" Ben asked.

"I wrote it down somewhere," she said, and found the note on the table next to her. "I'm so glad you all put this stuff where I can reach it. Oh, me." She was shivering. Ben sat on the bed next to her. "Son, I never knew you to clean a bathroom unless I stood right over you."

He blushed. "We just want to help."

She looked at him. "That's good. You're growing up, looks like." Her voice was almost peaceful. She turned to Ronny, with a bit of a smile, though she appeared more tired than before. "Did you boys tell Harley to get flowers?"

"No, ma'am."

She laughed. "What in the world is going on with him? He never bought a flower in his life. But I appreciate it. He was so tickled with himself."

Ben caught Ronny's eye across the room at one point, after giving his mother the cup again to take a sip more of broth. Ronny could not have described all he saw in Ben's eyes. Nothing soft or easy; maybe even more anger than before; but toward Ronny an admission, a yearning, even an edge of his own fear.

Later Ben found him in the kitchen, standing near the back door looking around. Ben was wandering aimlessly with a beer in his hand. They were alone. When he saw Ronny he moved forward; he poured part of his beer in Ronny's mouth, grinning. "I put your bag in my room."

"I saw. I was just upstairs."

"It's not too bad up there."

"No. I'll clean that bathroom tomorrow."

"I'll do it. I can make my lazy ass clean another bathroom."

"I really don't mind. I like to be busy."

Ben's face grew solemn and tender, and he looked as if he might say something. He ran a hand through his hair. "Man."

"Be careful," Ronny said.

"Don't worry." He put his hands up, and grinned. "I'm just glad we're both here."

He walked away with his beer in his hand. His mother called out to him, in the other room, "Don't guzzle down that beer like it's candy, son. It'll go to your head."

"Sure, Ma."

"The house feels a lot better. I think so anyway."

"I know it does."

"It's a good thing you listened to your mother yesterday, don't you think?"

Ben laughed. "You won't get any argument from me about that."

Mr. Nickelsen called from the backyard. "These steaks are just about ready, son."

"I'll be right out there."

Ben took a card table from the laundry room and set it up in the den, then went outside, to check on his dad. Mrs. Nickelsen was pleased at her son's idea, that he wanted the table set in the same room with her. She sat up in bed, touched the flowers, smelled them. Watched her husband with her hands in her lap.

"He's been better since Ben got home. He has a way of straightening his dad out." As though she were speaking to herself, almost. "His dad used to be able to do the same thing for Ben but not anymore. With Ben, you've either got to beat him or love him. Otherwise you can't even talk to him. His dad can't beat him anymore and he loves him but he don't know how to show it. The way most men are."

Ronny could hear that she was trying to tell him something in her roundabout way. "You think Ben's like that?"

"Probably. I can see what he's feeling most of the time so he doesn't need to tell me. But I expect he's like my husband, at least some. I know he feels a lot of love, when it's waked up in him. He has a big heart."

Ronny was quiet, watching the men pile the steaks and potatoes onto plates.

"Now you watch," she said. "That's dinner right there. You won't get anything green while my boys cook."

"That's fine," Ronny said. "I can live with it."

"Do you agree Ben has a big heart?" she asked, in a voice that drew Ronny's gaze back to her.

"I know he does," Ronny said.

They looked at each other. The sliding glass doors were opening.

"Ronny," said Mrs. Nickelsen, "there's one of these pills I need to take with food, could you look and see? That chicken and rice is ready, I can smell it."

After dinner Ben and his dad played nickel poker at the card table while Mrs. Nickelsen drowsed. Father and son each had a jar of nickels they kept for poker sessions with each other. They wore special poker caps—Mr. Nickelsen had a green hat with Thompson Farm and Feed on the front, Ben had a black cap with a Cowboys logo. They were role-playing, whether they knew it or not, some halfhearted saloon in which they were cowboys; father like son was still two parts boy. Mrs. Nickelsen had eaten some rice and kept it down. She closed her eyes. On the TV was some kind of crime drama, the sound very low. Nobody was paying attention to it. The boys at the card table were subdued, watching the woman on the bed.

"I'd sure like some lotion for my arms," Mrs. Nickelsen said.

"I'll get it, Mom."

"In my bedroom in there, on the dresser. It's a yellow bottle."

"Are you going to sleep out here, Ma?" Ben asked, as she started to spread the lotion on her skin.

"No. This bed's too high, I'd be afraid I'd fall off."

"She wants to sleep with me," Mr. Nickelsen said, "like always."

"You heard your father. Can one of you help me into the bathroom? I think I'm going to put on my nightgown and go to bed."

"How you feeling?" Ben asked.

"Not so hot. Better since I ate something. The pain is worse tonight but I took a pill and it's easing off."

"That's good."

"The doctors are going to be mad at me that I'm not drinking that milky stuff but I don't like it. Now I know why I wasn't eating, I just didn't have anybody to cook for me."

"We're mighty thankful to you boys." Mr. Nickelsen had been repeating this all evening, every half hour or so. "I swear. This is the first beer I have enjoyed in I don't know when." He had appeared to enjoy two or three before that, but Ronny took him at his word.

"I'll be up and around a little bit tomorrow," Mrs. Nick-elsen said. "On the days I don't have the treatment I feel better."

"She's telling the truth, too, son. It's like it knocks her flat and then she gets up. She's amazing, I tell you."

"Are you going to help me up?" she asked.

"Yes, ma'am," Mr. Nickelsen said. "That's my job, ain't it. To get you through the threshold again."

"You made a joke, Harley."

"I been known to. In my younger days."

Ben stepped behind Ronny and stretched. "I'm about ready, too." He laid his hand on Ronny's shoulder.

"You want to say good night?"

"I doubt they'll come back out," he said, though just at that minute Mr. Nickelsen stepped to the door.

"Good night, boys," he said, glancing in their direction, at Ben's hand on Ronny's arm. Nodded and listened, in the quiet, to a clock that was ticking with a deal of self-importance.

They packed away the card table. There was still one load of dishes to do, laundry to fold, and the upstairs of the house to clean. "It's starting to look more like it ought to," Ben said.

"I like your parents. They're good people."

Ben stepped close. "Yeah. I guess they are. I can't believe my dad."

"He was so cute with the flowers."

"Fucking flowers. My old man."

Ben walked around the house, checking doors. Barefoot, half lit, in his tee shirt and jeans, the reality of seeing him here in his house, so ordinary. He touched Ronny's hand and they went upstairs, climbing past an oval-framed picture of wife and husband, black and white, clouded at the edges. "I feel like such a dick," Ben said.

"What?"

"How much brains does it take to know my ma would like it if somebody would clean up her house?"

"Baby, you just don't think that way."

"Well, if I don't start, what's going to happen around here?"

They stood in the doorway of his room. Ronny put his arms around Ben's tough waist, ran his hands up Ben's back. "There are options," Ronny said.

"Like?"

"Like you and me figure out how we're going to get here as much as we need to the next few weeks."

"You serious?"

"I'm only working three days a week. So when I'm not working I can be here, too."

"I hope my sister comes tomorrow, we need to talk to her."

"No way these two should have to sit in this house by themselves."

Ben nodded, his hair brushing Ronny's cheek. "It makes sense. It calms my stomach down."

Ronny started to say something else and Ben put a hand over his mouth. He took a long breath. His eyes were full of pain but dry, nowhere close to tears. There was a sob in him that he had to keep in there, to prove that he could contain it. Pulling Ronny against him, chin in Ronny's hair, an intensity in his body, rivers of anger and confusion. "You got to me just in time," he said. "You know what I mean?"

"The other night?"

"Yes."

Ronny held still against Ben's shoulder, their fronts warming, Ronny standing in the doorway looking into the empty hall. Ben ran a hand through his hair. "She looked like she felt better. Did you think so? By the time she went to bed."

"She hadn't thrown up in a while."

"That's right. She ate."

"She kept it down."

Ben pulled him inside and they undressed. Ben walked to the stair landing and listened while Ronny brushed his teeth. Even now Ronny had a hard time looking at anything other than Ben, walking naked in the house, the hair on his legs, the smooth planes of his back, his strong arms. This is the only reward I ever want, Ronny thought, and felt in himself for the first time the stirring of another fear, that he could never pull back from this. That he would fall into Ben and drown.

They lay in bed in the dark. Streetlight here was duller or the night was darker; they had opened the window for the breeze, Ronny lying on top of Ben, as close as if they were still in Ronny's room on his single bed. Ben said, "Man, I was feeling so fucking crazy that last night I was here. I was afraid I was going to hurt somebody. I was up here with Jen, I couldn't get away from her."

"You had Jen up here?"

"She was staying the night."

"Well, I guess I should have known."

"Hey."

"We'll change the sheets tomorrow," Ronny said.

"You little bitch."

"That's me."

Ben chuckled, pulled Ronny against him. "That really made you jealous."

Ronny relaxed, knowing he had to, or risk a fight. "I'm all right."

"You know I'm not going to say I'm sorry."

Ronny stayed still, where he was, near the stubbled cheek and ear and dark curls.

"Can't you give me a little smirk?"

Ronny looked at him.

"That's better." Ben kissed him, opened him up, brought their bodies together, drawn down into each other, nothing had changed. Ronny tried not to expect anything at all and found himself soon enough as lost as before in the sensation, Ben gentle for longer than ever, which only made the turn to something fiercer more acute, more like a heartache that pierced them both at the same moment. Suddenly in the double bed they learned economy and hardly needed to move. Pleasure can burn, can sting, can cool, can heat, can do everything at once, and then soothe, and then rush forward, almost there, and almost there, as many times as it can be pressed, until there comes an end. They had that thought again, together and at the same time, that this was the thing they were, not what they were doing but what they were seeing, that what they contained was a big space, open, clean, belonging to no one else. Free.

"That's ending up, for you," Ben said in Ronny's ear, breathing heavily for the first time.

"Is that what you call a gut check?"

Ben laughed. "Probably so, from your point of view."

They listened to each other for a while. Ronny felt the day come down on him some, the length of it, all that had happened. Ben murmured something, rolled off Ronny, rubbed his cheek with a hand. "I got this impulse to say something stupid myself," Ben said. "What do you know?"

"Yeah?"

"You don't need me to, do you?"

Ronny shook his head. "Pretty much everything I need is right here already."

"That's my boy."

"We should go to sleep."

Ben grunted, rolled onto his back. "If you wake up, you know what to start doing," he said.

"Yes, boss. You want me to wake you up first?"

"No. Let it be a surprise."

Nina

BEN SLID OUT OF BED BEFORE Ronny, who watched him stumble downstairs after pulling on a pair of pajama bottoms that really didn't look like he'd slept in them at all. Moving like he wanted to be quiet. Big as he was, he could step light. Ronny drowsed awhile, got up a few minutes later and pulled on jeans and shirt, finding a pair of socks for his cold feet.

Ben's room was bare of anything personal, a small room, painted sheetrock, bright green, absent of ornament, as though its occupant could be anyone. It had the appearance of a shabby guest room in a house where guests rarely came. Ben had no heroes taped to his walls, no pictures of himself or his family, nothing that spoke about his past before Chapel Hill. If he had ever won any trophies during his sports career— he had also been a wrestler in high school—he refused to display them. A suitcase sat in the corner, clothes wadded and twisted; the closet, though, was bare except for a hunting rifle, what looked like a toolbox, half a fishing rod, and a stack of old board games: Clue, Monopoly, Parcheesi, Risk, The Game of Life, Twister. A backpack, a baseball bat, a catcher's mitt, a basketball mostly deflated. Oddly enough, he had no football anywhere to be seen.

Something prevented Ronny from looking in the drawers: maybe fear of Ben's temper; maybe some sense of honor about Ben's privacy; maybe just reluctance. He felt as though he had been here much longer than he had. Close to Ben, happy as he had ever been; unsettled by the circumstances, watching the family suffer, watching the mother fight for her life, the father bewildered, the son fearful, all of it laid bare.

Downstairs, father and son were at ease in the kitchen with the smell of frying bacon. Ben was cooking; he had already made coffee and it was perked by the time Ronny arrived. He poured a cup for himself.

Mrs. Nickelsen lay in the hospital bed, her eyes closed, the room darkened with the drapes shut. She was wearing a housedress and resting on top of the blankets, as if she had just settled there. Ronny stood in the door and watched and then went back to the kitchen table to sip coffee next to Mr. Nickelsen, who was already dressed for work.

"You going to run this morning?" Mr. Nickelsen asked.

"I think I'll skip it."

"Nice of you to make bacon."

Ben was gruff, staring at the frying pan, ignoring the rest of the world. "You don't have to say bullshit you don't want to, Dad. I know you appreciate food."

Mr. Nickelsen laughed. He turned to Ronny. "This is what I get, you see? This kid never wanted to be thanked for anything in his life. I never seen the beat of it."

"Thanks is just talk. People talk shit to death and what good does it do?"

"All I mean is you should let a person say thank you when he means it. You know."

Ben looked at him, tapping the spatula on the edge of the iron skillet. "I'm glad to do stuff for you even though I'm a rat-fuck son of a bitch to you most of the time."

"And vicey versey."

"We may be fuck-ups but we don't mind admitting it."

"You got to emphasize your good qualities, son. But I tell you, the world will be just as glad to fuck you for them as it will for your bad ones." Scratching dry skin from his ears, which were sprouting curly hairs along the edge.

Ben laughed. "Here's your eggs."

"Just in time. I got a goddamn sales staff meeting to get to."

"You want a piece of bread?"

"I got some. Sit down, eat yourself. Ronny?"

"It's too early for me."

"He'll sip coffee till it's fucking ten o'clock and then wonder why he's hungry," Ben said.

"Maybe you ought to cut out the language. Your mama don't like it."

Ben grunted, chewing like a machine. A half dozen eggs on his plate.

Mr. Nickelsen said, to Ronny, "You ought to eat something while it's here, boy. You're skinny as that coatrack."

Ronny bit into a piece of bacon and savored it, watching Ben across the table hunched over his food, glancing at his dad. The posture of a small boy, set to imitate every move his father makes. The clock showed the time as before seven in the morning, light still gentle in the windows. Ronny felt a sense of peace rising into him, replacing the anxiety. They were treating him like one of the family. He had wanted a feeling like this for a long time.

When his dad walked out into the fog of morning, the meal over, Ben rinsed the plates and poured off the bacon grease into a jelly jar. Ronny put the plates into the dishwasher, and they bumped against each other, Ben still shirtless, his body such a rich object, Ronny could barely see anything else. Ben grinned slow and pressed Ronny against the kitchen counter, held him there. "You think we could go back upstairs?"

Ronny laughed, shaking his head. His voice failed, having the guy so near. Ben looked disappointed. When Ronny started to move away, Ben pulled him back. Pitching his voice low. "Stand here for a minute. Don't be so fucking twitchy."

Ronny touched Ben's bare skin, stood close, and breathed, his hands on the broad back. "All right."

"Nothing needs doing right this second except me. All I want is you just standing right there."

"I can do that."

"Good." After a while, Ben chuckled. "Man. What does this feel like to you?"

After a moment, Ronny answered. "Like I'm tuning into you, kind of. Like my body knows you're there and the longer you stand there the more I feel you, the deeper it goes."

"Does it tickle?"

Ronny laughed a moment. "Yeah. Almost. Down here, in here, somewhere."

"I feel like I'm not going to be able to fucking breathe," Ben said. "Did you ever feel like this?"

"Before? No."

After a minute, Ben wet his lips. "You have to ask me, shithead."

Ronny's voice was shaking. "Did you ever feel like this?"

"Hell fucking no."

Ronny put his head down against Ben's shoulder. Ben touched a hand to each of Ronny's arms, held him.

"Don't even think about trying to move," Ben said. "I'm listening for Mom, if she needs us, I'll know."

A long while passed and they stood there. All golden. When they heard her stirring, Ben headed through the door, stepping away from Ronny, who was heated down the front of his body. Ronny's eyes filled and he wiped them and they filled again. He stood there trying to breathe calmly.

"Why is it so dark in here?" Mrs. Nickelsen asked. "Open those curtains."

"Yes, ma'am."

"I smell bacon."

"I cooked for Dad this morning."

"That smell. I don't think I could eat that."

"Are you hungry?"

Ronny walked into the room. Ben was watching him. Mrs. Nickelsen asked, "Did you sleep good?"

"Yes, ma'am."

"Mom—"

"I heard you, son. I think maybe I could eat a piece of toast."

"Is that all?"

"You know I don't want much of a morning."

"I don't guess you want any coffee?"

"The doctor says I can't have coffee anymore. To tell you the truth I don't miss it as much as I thought I would."

In pictures scattered around the house she was a tall woman with a hint of the stately in the way she carried herself, large soulful eyes, a mouth set in a perpetually sad line, a penchant for wearing flowered prints. She had a face a person would respond to, a spirit one would find easy to know, or at least this was the promise of the pictures. There was a slump of defeat to her shoulders, but her eyes hinted she was stubborn and would never much give in.

The same woman lay here now, the fine bones of her skull almost luminous, her skin translucent, the sad turn of the mouth suddenly become bemused, the soulful eyes peering deeply into every shadow and corner. A knitted shawl over her shoulders. She was more present today than yesterday, trying to sit up, eyes alert and open, turning from one part of the room to the other.

"Do you want that bed cranked up some, Mrs. Nickelsen?" Ronny asked.

"That'd be nice. I do feel like sitting up higher today. Overcast hadn't burned off yet, can't tell what kind of weather it's going to be. Listen to those birds."

A high flurry of trills and piercing calls was sounding from outside, vaguely overhead. Gray light suffused the room and the backyard, muting the colors of the grass and flowers. When it lit her face the lines of her skin were softened, and she looked younger, happier.

"It's that big pecan tree in the backyard next door," she said. "I love to hear the birds in it."

Ronny moved to the chair next to her. She was very different from his own mother, who was sharp in voice and personality, tight energy bound into her body from head to toe, as if she were one big coiled spring. Mrs. Nickelsen was gentle and subdued where Ronny's mom was strident and brazen. But there was some core of softness that they shared, a feeling that either could be hurt, easily, and maybe the sense that they had been.

"Where are your parents, Ronny?" Mrs. Nickelsen asked.

"My mom just moved to Nevada to get remarried. My dad lives in Richmond and works for a power plant. I really never spent that much time with my dad."

"Do you like the man your mother is marrying?"

"I haven't ever met him."

She gave no sign of surprise and asked no more questions. "I'm sticking my nose in everybody's business this morning," she said, looking pleased.

"I could pretty much tell you were feeling better." Ben said, his eyes luminous, the blue burning. They sat in quiet with each other. She brushed her fingers across the top of his hand. Ronny left them alone to talk and quietly continued with work in the kitchen. He had never heard Ben talk so much to anyone else: the doctors, the sickness, school, the summer, Dad, Nina, the hospital again, chemotherapy, the quiet embarrassment of it, being ill. Overheard as Ronny moved through the periphery, among the laundry and the trash. Ben resting his head and arm on the edge of the bed, Mrs. Nickelsen lying back in her pillows, murmuring something about the grass that needed cutting.

When she saw Ronny in the doorway to the kitchen, she said, "He won't tell you this, Ronny, but he's never had a friend he could talk to like he can you. He told me that. And I'm telling you right in front of him so you'll know."

"Yes, ma'am."

"This chemotherapy has loosened up my brain," she said. "I feel like I can say anything. Even to your dad."

"You need to take charge then," Ben said, "and make sure everybody takes better care of you. I would have cleaned the house if I knew it would make you feel that much better."

"Ben, son, let me tell you something. When you're sick you don't even hardly know to ask."

Ronny went upstairs to shower and dress. The first thing he did after was to change the sheets on Ben's bed. He took the dirty linens down to the laundry room, emptied the dishwasher and loaded the last of the backlog, then went upstairs to clean the bathroom. He was scrubbing the tile in the shower stall when he heard steps at the door and a young woman stuck her head in. She had dark, shining hair, cut short, just below her ears. Her skin was milky pale and bright, touched with three small moles on one cheek. She looked at Ronny in laconic surprise and he said, "Are you Nina? I'm Ben's friend Ronny."

"Oh, that's right," she said, in a kind of dreamy way. She had a dusky voice and spoke so slowly that it was almost affected. "I just came to sneak in my bag before I saw Ma. Was the place a mess?"

"It wasn't that bad but it was driving your mom crazy."

She rolled her eyes. "No shit. Miss Clean Freak herself. You need help?"

"I'm almost done."

Her expression soured and she looked at Ronny askance. Likely she was thinking about her mother. Cleaning supplies arranged on the floor beside him, the tub smelling of Comet cleanser, the toilet bowl bright. "You sure you're one of Ben's friends? I mean, you speak English and you clean bathrooms. The last friend Ben brought home would have been shitting in the corner." She shook her head. "Okay, I'll put this in my room."

He started to say something polite like, "It's good to meet you," but her face had the same set sharpness as Ben's, and she had a distracted air at the moment. She moved noisily into the other bedroom. On her way downstairs she stopped in the doorway again. She was pressing her palms against her face, her eyes red rimmed. "Oh, lord," she said. "I don't want to do this."

He stopped and studied her, shoulders rigid, jaw muscles visible. She was upset and it made her angry. Better to be angry than vulnerable. She truly was Ben's sister, he could see it now.

"How is she?" Nina asked.

"Seems like she feels better this morning. They're downstairs talking."

She nodded, looking at the ceiling. "Oh, this sucks so much."

He kept quiet. Stupid talk might make her angry, too. She watched him awhile. "How long have you been here?"

"We got here yesterday."

She took a deep breath, running her palms along her cheeks. "Can't be that much fun. Visiting a sick house where you have to do the cleaning."

Chose his words carefully. "Beats just sitting around."

She laughed, leaning against the doorway. Gathering herself. "Really? If you say so. Oh, well. Guess I have to face it. Thanks."

She hurtled herself down the stairs, as though it were a move she needed to make without hesitating or else she might run back into her room and close the door. Ronny rinsed the cleanser out of the shower basin, toweled it dry. Nothing left now but the floors. He could hear voices from downstairs, and everything sounded calm enough.

How would he feel if this were his own mother? The thought gave him a pain, a fear that was all the more real because she was so far away, and the idea of cancer was vivid now. Even in his imagination the idea was fierce and made him want to talk to her, to find out whether she was all right, to tell him he was glad she had found somebody who cared about her, that he hoped things were going well.

He finished the bathroom and ran the vacuum on the hall carpet. Ben stuck his head up the stairs to say, "Mom's getting agitated with you up here cleaning and all of us downstairs."

He turned off the vacuum and looked at Ben. "And?"

"Stop and come down."

Ronny shook his head. "I'll be done in a couple of minutes."

Ben frowned, walked behind Ronny, unplugged the machine. He wrapped his arms around Ronny and lifted him, carried him down a couple of steps. "I said it's time to stop."

Ronny could feel Ben's heart at his back, beating and beating. He said, "Well, fine."

"Just do what I say," Ben said, but calmly, even a little gently.

They went downstairs, where Nina and Mrs. Nickelsen were laughing together at something Nina had said. Mrs. Nickelsen pointed at Ronny with her finger. She was sitting up on the side of the bed. "Young man, if you don't sit down I'll tell Ben to knock a knot on you."

"I can do that," Ben said.

"Yes, ma'am, I'll sit, I'm done."

"Nina, he's been working since he got here."

"And, Ma, I know how much it tickles you to watch a man do the cleaning."

Mrs. Nickelsen laughed. "You know, I hadn't even thought about that. I do kind of appreciate it, now that you mention it." She reached for the stool with her foot. "I think I'm going to get dressed and walk around my house now that maybe I can stand to look at it."

Ben took her arm. "Let me help."

"Don't help too much, now. I need to do some things on my own. The doctor told me to try to get out of bed when I could."

Nina showed no signs of upset now; she was like her brother, practical and crisp, as though this were an ordinary visit home, and it was normal to have a hospital bed in the middle of the den. "Do you have a wig, Ma?"

"Yes, but I can't stand to wear it. The day of a treatment my skin hurts too much. And when I feel better I don't want it on my head. So you all will just have to look at my bird feathers."

"Oh, that's not what I meant." Nina frowned. "You look all right."

"Come with me in the bedroom and I'll try it on for you," she said. "I have two, I have one so blonde I look like Marilyn Monroe. I got that to scare your daddy with." She sniffed. "The house sure smells better."

Nina went with her mother in the bedroom. Ben came to Ronny, who was opening the sliding glass doors. They were quiet together, side by side.

Nina made a shopping list and sent them off with it, while she stayed to talk with her mom. She gave instructions with an emphasis toward Ben, as though she had to make things clear to him, and he scratched his ears and nodded. When they were leaving the house, Nina was trimming her mother's ragged hair. "I like your hair this color," said Mrs. Nickelsen.

"You never let me keep it as short as I wanted to."

"Well, you were so skinny, I didn't want you to look like a boy."

"You never liked my hair, you were always after me to curl it."

A sharpness to their talk, as if they were at the edge of a quarrel, as if they always were. "Let's get out of here," Ben said, "before they piss each other off."

People knew Ben in town and spoke to him as if he was still the star of the Turtletrack Trojans, as if time had stopped then. A couple of women made the same joke, looking Ronny up and down and saying, "Well, I don't think you're on the football team, are you?" then bursting into laughter and grabbing Ben's arm. The men mostly ignored Ronny altogether, preferring to talk a little Carolina football with Ben. Ronny shopped in the background.

Even that short trip into town yielded lore. There had been a big lumber mill here once, connected with a basket factory across the state line in Murfreesboro; a lot of people worked there until it burned down in the early sixties. A tobacco market had closed around the same time, and the town drifted into decline. Main routes of traffic had bypassed the village around the same era, and this part of Virginia never had much to offer as destination, anyway, being close to swamps, bordering the part of North Carolina where Quakers had settled, along Albemarle Sound. Since there were no big towns nearby, Turtletrack had taken on an isolated, ghostly feeling, storefronts boarded up or empty on the central streets, forlorn lines of rusty parking meters, traffic lights that blinked yellow over empty intersections. The little commerce that remained had moved to the outskirts of town. Ben told him about some of this. He had some nostalgia for his home, maybe some pride. Growing up here had been easy, he said, except for family stuff. He and his buddies played without fear in the yards and in the woods; nobody supervised them much. Now it was different. People had started to lock their doors, hover over their children like they were precious butterflies. He said this with a mocking smile. "I don't like kids much."

"Yeah. Same."

"Then let's don't have any," Ben said, and chortled, enjoying his own joke, slapping Ronny on the back.

Ben went for a run in the afternoon, lifted weights in the basement. Mrs. Nickelsen had a spell of nausea and went back to bed. Nina worked around the house with Ronny, dusting, cleaning her parents' bathroom and bedroom. She was silent while she was working, answering any question put to her but otherwise focused on the work. Cleaning was not something she cared to do, she said, and at moments she appeared irritated and indifferent. Later, when they went to her room to take a break, she showed no sign of reserve at all. She sat cross-legged on the bed and Ronny pulled off his shoes and joined her. She shifted a strand of hair that was hanging down in front of her face to behind her ear. "Man. I haven't played maid in a long time."

"It's kind of fun."

She looked at him a bit sharply. "What are you, Pollyanna or something?"

Ronny giggled. "Well, I don't really like scrubbing toilets, that's true."

"I always got stuck with the housework because I was the girl. I don't think Ben even knows how you use a sponge." She was tearing up buds of pot on a tray, the smell pungent.

"I don't know why I'm doing this, I don't want to smoke right now."

"Me either, not while I have to face your folks."

"I just fall asleep." But she went on cleaning the stuff, separating seeds from leaf. "We can have a joint when my folks go to bed. Ben wanted me to bring some." She was watching him, studying his clothes and hair; Ronny felt her gaze move from one part of him to another. "You're so skinny."

He laughed, and looked at her quizzically.

She shrugged. "Ben usually brings these apes home with him, you know? Football guys." She shook her head. "I don't like guys like that. I like skinny guys."

Uncomfortable, he changed the subject. She was in graduate school, so he asked, "What do you study?"

"I bet you asked Ben and he couldn't tell you."

"He said something about women's politics, but I couldn't understand it."

"I'm in history combined with women's studies. Greensboro has a new program."

"Oh. Well, that makes more sense."

She giggled. "Right. I personally am studying women's suffrage movements for my thesis. Comparing them from country to country." She licked the joint and sealed it. "I guess women's politics is close enough. I'm surprised he knew that much."

"He says good stuff about you."

"Really?"

"Sure."

"Like what?"

"You're smart. Like his mom, he says. And bad stubborn like he is. And you have a wicked mouth when you need it."

That did please her, in spite of herself. "Like Mom, huh?" She snorted a hoarse laugh and shook her head. "He would say that. I love my mom but I don't want to be her, married and stuck in a place like this. You do Ben's homework?"

"I help him with some of his writing."

"I thought so. That's Ben. He always gets people to do stuff for him."

Her room was full of pieces of her, the walls painted a soft, creamy white, bright rugs on the floor. A low bookshelf held copies of *The Feminine Mystique*, *A Room of One's Own*, Virginia Woolf's diaries, *Cities of the Interior*; there was a copy of *The Second Sex*, the book Ronny had read in class this semester; on the wall, posters of Gloria Steinem, Betty Friedan, Angela Davis, all taped on top of other posters: David Cassidy's showing the eyes, Davy Jones's mouth and chin, the side of Jimi Hendrix's face, the top half of Bobby Sherman's head. It was a collage of her obsessions, she said. He was staring at them and she noticed. "I had crushes on those guys when I was a kid. Except Hendrix. I've still got a crush on him."

"But you covered most of them up."

She giggled and rocked back and forth on the mattress. "I know. Isn't it great? You know who those women are, right?"

"I don't know who Betty Friedan is."

"She wrote *The Feminine Mystique*. Reading her changed my whole life."

She told him about the book, and he told her he'd read *The Second Sex*, and that impressed her; they talked about Simone de Beauvoir, Charlotte Brontë, books in general, writing. She was quick, like Ben, but she was also engaged with something, the idea of women and what they ought to do to be equal to men. Thoughts spilling out of her so quickly, it was hard to keep up. Whereas Ben was lazy-smart, his brain an adjunct to his body. Nina showed Ronny her collection of Barbie dolls from childhood, lined up on a shelf at the back of her closet, marked up with black marker, mustaches, S&M outfits drawn onto their naked bodies, their costumes slashed and bloody. "They're doing time," she said. "Paying for their crimes against women."

"Crimes?"

"These are their true inner selves." Smirking, tossing Leather Barbie back on the shelf.

They went downstairs again, sitting outside the sliding glass doors in the fresh air. Mrs. Nickelsen was still resting. Ben came up from the basement, sweaty, his body gleaming, tee shirt sticking to him; he said hello to Nina and they talked in hushed voices, to keep from waking their mother. She asked him what had happened to him that he brought home a decent person for a friend. He smirked and asked her whether she had any friends or if she still hid in her apartment all day. She threw a little rock at him. He ran upstairs.

"You want to teach this stuff you're studying?" Ronny asked.

"Maybe. Maybe go into politics. Maybe go to law school when I get done with my women's studies degree. I'm not in a hurry."

"Law school for me, too. Or else I want to work for a newspaper."

"It sounds like fun to me, being somebody's advocate in a court, or whatever. Knowing how the law works."

"My ma always wanted me to be a doctor."

"Mine used to say that to me, too, that I was smart enough to be a doctor and it was getting to where a woman could be one if she wanted to."

"Good that she pushed you some."

She was getting a little irritated again and frowned. "You know, you kind of overdo this find-the-virtue thing."

"She didn't try to make you settle down and get married, right?"

Nina nodded, considering. "I guess she never nagged at either me or Ben that way, that I remember. It was more neat-freak stuff than anything else around here. And general worship of Ben."

"Obnoxious?"

"Please. Try being the big sister of a football hero. You don't even get to do the hero worship or sneak peeks at him in the shower, like the little sister would do." She got out a pack of cigarettes and lit one. "At least I was old enough that we were only in school together one year."

"How were you guys before that?"

She shrugged. "We were mostly fine. We still are. He knows I don't give a fuck about football. Mom doesn't like it either, much, but she adores her son. But then he started dating these godawful girls that never used their head for anything but a makeup display." She was quiet, shaking her head. "Things calmed down when I went to college, anyway. I like him better now. The family kind of shut down this last couple of years. I don't know. Maybe Mom was getting sick and running out of energy. Or maybe it was both of us kids being gone from home."

"Seems like he goes to see you pretty often."

"We're so close together, why wouldn't he? He's my bud, even if he is an ape."

She got up to look at her mom, then came back and whispered, "I'm going upstairs to talk to Ben a minute, okay? You sit with her?"

"Sure."

"Sorry I'm running my mouth so much. I'm not usually like this. It's easy to talk to you."

The two of them were upstairs for a very long time. Mrs. Nickelsen woke and Ronny warmed some of the soup for her. She asked where her children were and Ronny told her they were upstairs. She remained quiet after that, lying on her side looking out the window. He helped her to eat the soup and she closed her eyes again. She appeared to be in pain so he simply sat in the room with her, left her to herself. At times it was hard to tell whether she was awake or dozing. After a while she said, "You know, I wish Ben could find a girl who makes him calm down like you do."

"Well. Maybe he will."

"But maybe that's not what he needs," she said. Ended with a fit of coughing, waving away the soup, closing her eyes, the pain rising and then subsiding. She went easily into sleep, a miracle maybe linked to the painkillers, and he watched, wondering where his own mother was, wishing he could call.

He took the dishes into the kitchen and met Nina coming down the stairs. She refused to look at Ronny at first and appeared shaken. Her eyes were red. She leaned over the kitchen sink and looked out the window. "Man," she said. "That hasn't happened in forever."

"What?"

She wiped her eyes with her sleeve and took the dishes from his hands. "Just talking." She looked toward the stairs and stood there for a moment. "About how to take care of Mom." She wiped her eyes again. She stood at the sink shaking, making no sound at all. He started toward her but she shook her head and sniffed. "I'm okay. But listen, go up there, all right? Look after my brother."

She said it so naturally, as though Ben were Ronny's charge. It made him wonder.

Upstairs he found Ben sprawled on the bed on his stomach. His eyes were red and swollen and he was breathing hard. Ronny stood in the doorway, watching. Ben shifted his face toward the pillow. "Don't look at me like this," he said.

"Don't be ridiculous."

"I mean it."

"Mean it, then. I'm not going anywhere." He closed the door and lay along Ben's back. He put his face near Ben's. Far from resisting, he reached for Ronny's arm and pulled it around him.

"Nina can still get me to cry," he said. "She always could. I hate it." He said the words between little gasps. His eyes were completely red, bloodshot, the lids swollen from tears. His face was flushed and his nose was running. Ronny went to get him a tissue and he wiped his nose and threw it on the floor. He turned over on his back and pulled Ronny onto him. "She sitting with Mom?"

"Yes. She woke up and ate some soup."

"Good." He pressed his hand onto Ronny's back, closed his eyes. "I'm fucking scared of this, Ronny. My mom's so sick."

Ronny kissed his chest, waited.

"She's better today but she'll be worse tomorrow."

"That's the treatment, Ben. You don't know how sick she is right now from the cancer."

He thought about it and nodded. But he couldn't manage to say anything.

They lay together, listening to the sounds from outside, children's voices somewhere, playing, the sound of a lawn mower, a few cars passing on the street. The day was warm but they kept close to each other anyway, and Ben stripped off Ronny's shirt and threw it on the floor, so their skins were touching. The quiet they felt with one another felt like something alive around them; sweet to lie still like that, to breathe together. Ben grew calmer, and Ronny pushed up from his chest, looked at him, kissed him gently.

"Nina says you're too much. Way too good to be true." Ben giggled, wiping his eyes on the back of his hands. "She's almost right."

"Almost?"

Ben grabbed him and they wrestled and Ben flung Ronny around a bit and fake-punched him a few times and felt all the better for it, judging from his satisfied grunts. He worked himself into a sweat. They fumbled together quickly for the rest, conscious that Ben at least needed to get downstairs to his mother again.

"By the way," Ben said, sitting next to Ronny, who was still lying in bed while Ben pulled on his underwear. "We're busted."

"What?"

"Nina hangs out with a lot of gay people in Greensboro. She spotted you right away."

"She didn't say anything to me."

"She knows I'd get pissed if she did. She won't make you talk about it, unless you bring it up."

"You told her the truth?"

He chuckled. "She asked me if I really wanted her to believe I was sleeping in my room with a gay guy and not having sex."

"Man."

"I didn't actually admit to anything, and she didn't push. She just wanted me to know."

"Jesus."

"I don't feel too freaked about it," Ben said.

Ronny lay there quietly after Ben had gone downstairs again; there was a sense that he was brimming over, that he could scarcely contain all this feeling. Afternoon light and heat dazed him; he was actually warmer when Ben was gone, even though they had lain so close together, their skins touching. He fell asleep, and Ben came to wake him later, around five, when Mr. Nickelsen came home. He opened his eyes to find Ben there, sitting on the edge of the bed, hand in Ronny's hair. "Wake up, sleepy."

"Oh, man. That was cool."

"We want you to come have a beer with us. You lazy fuck."

"Nice nap," Ronny said.

"I hope so. You were up here two hours."

"Man."

"You ready for me to pull you up?"

"Well—"

Ben pulled him up and Ronny grabbed his shirt.

So in between moments with the family—with Ben mowing the lawn, with Mrs. Nickelsen watching the squares of the world visible through the window and the sliding doors, her husband next to her, asleep; with Nina reading in the kitchen making more broth, to freeze for later—Ronny tried to process it all, to understand his part in it. Nina knew their secret, and yet acted as though it did not signify, and kidded her brother when he took off his shirt to mow, showing off again, she said; and winked at Ronny, and licked out her tongue, and giggled, walking quickly back to the kitchen, enjoying her secret far too much. Mr. Nickelsen talking about the stupid Democrats and why it was he would never vote for them again, with the integration, and the way they did the Watergate, trying to impeach that poor Nixon fellow, and they were all crooked, and his wife telling him to hush, that he didn't know anything about that mess and he ought to just let it all alone. She lay in bed and stared dreamily into the room; whether she was content or in pain, peaceful or queasy, impossible to tell, because she rested so completely within her moment. As though to say she was ready for whatever might follow. Only now and then, when Ben was in the back-yard and walked the mower where she could see him, a spark of worry; Ronny felt in those moments that he saw the whole history of the family, the mother fretting over the son, maybe not sure why, exactly, but understanding that he was where she needed to place her concern. While on the surface he was the star, the athlete, the boy doing what so many boys dreamed of doing, starring on the football field, going to college on a scholarship. Ben with his roughness, his frantic energy, his anger, and now his hurt.

But he was made for something bigger, maybe? At least a little bigger than a fertilizer salesman who had the raising of children as all he could do. No matter whether he was gay or straight, no matter whether he found a woman, no matter what.

Nina added a contrast, a finished person even at her age, already seeing beyond her present to the life she believed she should have. Aloof beyond her sarcasm, watching everyone else.

The evening passed well, notable only for the fact that Nina pulled her father aside and told him sometimes he was looking at Mrs. Nickelsen like she was already dead, like he was completely terrified—this had been more and more true as the evening wore on. She told him he had to stop doing it right now, and he nodded his head and ran his hand through what remained of his hair. Nina had something more of a hold on her father than Ben. He said it was easier now that the children were around to help.

The next day was chemotherapy day. The whole family went, Ben and Nina wanting to talk to their mother's doctor. Ronny stayed in the house, reading, freezing the broth Nina had made, making dinner for the family. He tormented himself with the fear of his own ultimate iniquity, that he might be doing good for all the wrong reasons, merely to ingratiate himself, and was certain to be punished. He was focused on the thing he wanted.

The afternoon was hard. Nina and Ben tended their mother through the nausea. Mr. Nickelsen paced from his bedroom to the sliding glass doors, gradually returning to something like his normal color as the memory of the chemotherapy unit faded. He smoked a cigarette outside, with the clouds gathering to make more rain. Ben tried to convince himself the nausea was better this time, mentioned it twice, until his father shook his head and said, "No, it's not, son. It's just like it always is."

That night after dinner Ben drove Ronny back to Chapel Hill.

They were quiet at first, overflowing from the visit, Ben shocked at the look of his mother after chemotherapy, lifeless and gray. About the time they crossed into North Carolina, Ben started talking. "Nina says she can be at the house on weekends, to give me a break. She'll get there on Friday. Dad will just have to be alone if I take you back Thursday morning and decide to stay with you."

He meant that the two of them would do this every week, that Ronny would be there. "That sounds good. We'll have some time together that's not at your house. Or maybe we'll be able to."

"What's up? You feeling all fucked up and doubtful again?"

Ronny shook his head. "I'm just thinking that anything can happen from here, that's all."

Ben nodded, grinding his jaw, staring at the road, headlights playing over his face.

"It's been intense the last couple of days. Maybe I'm just wiped."

"Rest up in the car, then," Ben said. "You don't need to keep me company."

"Seems a shame to sleep."

He chuckled. "Why? I'm not going anywhere. Lay your head down on the seat."

He did, and closed his eyes. His head was actually on Ben's thigh, which was spread to its usual position for driving. The engine ran through them both like a song; now and then Ben lay his arm on Ronny as they drove quietly through the countryside in the dark.

"You asleep?"

"No. I'm listening."

"I'll probably stay in town tomorrow night since Nina's at home. I want to party with the boys some. I think I need to blow it out a little bit."

"That sounds smart."

"So I doubt I stay at your place tomorrow night. I'll crash in the room with Tate or something."

"Or pick up some girl."

"Well, it's possible, if I get drunk. I cannot make any promises." Ben pulled Ronny closer, shifted his thigh some.

"If you were a girl you'd be quite a little cat bitch. I'd hate to cross you."

"I would, too. In fact, if I were you, I would hate to cross me now."

Farther along the road, Ronny asked, "You don't get jealous, do you?"

"Only once or twice. Not much." He rubbed his chin, rested his hand on Ronny's side. "I don't know, though, if I was to catch you with somebody. That would be ugly, right there."

"But you can do what you want to do and I have to put up with it."

"Well, you don't fucking technically have to."

"Yeah. Right. But you know what I mean."

"I'm just telling you what it would be. If I caught you with anybody I would have the same flash of jealous shit you do, but mine would have my fist behind it."

Ronny thought about it. All in all he was not unpleased. "I suppose I have to concede the justice of that. You are whatever the fuck you are."

"The cussing is getting almost excellent for a sissy such as yourself."

"Fuck you."

The moment had made Ben light, forgetting all about the trouble, and he ran a hand along Ronny's side. "So, bitch, the answer is you don't want to see me with anybody or hear about me with anybody and I have a similar hankering for myself where you are concerned. I would never say to you, I do not want you to screw anybody but me. Well, I would say that, but not with any expectation you would have to listen. But I would say to you, very honestly, that if I ever catch you with anybody, I will beat the shit out of whoever that poor unfortunate motherfucker may be. He will not be sleeping with anybody for a good long time after that."

"Is it sick for me to say I find that oddly exciting?"

"No. As long as you don't think for a second I'm joking." Ben's tone had become serious, but lightened now. "So when you are with anybody else you're risking his good health. Not to put any pressure on you."

"But, you know, I just don't see it happening anyway. I'm the loyal type. And if that changes I'm not stupid enough to let you catch me."

"Good move," he said. "It's always good to leave some room for doubt."

"Why?"

He shrugged his shoulders, cocked his head. "You don't want me to be too sure of you. And I kind of like the thought of totally beating piles of crap out of your back-door boyfriend, too. Makes me tingly."

An Elegy

RONNY WOULD ALWAYS WONDER, HAD MRS. NICKELSEN lived, whether he and Ben would have managed to survive that summer with more knowledge of each other than they got. Whether, indeed, they might even have survived it intact. But she died very suddenly a few days later. The cancer had invaded too much of her body; she caught pneumonia in her weakened state and that was that.

By Sunday morning, her decline was beginning, fluid in her lungs, crackles in every breath. Ben still drove to Chapel Hill to pick up Ronny, as planned. In the boardinghouse he told Ronny to bring clothes for a funeral just in case, and Ronny's heart sank. All the way to Turtletrack he could feel the tension in Ben, the curtain of an awful, undefeatable silence coming down, not simply between them both, but between Ben and the world.

"You know I'm not going to try to say anything dumb," Ronny said.

Ben nodded, tightly, lips clamped together. "I couldn't take it."

"Can I put my head on the seat again? I just want to be close."

When he nodded again the movement was small and quick. A moment of softness passed over his face. "That would be nice."

As soon as he did, Ben settled an arm over him.

Down the road, Ben asked, "What am I going to do?"

"You think this is bad, don't you?"

"I know it is. I can see it."

There would be an ocean of sorrow in Ben now, if this were true. He would go wild.

"Is there anything I can say?" Ronny said. "Whatever you do, I'll be here."

Ben gripped Ronny tight; they said nothing. "I feel like such a shit I let her sit in that house like that. Thank God I did something right—" He stopped there, at that word. He would have said, "at the end." In his mind, it had already happened.

That time Ronny thought it better not to contradict him, to let him pound on himself, knowing he would not accept anything else.

"We have to try to talk about stuff," Ben said, that coiled quality to his voice making Ronny ache. "I don't think we're going to have a lot of time when we get to Turtletrack. Nina and Dad were taking Mom to the hospital, I expect we'll find out she's admitted when we get home."

"It's that bad, so fast?"

"It's got to be pneumonia. The doctor said if we could hear her breathing hard to bring her in. We heard her last night but she wouldn't go."

233

"After we talked."

"Yes."

"I wish you'd called me back."

"I started to. I just felt so wrecked. Then I got up this morning to come for you. I should have just come on last night. Mom was up and so was Dad and she was having to sit up to breathe."

"I know you didn't want to leave them—"

"Sure I did. I had to get you. Don't start anything like that. We're going to have a hard enough time."

Ronny put his hand on Ben's thigh. Ben reached for it with his own hand. "That's how we started out," Ben said. "Holding hands, kind of."

"I remember that game. Acting like nothing was going on." Ronny swallowed. "You're not getting ready to tell me to go away, are you?"

"I knew you'd think that."

"Sorry. I should have kept my mouth shut and waited."

"No." His voice was husky. "I am going to have to go away. I'm not going to be able to have you around right now."

Ronny felt a sound come out of him, low. Ben held him in place and when he struggled held him harder. "Don't make me smack you."

"Let me up."

"No. Listen. I don't mean what you think, so listen. I'm just going to tell you what I want. I want you to stick with me as close as you can till this is done one way or the other. But if she dies, baby, I'm most likely to bolt. I don't know what I'll do. You can't be around. Not when I'm like that. And I know it's coming if she dies." He drew a long breath and went on. "So that's what I need to know. Can you stick with me as tight as you can till we know what's going to happen, no matter what any fucker tells you, no matter who it is? And then can you let me run?"

Ronny swallowed, easing against the seat. The sense of panic subsided. "I can do that."

He shook his head. "It's like you always said, and I fucking wouldn't listen. There isn't going to be any time. We got every fucking thing else, but we didn't get that."

"As long as I don't have to think you're gone for good, I'll be all right," Ronny said.

"I don't know how long."

"When you know, call."

"That's my boy," he said. "I will."

He was quiet, holding Ronny's hand, driving the Impala. If he had any hope that his mother was going to live, he was speaking from another place.

"I know I'll be back this fall," he said, "and maybe before. I'm not going to miss that last year, not after being a redshirt. If there's any time I ever wanted to play football, it's now."

"Why?"

"I'm going to want to smash some things. I'm going to need it."

"What about the sticking-by-you part? Don't you already know I'll do that?"

He ran his hand over Ronny's cheek. "I might have team-mates at the funeral, and coaches. They're not all very bright, but some of them are. Tate is, for one. Some of them are going to see us together and know. I know it. There's no way I'm going to be able to keep from leaning on you. So you're going to have to stick with me with all that happening."

"I'll do it. They can't kill me at a funeral."

Mrs. Nickelsen died in the hospital the next day. Ronny was faithful to his promise and stayed by Ben, sitting in the next chair in the hospital, waiting while things worsened. Ronny never went in to visit Mrs. Nickelsen; she sent word to say hello and Nina said she had been asking about him. She was thinking about her son to the end, wondering how he would manage without her, who would take care of him.

They went home in a daze and Ronny lay beside Ben on his bed. Nina took charge of the funeral arrangements. She came once and asked Ben to go with her so they could talk, and he came back and collapsed again, grasping Ronny, terrifyingly silent. He worked himself into a state and broke the chest of drawers in his room, smashing every piece of it, leaving only a pile of wreckage mixed with the clothing it had stored. Nina came to the door but Ronny shook his head at her and she went away, frightened. Ben raged and stood there, face a mess of snot and slobber and tears. When he was simply breathing Ronny brought him back to bed. At first he grabbed Ronny, lunged at him, dug his fingers into Ronny's shoulders, but then he collapsed and cried and Ronny eased him onto the bed and held him. He sobbed until he was empty.

Ronny got a cloth and washed his face. "Just lie back and let me do this."

Ben gazed at the cloth. He took a breath and nodded, lay back, closed his eyes. Ronny wiped his face slowly and carefully with the cool cloth until it was clean. He kissed Ben's forehead and his mouth.

Ben's hand came up to his neck. "Lie down with me."

Ronny climbed beside him. They lay there into the night, sometimes talking. Once, when Ben appeared to be drowsing, Ronny went downstairs to see Mr. Nickelsen passed out on the couch, Nina in the chair. He touched her arm. "Don't you want to go to bed?"

She looked at him, bleak. "I'm all right. I'm with Dad."

"You want a blanket?"

"I wouldn't mind that."

He brought one from the bedroom, got another for Mr. Nickelsen. Nina put it over him. "How's Ben?"

"Quiet now. After he busted up that chest he cried for a while. I need to get back up there."

"Did he hurt himself?"

"I didn't even think to look at his hands."

"I was scared shitless, I thought he was freaking."

"How are you?"

"Holding up. I cried and cried and now I'm too tired to think."

"He wore himself out pretty much the same way."

"Go back," she said, "before he gets like that again." She yawned and closed her eyes. "I told people to stay away from here but they'll all be at the funeral home tomorrow."

Upstairs, Ben was standing by the window, his jeans shoved partly down his legs. He'd started to undress and gotten caught by his own thoughts. His face looked better, but still like a wasteland. Ronny took off his own clothes by the bed, assuming they were going to try to sleep, or at least to lie still. Ben did the same and they crawled into the sheets and lay quietly. "How's everything down there?" he asked.

"Your dad's on the couch in the den. Your sister's on the recliner. She says she wants to sit with your dad."

"He won't go to bed without Mom," Ben said.

"He's asleep, though."

"Drunk?"

"I don't think so."

"Me neither. I never drank a drop." He was looking up at the ceiling, speaking to someone there.

Ronny ran a hand through Ben's dark hair. "Show me your hands."

The fingers and knuckles were cracked and swollen, bruised, partly clotted though still bleeding a little, from the chest. "Do you want me to clean these?"

"No." His mouth was set, his jaw grinding. "They're fine."

Ronny kissed the fingers gently and settled against Ben again. Ben lay his arms against Ronny's back. "It's a miracle you don't argue."

Ronny had no answer, just lay still, touched the hands gingerly, waited.

"My ma wouldn't be too happy I busted a piece of furniture."

"She'd probably be glad you didn't try to hold your feelings in."

He snorted, pulling Ronny tight. "There goes that fucking Pollyanna gene again."

"I don't mean to be stupid."

"You sound just like her," Ben said. "Just as calm. And always coming up with something I don't expect. And always finding a way to make something out of my mess."

"You're going to break my heart."

"You better fucking believe that. I'm going to tear it to pieces before it's over."

Neither of them had expected it but when it came it seemed natural and easy to touch each other. Ben was too carnal to have any qualms. He was too conscious, too, that time was running out.

Ronny kept his promise when some teammates arrived at the funeral home and later at the service. Nina helped to keep Ben in the family circle and Ronny's persistence did the rest. He was as close to Ben as anyone could have been, and he could feel the difference it made. At times Ben put a hand on Ronny's shoulder, or leaned into his side.

He would in later years think that all funerals merged into one, the bleak shock of dying, the loss, all in the same bland chapel, the same spectators sitting in a daze, the music and words and prayers to pass time. Conscious of Ben next to him. The funeral director speaking discreetly into Nina's ear. Mr. Nickelsen shocked into pallor, almost curled in a ball on the pew, holding a handkerchief to his eyes.

Outside they walked to the car. One of the coaches came up, scratched his head, and told Ben he had their good thoughts and prayers. Ben was drained, breathing with effort, gazing blankly at the seat. Someone from the funeral home drove them to the house.

Visitation at home, faces blurring, coming in and out of the field of vision, saying words, repeating words, trying to think of something appropriate, relieved when it was done, withdrawing. Tate sat with Ben awhile. The other guys hung back. Ronny stayed within sight, caught Ben's gaze now and then, and waited through the whole ordeal. The last person left after dark. Mr. Nickelsen sat in his chair, blind to everybody else. In the light of one lamp they sat with him.

Ben was shaking more now, started to sob again. Nina asked him if he wanted to go upstairs. He nodded, and Ronny took him by the arm. They climbed the stairs, step after step. Ben sprawled on the bed and Ronny slid close; Ben closed around him. Ronny lay his head close to Ben's, holding him, saying nothing. After a while the shaking eased some.

"Do you want to get into bed? I can get you warm then. We can stay dressed."

He nodded and Ronny moved him and covered him with blankets and lay next to him. He turned out the lights and locked the door. The air-conditioning upstairs hardly worked to begin with but Ben was shivering as if he were on ice. Ronny held him until the shivering stopped.

A long while later the house grew quiet. Ben took off his clothes for bed and Ronny undressed, sliding beside him. The feeling of stillness and separation had settled into Ben more deeply. He was aware of Ronny and lay against him, touched him, but there was something absent, gone from only a moment ago. Ronny felt the first touch of his own loss, the first ache of his own grief. It caught in his throat and he pressed against Ben, who pulled him closer, once he understood. "I'll take you back early in the morning, I guess."

"Then what?"

He shrugged, grinding his jaw. He put a hand on Ronny's shoulder to show him it was all right. But he stared straight up at the ceiling.

"Is it like you told me it would be?"

His eyes were brimming, tears streaming out. He let Ronny lie there but Ronny knew better than to do more. After a while, Ben exhaled, heavily, as if he had been exerting himself. "Nothing's changed, Ronny. Not between you and me. Okay? Just let me go."

"Can you call me? Let me know you're all right?"

"Yes." He swallowed. "I'll try. You're not coming back to the dorm, are you?"

"No. I can't."

"I could never have done this without you here." Wiping at his face. He looked as if he were strangling. He let nothing out, building it all toward whatever release he meant to have, that had nothing to do with Ronny or anyone else.

"Do you want to leave now, drive back tonight?"

"I want to stay right here as long as I can."

Fall

MRS. DELACY TRIED TO MAKE COOKIES THAT morning, the burn smell filling the upstairs, guys coming to their doorways looking at one another. Ronny put on his shoes and hurried down the steps into the kitchen, where she was standing with a smoking cookie sheet, pot holders in her hands, looking at it as though she was not sure what it was, as though she was not sure where she was, turning when Ronny came into the room. He took the pot holders and carried the cookie sheet to the back door. Charred cookie shapes smoking, a ruin. He threw the little charcoals into the garbage, left the pan to cool on the table with the back door open. She was standing in the doorway, watching. "Oh, lord help me," she said. "I messed it up again."

"Don't worry about it, Miss Dee."

"I didn't even remember I was baking anything."

This was November, a chilly morning after a storm swept color down from the trees, the yard golden and bronze, wet leaves clinging to the steps. A beginning of the fall of leaves in the canopy overhead, trees in every direction. One must have a mind of winter. He was reading Wallace Stevens in a class, "The Dove in the Belly," the first time he had felt a poem in his marrow. "The whole of appearance is a toy. For this, / The dove in the belly builds his nest and coos . . ." It made him shiver. The nothing that is. Miss Dee was standing at the door from the hallway. "Is the kitchen on fire?" she asked.

"No. It's fine."

"But I smell smoke."

"There was a pan of cookies burning in the oven."

Jamal had entered the kitchen behind her, and stood there scratching his chin. He was trying to grow a beard, mousy hairs splattered here and there, almost comical except he took it so seriously.

"Who was trying to bake cookies?" she asked. "You boys aren't supposed to use the kitchen."

"I don't know, Miss Dee."

"Lord. You could have burned the place down."

"Somebody could have," Ronny said. She looked up at him.

A moment later she came back to herself, walked to the bowl of cookie batter, and stirred it at little. "Is that you, Jamal?"

"Yes, ma'am."

"Taste this cookie batter, let me know what you think."

"You want to bake some cookies?"

"I thought I would. I'm in the mood for something sweet. You want to help me?"

Jamal looked at Ronny, who shrugged.

"Sure thing," Jamal said.

"Look around for my cookie sheet," she said. "I know it's in here somewhere."

"That cookie batter is really good."

"It's for sugar cookies," she said. "My grandma's recipe. You know. She gave it to me." She turned and looked at Ronny. The cookie sheet had cooled enough that it wasn't smoking anymore; he was scraping the remains of char off it into the garbage, and carried it to the sink. He started to wash it, as Jamal stood next to Miss Dee, hands on her shoulders.

"Ronny found the cookie sheet, he's washing it."

"Oh, that's good! I haven't used it in so long, it probably needs it." She was peering toward the sink, wooden spoon in shaky hand, blinking. "You said Ronny was washing it?"

"Yes, ma'am."

"Oh, I remember him. Ronny upstairs. He lives in that little room that used to be a closet."

She remembered Jamal more consistently than anybody else. No one understood why. Some of the other boys from upstairs were looking in the doorway. No one spoke. She had gotten feebler in the past few weeks, and there were spells when her memory came and went—followed by spells when she was herself, and everything was fine. They were all trying to take care of her—well, most of them were. A couple of the guys were asses and just thought it was funny to watch her plodding around, trying to think what she was doing or remember to whom she was talking. But there was nothing to do about people like that. Miss Dee never appeared to notice.

She started laying out the cookies again on the sheet, after rubbing it down with butter slowly, moving at her own pace, as she had always done. The work appeared to bring her more fully into herself, and she said to Ronny, as the smoke cleared from the kitchen, "We had a good rain last night."

"Yes, ma'am. It was a big storm. You see how the leaves are coming down?"

She patted the cookie batter carefully onto the sheet. "I don't see much, but I guess I'll take your word on it. Are you working today?"

"Not till late."

"What are all these boys doing peeping in the kitchen like this? Did something happen?" She thought about it for a minute. "Oh, that's right. I burned the first batch of cookies. But the smoke's clearing out."

"You want me to shut the door?" Jamal asked.

She shook her head, washing her hands at the sink, carefully soaping and lathering each finger. "Oh, no. If they don't have anything better to do, they can stare at me, I don't really care. It's my house. I can burn all the food I want to as long as the house don't catch fire." She laughed at her joke, and looked at them, and they looked at one another.

Jamal stayed in the kitchen while she worked. Upstairs, Ronny left the door to his room open, listening. Diego stuck his head in the door, hair still wet from the shower, shoulders bare; "Is she okay?" he asked.

"She's fine, now. She knows where she is and what she's doing."

He shook his head. A nice guy, chemistry major, hoping to get into medical school. Pudgy, short, and flatfooted. He nodded, hurried off to his room, saying, "I'll leave my door open, too."

"Jamal is with her right now."

When Ronny was alone in the room the feeling of emptiness settled over him, that he was awake on a Saturday, that nothing had changed, that it was months now, that he was still here, and the awful waiting went on, refused to leave him no matter what he did. Today was a game day. No way to escape knowing; the football team was playing at the University of

Virginia. Ben was there in Charlottesville, a starter on the defense; across campus people would be listening to the game on the radio. Later today at *The Chapel Hill Newspaper* the sportswriters would be talking about the game, typing about it, the photographers would print their pictures, Ronny would assemble the pages and read the stories and remember. The whole day he would be reminded: Ben had come home, but from where?

JULY

Ronny had spent the latter part of June and all of July stunned and restless. Ben had disappeared after his mother died, and no one knew where he had gone. He had not heard from Nina since the funeral and finally called her in July: no, she didn't know where Ben was, selfish fuck to leave them all to deal with Mom's death, Dad just sitting in the house in shock, the two of them frantic—no, she didn't expect to hear from him, the sorry bastard, and what good would it do anybody if he called? She told Ronny to forget it all, let it go, move on. Ben wasn't worth anybody's time, was he? She'd never forgive him. Leaving her alone to deal with all this shit. She broke down in the end. She hoped he might have heard something. Rage poured out of her, as though Ben had stabbed her in the heart. "You'll tell me if you hear from him, right?" she asked. "Send me a note or something."

"I will. But I don't think it's going to happen. Not soon."

"Yeah. I know. But he'll be back for fucking football. You can bet on that."

*

AUGUST

And when football practice started in August, there he was, late in the month, just before classes started, trudging from the field house to the practice field. Ronny was on his way to Ehringhaus to see if Sheria had returned and there was the team. Ronny had been waiting for the phone to ring, heart-sore, anxious, a constant flutter in his midsection. A shock, that moment of seeing—Ben marched through the pines with his helmet in his hand, had not known Ronny was watching—followed by despair, because Ronny could feel the wall between them. Ben had promised to call, but he hadn't. He had said they would see each other in the fall but they wouldn't. So it was over, whatever it had been.

Ronny walked back to Mrs. Delacy's house, sat on his bed—he had kept the room when its former occupant decided not to return to school—and felt himself sinking. Ben had managed to come back for football. Whatever grief he had felt. Maybe he reconciled with his father, his sister; or maybe he just showed up at the door one day, and said nothing, just walked up to his room. Packed his clothes to return to campus. But he never called Ronny, not once, as, hour following hour, the days trickled past.

SEPTEMBER

In September there were classes. Ronny still needed to work if he wanted to pay his room rent and buy food. He had to study. That meant he had to leave the room. Moving like he was hollow, clutching a backpack, walking through the late summer, the early fall, avoiding the brick pathways, afraid to look up from the ground. Only in the *Daily Tar Heel* office did he remember who he was, do his job, keep the paper running, laugh, tell a joke, throw out an insult, a kind of performance, but it helped, because he could at least act it with conviction. That brought him back. In class he struggled with the long prosiness of *Ulysses*, the spare comedy of Muriel Spark. He had always been able to absorb hurt. A spark of anger, a feeling that Ben had wronged him, made it easier.

At dinner with Lily, he picked at his food. He had no appetite. He read nothing outside his class assignments, and struggled with interest in statistical analysis and news editing classes. He received his first C on a paper and he hardly cared. He wrote a long letter to his father, then destroyed it. On the phone, his mother told him in a raspy voice, "Love is stupid, honey, but so is sitting alone in your room."

OCTOBER

At the South Carolina football game late in the month he stood in the student section watching the Tar Heels defending against the Gamecocks, the line of bodies on the emerald turf, the ringing of the announcer's voice, the roar of the host in the stadium, a Saturday of blue skies and crisp air. There Ben was, doing the thing that he wanted. He was having a good day until he intercepted a pass and was knocked flat by a fellow on the other side who moved like a fighter jet; the tumble was vicious and Ben was a long time getting up, holding his rib cage and strolling off the field, his teammates hammering his back for the turnover, the crowd screaming, students standing on their seats, faces painted blue, the cheerleaders performing their pom shaking and leg lifting, the band striking up a measure of drums and trumpets. Ben hurt but shaking it off, trudging to the sidelines, breaking into a pained trot just at the last.

Ronny visited Sheria after the game and she laughed at him for attending in the first place. "I never pictured you as a sports person," she said. "You know I think that's a mental defect."

"Oh, that's fine. We all have our defects."

"You should pursue one that's more interesting."

"Like what? Schizophrenia? Or agoraphobia?"

"Hey, watch it." She was still mostly a recluse, never straying very far from her bed.

Her friend Sara, who had been listening, added, "I never liked football that much, I never can figure out what's going on."

"You like football players all right," Sheria said.

"Not really. But a lot of girls do."

On the walk home Ronny scanned the crowd, in case. He let the thought go no further than that. He had been in fair spirits, but in the late afternoon the mournfulness descended on him again, and he lay in bed wishing he could stay there. But it was time to go to work at *The Chapel Hill Newspaper*, to do pasteup, stories about the game, sports reporters chattering in the composition room. There would be constant reminders all night. But still it was a good thing to have no choice but to move.

So, today, November. Ronny sat in his room, waiting to hear someone turn on the radio. Dullness had settled into him, replacing the scalding despair of June and July, the fury of August, the quiet wish of September, the silence of the weeks after. He had tried to avoid Ehringhaus but found himself drawn there sometimes, hoping. As if part of him had never given up. It should have felt like an ending, shouldn't it?

In the afternoon he found Miss Dee on the porch. She was sitting with a blanket on her lap, a plate of cookies next to her, a cup of tea. "Sit with me," she said, and smiled. She was herself, the same woman he remembered from earlier in the year when he had rented the room. "My cookies came out good," she said. "I left a plate for the boys to eat. Just so they would know I haven't lost my mind yet."

He smiled and sat with her, putting his feet up on the railing. "No, you sure haven't."

"I can feel it all slipping sometimes, though," she said. She was looking up at the trees as though she could see them clearly, but she had taken her glasses off and laid them in her lap. "This wind makes me feel like I'm still here. Feel that cold bite right into you."

"It wakes you up," Ronny said. "You sure you're warm enough?"

"What's a little cold?" Miss Dee asked. "Oh, lord, I've always loved it. My husband and I used to go up north for the winter. The first time we did it because we figured it would be a cheap vacation to drive up there. We went back over and over. We had some of the best times."

"You never said anything about him before."

She glanced at Ronny. Without the glasses, her face showed more of what she felt, and he could see the person who inhabited the aging, the frailty, an echo of what she had been, what she carried inside. Sadness somehow made her look younger and more vital, because it was human, maybe; because it meant she remembered. "I don't like to talk about him too often. It makes me want to cry even twenty years later. I guess it's twenty years." She thought for a moment, then shook her head and waved her hand. "That doesn't matter. I usually start thinking about him pretty steady along about now, when the leaves are coming down. He died about this time of year."

"Oh, me."

"Everybody has memories like that," she said.

Ronny was silent.

"You heard from your mama?" she asked.

"We talked a couple of days ago. She's doing pretty good, I think."

"That's nice. Because, you know. You been mad at her, you told me."

"I know." He shook his head. "But things worked out. Her husband is a nice guy, this time. I think she really likes him."

"When I met her I thought she was a real fine person." She said this with conviction. But it had to mean she was straying again; she had never met his mother, though he had shown her pictures. They'd become friends, he and Miss Dee, as the summer passed, and she'd been happy when it turned out he would be staying in the house. He looked at her now and figured it was no use correcting her.

"Mom thought you were really great, too. She told me to tell you hello."

Her smile had such a sweetness. Though maybe that was just the way he saw her; maybe that was just the way people saw older women, full of gentleness, when it was really something altogether different.

"I saw your friend's picture in the paper again," she said after a while. "Seems like Carolina is having a good year. I never did like the football, though."

"Yes, ma'am."

"They ought to be playing a game today. It's Saturday, isn't that right?"

"They're playing at Virginia."

She had often brought up Ben in the past weeks. He was part of a memory that clung to her; trust him to make that kind of impression. But she had no idea that the friendship was over. She asked, "Are you proud of him?"

"Yes, ma'am."

"I was so surprised when I saw that first picture. He was handsome, you know, so I remembered. You never told me he played football."

"I don't see much of him anymore."

"I saw him just last week," she said. "I never told you that, did I, now that I think about it. He stopped by to say hello. He was walking by and saw me in the yard looking at my pitiful roses."

Ronny felt hollow all through, but sat there, opening his coat to the cold.

"To tell you the truth, I thought he'd been drinking. I meant to tell you about it, too."

"He shouldn't be drinking during the season, not on a weekday."

"Oh, I don't know what day it was. And the young people, you know. You all do what you please."

Maybe this was a phantom, like her memory of meeting Mom. He shook his head, tried to forget it, but felt himself sinking again. She was talking about planting more roses now, as though she had already bought them and only had to dig holes in the ground. "This is the right time for planting," she said. "They can root through the winter, you know. While the world is all cold and dead like."

She sat quiet after that. Pretty soon her niece showed up— the one family member she had left, Miss Minette, who looked almost the same age as Miss Dee. She said hello to Ronny and he stood up so she could sit. "Oh, you don't have to do that," she said, all the while settling into the rocking chair, her girth filling the seat; she let out a heavy breath. "Lord, that walk gets to me anymore. I can't get my breath like I used to."

"It's cause you're so old," said Miss Dee, and laughed.

He left them to talk and went upstairs to get ready for work. It had set his mind to racing, the thought that Ben might have talked to Miss Dee, might have walked by the house; but that made him feel desperate and stupid, and he tried to stop the whole chain of imaginings that followed. The idea preyed on him. But what did it matter? If he had visited Miss Dee, he hadn't come upstairs to see whether Ronny was in his room; he hadn't left a note; he hadn't called, even though he had the number—even though he was the one who had given Ronny the money to put in the phone. For such a long time they had talked every day. That had been real, hadn't it? What had happened between the two of them, that had been real? He hadn't made it up. But here he was in the fall, listening to the echoes of the football game on the radio, Carolina leading Virginia, those boys playing hard today, the ones he had known in Ehringhaus, the ones he had written papers for, cheated for, watched, out of obsession—he felt sick to his stomach but nothing would come up. He stood at the bathroom sink and looked at himself, wondered what would become of him.

He went to work, pasted up the newspaper, did his job, played and joked with Fred, who spelled his name Phr3d; "Transcendental Pasteup," they called themselves. Pages assembled while you wait. The work eased him and he forgot. But when he stepped into the room that night—the house quiet, Miss Dee's room closed—it all came back to him, and he collapsed onto the bed, lay there until the sorrow welled up in him, took off his clothes, and slipped under the blankets, pulling them over his head, surrounding himself with the dark.

Some Meetings

HE WAS MANAGING EDITOR AT *THE Tar Heel* now, in charge of
the other editors, scowling at them when they appeared likely
to miss their page deadlines. Enjoying the force required of
him, he found he had a knack for it, and could perform a convincing scowl when necessary. The job took up his weekdays
from late afternoon until nine o'clock or so; he juggled it with
his pasteup work, and with so many hours taken up by work,
he was left with less time for brooding. The *Tar Heel* office
looked a wreck with reporters hanging over their typewriters, yellow copy paper everywhere, desks jammed together,
phones balanced precariously on stacks of old newswire stories, rolling chairs falling apart, some of them missing a
caster. One day he saw Otis at the end of the line of desks; he
was talking to the sports editor. Ronny threaded his way
through the bodies and objects to say hello. He offered a
handshake and grimaced at the way the big fellow squeezed
his poor metacarpals. "There's the guy I was hoping to see,"
Otis said. "I took your advice."

253

"He wants a writing job," said the sports editor. She was dainty only in appearance and was very frankly eyeing Otis from head to toe. "Should I try him out?"

Ronny said, "Oh, sure. Otis is getting pretty good. We had a class in J-school together."

"I'll do anything," said Otis. "Sports, I mean. Even the chess club."

"Do we even have a chess club?" she asked.

"Otis and I put together a good article about Title IX for the long-form class," said Ronny. "You already covered that a while back, though."

"Yeah," said the sports editor. "But we'll figure something out."

"Good deal. Make sure to get your page downstairs by the deadline. Later, Otis."

Tempted, for a moment, to ask about Ben; but he packed the thought away.

His mother called on her wedding day, which surprised Ronny, because he thought the wedding had already happened. She had never mentioned this before when they talked but she had decided to wait to marry Rayford Placid. She and Ronny had been talking off and on, once she found out he had a phone. Sometimes when she called she reversed the charges. But it was all right. He had money now: two jobs, and his rent was cheap.

She told him about her honeymoon, which they had before the actual wedding. "Rayford took me to Las Vegas to one of the big hotels, and oh, Ronny. The lights were like stars and stars and stars, like a whole cloud of them."

"Did you go gambling and stuff?"

"Oh, no, honey, I don't waste my money. Ray wanted to but I told him what. You can bet I did." Dragging on a cigarette, the small sharp puff.

"I can hear you smoking."

"Please don't worry me about that, I'm a newlywed."

"Oh, Mama."

"Just don't start, is all. Are you doing all right? Your daddy said he called you."

"I didn't know you were still talking to him."

"Honey, that is all the bygone days. I'm three husbands past him, now."

She went back to descriptions of Las Vegas, the time of her life, and on and on. Wayne Newton could sing like anything, and the showgirls! She might be one herself if she could start all over again, that was the life, spangled half to death and kicking up your heels, twitching your butt around, serving cocktails and selling cigarettes. It might have sounded the same as always. But she had a quieter tone to her voice, and when she mentioned Rayford there was hardly a complaint. It was early, of course. Anything could happen. But Ronny could hear Rayford in the background, the low gruff sound of his voice. "Where did my buck knife get to, sweetheart, did you put it up somewhere?"

She said, "You dropped it in your boot, didn't you? I saw you do it. He keeps his knife in his boot so he'll know where it is," she said into the phone. "And then he forgets it, or he sticks his hand in there and he can't find it and he thinks I lost it in a drawer." Her voice easy, a bit of laughter, another puff.

They had less strife when they spoke these days, maybe because of the distance, or maybe because Ronny understood better the whole craziness of that feeling—how it had drained out of him—after he left the bubble that had encased him with Ben, the ecstatic certainty of each other followed by nothing. Nor could he even feel any anger about it, because

Mrs. Nickelsen had died, after all, and she didn't deserve it, so who could blame Ben if he took himself out of sight, and who could blame him if he came back to play football, to throw himself into the game—who could blame him for anything, really? Mom had gone through that kind of thing with men, of course the same thing would happen to Ronny. So he listened more patiently.

He would remember it later: he hung up the phone on her and walked across the changing colors of the autumn campus, threading his way through buildings, crossing the gravel parking lot all the way to the student union, then upstairs to one of the narrow-windowed meeting rooms. A discussion was under way when he walked into it. Some of the other people seated in the chairs acknowledged him, a thickset girl with short, bleached hair; a pale boy with long, thin arms. She was wearing a button that said, "How dare you presume that I'm heterosexual!" He thought it was silly but it made him smile. This was his second time coming. He dreaded it. But he had to try, he couldn't go on hiding, so he dragged himself to the meeting room, opened the door, slid into the seat. Anybody could have seen him. If they saw him they would know. The Carolina Gay Association. Attendance could only mean one thing.

Gay. He had to accept the word and the fact. It was his nature, he had to stop denying. Remembering the times he'd told Ben he never could be attracted to a guy who was gay, which meant, effeminate, or obvious, or flamboyant; which meant honest, open, brave enough to come out of the closet. He hated the idea of being labeled, he had said; he was more than just a gay person, he had said; he wanted to be attracted to a man for what the man was, he had said. So much crap he had said. The conviction had swum up through his thinking during the awful summer, in the echo of Mrs. Nickelsen's death, when Ben was God knows where. If he was too afraid for people to know he was gay, then what did that mean about his character? What hope could he have? Doomed to be obsessed with straight boys. Doomed to nothingness. But even that wasn't fair. Because he had no idea what had been inside Ben. Because he had no idea what was happening to Ben right now. Silence told him nothing, after all.

Never mind all that, though. He was gay. He came to the meeting. The association was three or four years old by then, and there had always been a lot of ugly stuff said about it, articles in *The Tar Heel*, snide comments from students, a debate over student government funding, all the things you would expect. But here he was, and here were these other people—maybe twenty, mixed men and women. They were arguing about the group's purpose, its identity. Did "gay" include women? Were black students as welcome as every-one else? A discussion that went round and round. Some of the boys looked sissy in an exaggerated way. But that might just have been the way he was seeing them. Others just looked like boys. Same contrast with the girls. A room full of people.

A guy named Judson was sitting near Ronny. During a break he tried to talk. What year was Ronny? What was he studying? "I think we had a class together," he said. "Shake-speare? Last fall."

"Oh, right. Maybe. I don't remember you."

"I remember you." The guy was smiling. Maybe he liked Ronny. Maybe he was trying to start something. "You raised your hand and talked some, nobody else did. When we were reading that *King Lear* play."

"I liked that one. That poetry."

"Yeah, pretty creepy. Ripping that guy's eyes out." He moved toward Ronny by one seat, leaned toward him. "You been coming to this group for long?"

"Second time."

"So you're not a regular."

"Nope. I'm just trying to figure stuff out."

"Yeah." Judson played his fingers over the chair seat. He had a nice face, regular features, dark skin, dark hair. Lanky and tall. His voice was reedy, and he had an odd laugh—he laughed now, uncomfortable. "Who's not? Trying to figure stuff out, I mean. Are you out to your family?"

The question made Ronny uncomfortable, are you out? "No. I'm out to some of my friends, though."

"I'm out to my friends. A little. But my parents would kill me if they knew I was sitting here."

The meeting started up again. Ronny was relieved, both at the fact that he didn't have to try to talk to Judson anymore, because it felt so awkward, but also because he had said words aloud to somebody. No, I'm not truthful to everyone, not yet. But I know who I am, that's why I'm sitting here. He had been scared of the admission in the moment. He was giving himself more credit than he had earned. But he had talked to Judson, who was a decent person; he knew Judson was gay, because he was here; he was wondering whether Judson liked him, whether he might like Judson. He took a deep breath, tamping down a feeling of panic, an urge to sneak out the door, to pretend he had never come. He kept himself perfectly still.

At the end of the meeting a lot of the people hung around, talking about a picnic they were planning, a dance that might happen in the spring; some of them were going out to the Clown's Inn later. Ronny headed for the door after listening for a couple of moments, looking at them all, wondering. He took a deep breath outside.

Judson had followed him. So he waited. They stood together awkwardly. Judson started talking. He was in business school, he said, but he hated it sometimes. He wished he had the guts to do an arts major, maybe acting. Or even English, like Ronny. He liked to read. But his parents wanted him to do business. He did what his parents wanted. They lived in Greensboro, they came to see him sometimes. He was just rambling, wasn't he? He talked like this when he got nervous. "Do you want to go out for a drink sometime?" He stopped there, waited like he was holding his breath. "I mean, not like a date or anything. Just, you know, talk."

Ronny felt for a moment as if he were contemplating an act of betrayal. But that was crap. He said, "Sure."

He gave Judson his number. The guy looked unaccountably happy. Maybe Sunday, Ronny told him, explaining that he had two jobs, and not much free time. But maybe Sunday.

Judson flushed red from the neck up, stuck the number into his notebook, stood there clutching his books in front of him, terrified. There was something sweet about it. Ronny said, "All right, nice talking to you."

"Same." The guy ducked his head, pushed his hair out of his eyes. "I'll call you." Walking away quickly, small steps, cautious, looking down the whole time. That was the moment that made Ronny like him, that timid turning away, the scurrying quality of his exit. Maybe they could be friends, he thought.

But he didn't like to think of himself as timid, or scurrying, or hiding. When he wondered how much he was like Judson—or like his impression of Judson—he was troubled by the question. Because there were people in the gay association meeting who were not afraid, who declared themselves, who dared anyone to criticize them.

After *The Tar Heel* was put to bed he went for a late supper with Lily. She drove him to an all-night breakfast diner, a different place than the one he remembered with Ben; her car was a battered old Volvo, rusted and creaking, but she kept it neat as a pin, not one stray piece of paper, and it smelled like flowers inside, a hint of rose and honeysuckle. When he asked, she said, "Oh, I can't tell you my scent secrets. We're not that close." Then she laughed, full throated, delighted with herself. "It's such a disaster of a car. I had to do something."

"At least it runs."

"I suppose. I'm not sure how much longer it will, though. I think it's the rust that holds it together."

They'd been friends since freshman year, and they were seniors now. That counted as a long time, in college. In the restaurant, after they ordered, he took a deep breath and told her about the meeting he had attended, simply, without allowing himself to hesitate. She sat there for a minute. She had been telling him to do something like this for a while. But she appeared more perturbed than he had expected. He busied himself with unrolling his silverware, arranging it on the napkin, studying the other people in the restaurant. "So have you heard from your football player? Are you giving up on him?" She referred to him in that way, "your football player," with scorn, whenever he came up.

"No, I haven't heard anything."

They sat quiet. He tried to eat. The eggs were getting cold.

She lifted her fork, stirred hot sauce into her eggs. Her appetite appeared better than his. She was thinking hard, he could see it. "You said he's back."

"Yes. He's still playing for the football team."

"Why are you so sullen? I'm just trying to talk to you."

"You remember how you acted when I came out."

"How many times do I have to apologize for that? You do know I liked you myself, don't you?" She flushed, disconcerted. "I didn't mean to sound the way I did."

He had not known. He should have. But that didn't make the memory any different. And the memory didn't change the fact that she was his friend. "I told you about Ben, not so you could interrogate me about him. I wanted to be honest. I know what you think of it."

"How do you know what I think?"

"You make it obvious."

"Ronny, it wasn't pretend. That was what I was worried about, that you were chasing something that wasn't real. But it was real. Something happened with him. You said that yourself."

They let the subject go. So easy to watch the thoughts flicker over her; feeling flowed right through. She had something more to say but she willing to wait, so there was other conversation. They talked about Doris Betts, who taught writing on campus. Each had taken a class with her. Lily wanted to talk about a book of hers she had read, *Beasts of the Southern Wild*, an important short story collection, she said. She enjoyed making statements like that, and Ronny enjoyed hearing them; it was a measure of their adulthood, an assertion of a worthwhile opinion. Mrs. Betts was a beautiful writer, Ronny said. She was also a beautiful woman with sparrow eyes and long dark hair; it always came down to beauty. They discussed their friends, the coolness of Lily's sister, the stuffiness of Rushmore, the pretentiousness of

Sfarlien, the beauty—there it was again—of Roxanne. Her thighs, trained as a ballet dancer, like so many girls. Who had she slept with? Random talk. But Lily moved toward her subject in a meticulous way. Setting down her coffee cup just so.

"So he's back and you haven't talked to him? Do you need permission?" She waited for an answer, then shook her head, opened her palms, spread them, made him look at her. "Don't you have a brain?"

"What?"

"It's not all about you, stupid. Don't you even want to know what's going on?"

"He was supposed to call me."

She was leaning toward him, all feeling and fervency; all Lily's feelings were enormous, like this one. "Well, duh. His mother died. All right? Do you even know how that feels? I don't."

He ran his hand through his hair. For a moment he felt as if he might come to pieces. He had thought he was getting better. You could protect yourself to death. And that was only the first layer. She thought he was supposed to do something. But what? Walk to Ehringhaus, risk getting beat up by half the boys in the dorm, risk Ben being one of them? That sounded so dramatic. Was that an excuse to do nothing? Would Ben hurt him?

"You better eat your food, you said you were starving." Lily had asked for more coffee, and tapped on the table. "I can almost see your brain spinning."

For the rest of the meal they were quiet. They paid the bill and she drove him home. No advice, just good night. She wanted to borrow a book. He would find it in his room. That was all.

When he opened the door to his room the curtain moved, and for a moment, so breathless, it was as though Ben were there, coming in through the window, same as he had a few months ago, full of himself, sitting on the bed, waiting to be adored. It caught at Ronny, a pain at the base of his throat, a physical longing, emptiness, the room dark and silent.

Then in Rain

SO HE WALKED OUT OF THE house, onto campus. Silver dark, lights bursting, a fog, like a movie set, a feeling that it would rain, followed by rain, drizzle, mist, the finest distillation of water, as he followed the brick path. He would lose his nerve, the sensible plan made no sense, but he would never be able to wait, he was too sore inside, he was hoping for something, and trying to kill the hope, breathing in and out, first past the business school, then in front of the domed library, a few people out, walking as he did without an umbrella in the bits of rain. The path felt so familiar. How late was it? Late enough. The guys had a curfew. He would go, he would. He was afraid but he would do it anyway. So, past the bell tower, into the forest around Kenan Stadium, where he had come, so faithfully, so pathetically, every Saturday when there was a home game, sitting in the stands, looking at that tiny figure, shoulder pads and knee pads, helmet, the number all anybody could see from that distance but there he was, darting in and out, leaping, diving toward receivers; hardly any of it made sense; why would Ronny go to the game to watch? Why torment himself when the space between them had gone dark and silent months ago. Anyway, the images tumbled regular as his footsteps tonight, wet pine straw on the bricks, leaves slicked and wet. He was descending the hill now, the squat brick form of Teague through the trees, the scattered lights of Avery, the hill still descending, past Bryson Field, floodlights dark, the baseball diamond covered, grass of summer in hiding, and how many times had he walked this way looking up at the balconies of Ehringhaus, counting the floors and the windows to find the room where he used to live. The drum in his chest, the beat that drowned out everything, blood rushing, the rain falling heavier now. He had to keep moving, no matter how wet he was. Into the lobby, empty, the snack bar closed; he was dripping, but in the elevator he felt calmer, took a deep breath, rode up to the lobby, and then, there it was. He was on the balcony, all quiet, and walked to the room, anybody could see him now. Taped to the door a picture of Tate, a sign that said "Planet of the Apes."

Before he could knock, before he could take a breath, as though the world meant to give him no time at all, the shock of sound, the door opened, and there Ben was in his pajama bottoms, hair a mess, scratching his head, and Ronny started back, and looked again, and shock washed over him. What was this expression, anyway? Not happiness or welcome. Blankness. He shoved Ronny to the door of the suite, looking back at the other rooms. Running a hand through his hair, barefoot, cold. "Fuck, you're soaking wet," he said, and stood there. Went back in his room. Came out with a blanket, led Ronny to the stairs, wrapped him in the blanket. "Jesus."

They sat on the steps in the dark. Music adrift from the other wing of the dorm, where there was no curfew. Breathing, both.

It was too much to believe. Felt so ordinary sitting side by side. Ben hawked and spat onto the concrete. He had brought a sweater and put it on. Started to say something. But he was in the same state as Ronny, had no voice. So they just sat there. It took a while. Ben said, "Fuck, Ronny, you couldn't bring an umbrella?"

"I wasn't thinking about rain. Just started."

Ben cleared his throat. "I can't believe you did this."

"Why not?"

"Because I told you not to."

"You told me a lot of things."

Dim night lights burned in the walls. Rain multiplied, falling in long, gray sweeps, refracting the lights in the parking lot, those visible through the trees, beyond the black railing of the balcony. As though he could not help himself, Ben moved closer, wrapped his arm around the blanket. The weight of him, so warm. Ronny closed his eyes. What rushed out he could not help; he wiped his face. He asked, "How are you?"

Ben's voice broken, a sob. "I don't know right now."

"I just couldn't wait anymore. It was like I didn't know whether you were dead or alive."

"You knew I was here. Didn't you?"

"Oh, I knew that, all right."

"She's so mad at me."

They sat still. Ben rubbed an edge of the blanket over his eyes. Across the courtyard space a door opened, closed, along the opposite wing. Lights everywhere smeared with rain. Inside Ronny was sore, tired. He wanted to break down, to let go everything he felt, to throw off the blanket and scream in the stairwell, to the point that the silence echoed as if he had done it. Ben shifted away again. "You're mad at me, too." He spoke as though nothing had happened, as though they had only been apart a day or two.

"Miss Dee told me you came to the house."

"Yeah. I did. I was too chickenshit to go in."

"She said you were drunk."

"Probably."

They couldn't face each other, they couldn't stand up and walk away. Ronny could feel it for them both. Their plural. It made him ache, such a piercing fact. He said, "I'm sorry, I shouldn't have come."

Ben made a low, choking sound. Ronny stood, let the blanket fall.

"Let me take you home," Ben said.

"No, it's fine. It's just rain. You have curfew."

"Ronny, please—"

"No. I'm fine."

Ben was shaking now, sobbing. Ronny watched and let it happen. He wrapped Ben in the blanket. "I came to every game," he said.

Ben took a long, ragged breath. "Did you?"

"Yes. You had to have known I would."

He nodded, mouth quivering. So tempting to slide beside him, to pull him close. But not here. "You coming to Duke?"

"Can't get a ticket since it's in Durham."

He nodded, Ben did. He was collapsing. In the moment it felt as if he had needed to collapse. They were locked together like that, not touching, distant from each other, but frozen, unable to separate. Ben releasing something, shaking. Enter someone, though. There had been no sound. But someone was there, a bulk of shadow, and Tate said, "What the fuck, Ben? Who's that?"

"Me," said Ronny.

"Fuck me dead. It's the Brainhead." Tate looked half awake, not sure of himself. "Where you been, boy? We need you down here."

"Just here for a minute."

"What?"

"I have to go."

Ben was sobbing, collapsed, and Tate was staring at him. Nothing of his swagger, nudging Ben with his foot, kneeling down. "Jesus, Ben." He looked at Ronny. "What did you do?"

"Nothing. I haven't seen him since the funeral. I guess it all came back."

Tate helpless, faced with a problem he could not beat down. "Help me get him to the room."

Ronny shook his head. "You can do that. I need to get home."

"You should let me drive you," Ben said, between sucking sobs, "I told you."

"It's okay." He took a step toward Ben again, looked at Tate. "I wish I could see you guys Saturday."

"Yeah. It's going to be sweet."

He knelt, looked at Ben. To feel all this, too much; he had to be cold; he was cold, his clothes soaked. "It'll be okay," he said, and Ben watched him. "Just beat Duke. Okay?"

He nodded, small and broken. Ronny walked away, down the stairs, the two of them still there, Tate still kneeling. Flights of steps between him and them and he could still see the picture, even when he stepped into the washing of the weather, a cold enfolding, so sharp and yet so numb. It was the right frame for the night. He set out across the rugby field, through the mud and wet, where they could not see him; crossed into the woods, followed the path, step after step. Toward the boardinghouse. It was done; he had gone to Ehringhaus. Ben was barely there. But they were not finished, he and Ben. It should have brought him joy. Instead, only rain, sorrow, and night, sleepless, wondering what would follow.

Beat Duke

FRIDAY MORNING JAMAL BROUGHT RONNY A manila envelope, battered and wrinkled, the old address label struck through with a pen, UNC Athletic Department. Ronny was dressing for class, dazed from lack of sleep. Jamal said, "Guy dropped this by the house for you yesterday, while you were at *The Tar Heel*. Big dude."

"Yeah?" Ronny tore off the tip of the flap of the envelope. "How's Miss Dee, you seen her yet?"

"I don't think she's doing so good this morning. She called me Henry again." He grimaced, standing with his arms folded.

"Her niece is coming by this morning, I think."

"I hope so. I can't hang around. I don't want her to set the kitchen on fire."

"She won't." A ticket to the Duke game fluttered onto his desk. A note that said, "Beat Duke." Scrawled, block letters.

"Oh, nice," said Jamal. "You're going to the game on Saturday?"

"I guess I am." He took a deep breath.

"Shit, dude, you couldn't have got two tickets?"

Ronny scratched the back of his neck, stared at the ticket. "It's a gift. One of the guys at Ehringhaus. I used to tutor them."

Sheila was at the doorway, toweling her hair. She'd become almost part of the household, visiting Jamal so often, occasionally staying overnight. She said good morning, sullen posture, looking everywhere but at Jamal, and he grew wary at the sound of her voice; they were sore with each other, and looked like they hadn't slept. "Did we keep you up last night?" she asked. "We were trying to be quiet."

"No," Ronny said. "I couldn't sleep anyway."

"He tell you?" she asked, indicating Jamal. "His bright idea?"

"Come on, Sheila, I'm not doing it to hurt you."

"Oh, fuck you for that. He wants to take a break, he says."

The statement sank into the room, silenced them all; from outside, one of the other guys could be heard lecturing about the greatest guitar players in rock history, had to be Eric Clapton; no man, had to be Jimi Hendrix, he really had the licks, that sound; back and forth. Jamal said, "Please, Sheila, don't do this."

"Why not, is it a secret?"

"I just need some time to think, that's all."

"Who are you going to think on top of?"

"It's not like that."

Sheila was breathing heat if not fire, and said to Ronny, "Great guy, huh? I thought we were doing so good."

"This is none of Ronny's business."

"Really? So it is a secret?"

"That's not what I mean."

"I need to get out of here." She was still rubbing the towel against her hair, angry, and turned, walked away.

Jamal shook his head, mouthed, "Wish me luck," and followed her. They closed the door.

He stared at the handwriting. Ben's print-scrawl. If Ronny wasn't careful he'd be late for class, and he had to work at the pasteup job in the afternoon. Grabbed his books, belted his jeans, and the phone rang. Dread soaked through him, fear of answering, but he picked it up. Ben said, "Hey. Did you get the ticket?"

"Yeah. I did."

Silence for a long while. Ronny held the receiver and closed his eyes. Ben said, "Okay. You coming, then?"

"Sure."

"Nina's going to pick you up. I called her."

"Cool." Trying to feel this as little as possible. From next door the sound of a quarrel, low voices, intense. "You all right?"

Ben coughed, making a low sound. "I'm trying not to think about anything right now. Just the last game. That's all."

"Okay."

"You? That rain was pretty nasty."

"A little sore throat. Nothing to worry about." Ronny picked up the ticket. "Thanks. For getting me in the game."

"Yeah." His voice was changing, cracking a little. "Look, I can't do this on the phone, okay? We'll talk?"

"Sure. If you want to."

"What the fuck does that mean?" An edge of frantic. "Do you want to?"

"Yes." Ronny broke a little himself, then. "Yes, I do. I'm sorry."

"Okay. Let's just stop. I got practice today."

"I need to get to class."

"Okay. Okay." But it took him a while to hang up the phone.

When the connection broke, Ronny sagged to the chair, sat there with his head in his hands. His body was exploding and imploding at the same time, slowly. He threw the ticket onto the floor, let it lie there.

He got through the class by fixing his attention on the book they were discussing, James Baldwin, *Tell Me How Long the Train's Been Gone*. He made himself speak. The acts of breathing and speaking restored a sense of the normal. By the time he reached *The Chapel Hill Newspaper* he was all right; he talked to his supervisor Earlene, asked for Saturday off; he'd stay late tonight and get the Sunday paper as far along as he could, since most of the back sections could be pasted up now. "You're crazy about that football crap," she said. "I don't get it."

"I lived with those guys, I just want to see them play."

"It's a football game, it's just like every other football game. What's the use of watching it?"

He crossed his arms. "I've worked here since June and never been sick and never took a day off. Can't I have this one little favor?"

"Yeah. Well, your favor is a pain in the ass."

"Fred can handle it. Can't you, Fred?"

Fred, who was probably stoned, flipped a salute from the page boards. "Oh, sure. No job too big for me. Stop the presses and shit."

Earlene sighed to let him know how tremendous the favor was. She said she would be there anyway working on ads, she'd help out, but fuck if she thought she should be encouraging anybody to miss work for a shitfuck Duke football game. He was right, he'd probably earned it, but what a stupid shit to use your day off for sports.

Early Saturday morning the phone rang again; he figured it would be Nina, and he was right. She had no phone and was calling from a neighbor's house. She'd been angry at Ben the last time they talked. She was calmer today. "So you went to see my brother, he told me. In the middle of the night."

"It wasn't that late."

"Yeah? Sounds like you scared the crap out of him." She wanted to know more, clearly.

"You still mad at him?"

"Yeah. He's still shit in my book. But he's also my brother." She sighed. Joni Mitchell in the background, *I could drink a case of you.* "Are you going to make me ask how it went?"

His stomach was still in knots, same as it had been for days now. "I don't know. He just started crying and couldn't stop."

"Well, anyway. If he cried, that's something. You going to talk to him again?"

"Maybe." He had picked up the ticket, tapped it on the desk.

"Well, I guess I wish you luck. Listen. I'll be over in a couple of hours. Kathy's coming with us. You remember her, right?"

He sat on the bed, almost hurled himself onto it. Kathy. The old girlfriend. The moment stretched out. Facts settled into place. If she was going to the game with them it could only mean one thing. So she was back. So this was what Ben was not telling him, why he had never called. He fought the panic, the urge to throw the phone across the room. Something howling at the idea, Ben with Kathy, riding in the car with Kathy. "Oh, right, the game," he said, trying to hide the quaver in his voice. "Listen, I couldn't get off work. So I can't go."

"Really?"

"No. It sucks."

She was uncomfortable, she didn't believe him. Nina was too smart for lies. "Is something wrong, Ronny?"

"No. It's just I work Saturday afternoon and night, you know?"

She sighed. "Well, I know how that is. What do you want me to tell Ben?"

"Nothing. I mean, I'll probably call him."

"Probably?" She laughed. "This is my brother we're talking about, Ronny, do you want him breaking into your house to find out what's going on?"

He tried to laugh; but it hurt so much, the thought of Ben and Kathy again. "Listen, I have to go. I'm really sorry for the trouble. Tell Kathy hello for me."

He hung up the phone. It was more than he could take. He must have started hoping, this hurt so deep. He had liked Kathy, she was smart, she was the girl who maybe would be good for Ben. But the idea of it, now. He sat still for a long time. His stomach was hollow, he felt as if he would fly apart if he had to sit still. He picked up his backpack, shoved a book into it, grabbed the ticket at the last second, ran down the stairs and out the door. Images of Ben with Kathy tucked under his arm. Who was your best girl? Maybe Kathy, he had said.

Ronny was walking, but not toward the campus. Because he couldn't bring himself to miss the game. To the bus station. An hour later he was on the way to Durham on Continental Trailways. Looking out the window, trying not to think, bar after bar, strip malls end on end, fast food, a scattering of old houses that nobody had bought or torn down yet. The bus smelled of piss. The bathroom door banged open and closed. An old lady with ringworm on her shoulder, sleeping. A fellow with the lower part of his arm missing. Two girls popping chewing gum, talking about somebody they knew. Sitting still made him crazy, he couldn't shut off the thinking. When the bus arrived he burst through the door. He had cash for a taxi to the stadium. By early afternoon he was walking through the gates of Wallace Wade, ticket in hand, concentrating on the faces around him, the shapes of hats and sunglasses, women in their sweater wraps, stout men wearing fake athletic jackets. Beat Duke, he thought.

In the crowd he lost himself, waiting near a concessions area until just before kickoff, approaching the seat number assigned to him, counting down the row till he saw them, Nina with her dark hair tangled over her shoulders, Kathy copper haired, cut short and practical, smiling, the two of them with their heads together, surrounded by other Carolina fans. He was close enough to see them and recognize them but only because he knew where to look; he climbed past them, to the top of the stadium, where he stood against the back barricade. An usher came up to him, asked, "Do you need help finding your seat?" Bright as the day was, the usher used a little flashlight to check his seat number, told him where it was, and he nodded.

"I get restless," he said. "I'll probably just stand here or walk around."

The usher shrugged. "Suit yourself."

After that he felt frozen, a newly dead creature at the summit of the stadium, aerial view of a lake of tiny faces, bodies, and on the field, at last, the sky-blue uniforms of the Tar Heels, one of them Ben; he could pick out the number. Ben stamped one foot and then another on the sidelines, stretching, looking at the sky. Hard to stare at him and think of the facts of the matter. Kathy will be riding with us, Nina had said, and she would only be going to the game because of

Ben. She was the one he had called. Sometime since he got back to town; she was the one he had talked to, they had gone out together, he'd opened up to her, and she had helped him get through his grief. The two of them hand in hand under the trees of McCorkle Place, walking and talking in the moonlight, the twilight. Ben found the strength to call Kathy but not Ronny, who was nothing, after all, just an episode, something Ben had to get out of his system.

But the other night. Ben so broken on the stairs. What was that about? Guilt? Ronny tried to stop thinking, climbed down from the top of the stadium, moved along to another section of stands, into the Duke section; cheers for the kick-off, then silence. He descended as far as he could go, nearly to the fence, joining a smattering of people there. He watched Ben as though he were a stalker; nothing mattered but fixing his eyes on that figure in his uniform; like the other games he'd seen this season, breathless at the fact of him, at being in the same space again. Ben charged off the defensive line, hurtling toward a receiver on the Duke team, taking him down, thud, onto the turf, then picking himself up, trotting back, doing it again; on the sidelines sipping water, talking to the other guys, often to Tate, or the other defensive linemen. He was closer today than he had often been. Worried that Ben might see him—pick out his tiny, unimportant face among so many others. Halftime, the team trotted into the visitor part of the field house, leading on the scoreboard, and Ronny wandered along the fence where the photographers were standing around, some of them snapping pictures of the crowd.

Somebody there called his name, Maggie from *The Tar Heel*, carrying her camera bag, trotting toward him. Waving wildly. "Look at you!" she shouted. "Did you come here to yell at me or something? I'm not going to miss my deadline."

"Your deadline is not until tomorrow," he said. "I just came to watch the game."

"Cool. You having fun? You drunk?"

"Nope. Sober as anything. Game's okay though."

"Where's your seat?"

He pointed to the upper section of the pond of Carolina blue. The Duke band was high-stepping onto the field, playing something martial. "Way up there."

"Yeah. No wonder you're down here."'

Chatter, easing after a fashion, his insides feeling less twisted. Was she getting any good shots? Amos Lawrence was not having his best day, the game was all about defense, but he was still giving her good pictures, he was really something to see. That quarterback looked too skinny to be on the field but he was surprising people. Did people ever hassle her because she was a girl, the other photographers, he meant? They tried to sometimes. But she was pretty tough. Not every guy was threatened by a woman who knew how to take a picture. Gossip about the office. The sports editor, what a trip, sarcastic bitch. Not nearly as sarcastic as you are, she said. You know you scare the shit out of people. Well, somebody has to. You slack assholes think a deadline is an approximation. He'd grown so much better at cursing. Cold wind, huddled against the fence. Came out that he'd taken the bus to Durham. She offered him a ride home in the end, told him where to meet her. Relief, since he had no idea how to get back to the bus station. He hung around the fence for the rest of the game.

The hurt of it all eased up in the cold, in the noise, in the fact that Carolina won the game, the conference championship, a decent national ranking, probably a good bowl bid, too; the team was pretty jubilant at the end, jumping onto one another's backs, pouring Gatorade over one another, grabbing butts, knocking helmets. The shit of it was he liked Kathy. He followed the crowd through the entrance, found Maggie, carried her camera bag to the car while she fiddled with her camera and her film case. I burned some good film, she said. You usually do, he said. Driving to Chapel Hill through the slow-moving traffic. What a good day, she said. I suppose.

He's Not Here

JUDSON CALLED IN THE EARLY EVENING, anxious, breathy voice, remember me from the meeting the other day? Do you want to go for a drink tomorrow, like we talked about? Let's go tonight instead, Ronny said. Trying not to calculate what might happen. Turned out Judson didn't have a car. They decided to meet at He's Not Here. I don't really want to go to a gay bar, Ronny said. I don't either, said Judson. Besides, you can't get to one without a car. He's Not Here is fine, I've been there before, if you don't mind the jocks. Ronny set the time, nine or a little after. He had to check in at the paper, he said. A lie. When he hung up the phone he felt he had done something wrong.

But it wasn't calculation. No reason he couldn't like Judson, hit it off with the guy. Nice enough, decent, quiet, looked all right, maybe a little awkward. Ronny couldn't remember the face very well. But a pleasant guy, anyway. Why couldn't he like somebody like Judson, who called when he said he would, who talked like a sane person? He might as well try. Because Kathy and Ben. Because.

He rose off the bed, left the house, walked and walked, until dark, and after dark. A restlessness ate at him. Did Judson think this was a date, did he think something was going to happen? Was something going to happen? They could go somewhere quieter. Somewhere safer. Not fair to use poor Judson like this. But anyway, Ben probably wouldn't go to the bar. Kathy didn't like bars that much. He would probably cuddle up with her in her apartment, or in his room, and they would talk and giggle and she would kiss him on the mouth and they would do all that stuff, snuggly and cute; Ronny was heartsick thinking about it, burning more and more in his gut, and the chorus played again, that Ben had called Kathy, that they had been together this whole semester, probably, and why couldn't he stop thinking about it? He wanted to stop, didn't he?

When he reached the bar he was hungry, his stomach was empty and the beer hit him hard. He was sitting on a stool and Judson slid in beside him. His nice, open face, a sweet smile, nervous, eager, shy, all at once. He ordered a beer. They tipped glasses. "This place is packed."

"People come here after a game. I guess."

"Yeah, that was pretty cool. I hear we won."

"Fuck Duke," Ronny said, and they touched glasses again.

Judson was trying hard to show some energy, looking around. "I'd rather come here anyway. Gay bars get on my nerves. Unless I'm feeling cruisy. You come here much?"

"Not really," Ronny answered. "I guess I don't get out a lot."

"So you don't have a boyfriend?" Judson lowered his voice a bit for that.

Nevertheless the question unsettled Ronny, because of the chorus, the thought of Kathy; and he glanced around. "I thought I had one," he said after a while.

"Breakup?"

"I guess that's what it was."

"I shouldn't be nosy. It's none of my business."

"What about you?"

Judson had ordered the cheapest beer on tap, foam on his upper lip. "I had a girlfriend. Up until a few weeks ago. But, you know. I knew what I really was. So I called it off with her. That's when I started, you know." Pitching his voice lower. "Coming out."

Talk was easy, like two old pals. Turned out Judson really was a nice guy, friendly if a bit tense. Moving to a table when one came open. Judson ordered food. Ronny just drank. He was tipsy and talked freely, and so did Judson, about growing up, feeling different—but everybody feels different, don't they? Does anybody really think he's normal?—especially in high school. "But we are different, aren't we?" Judson asked. They had ordered a pitcher and were drinking it fast. Judson was refilling their glasses. Trying hard to make eye contact with Ronny. Hands fluttery on the edge of the table, like he wanted to play fake-drum or fake-piano.

"What kind of guy do you like?" Ronny asked.

Judson grinned, stretched his arms, shook his shaggy head, looked around. "I don't know. My best friend, you know. This sweet blond guy. Kind of like a basketball player but not too tall. I liked him a lot."

"Where is he now?"

"He went to State. I used to see him sometimes."

"You out to him?"

The beer had given Judson a sleepy cast. He had a tic; one eyelid fluttered from time to time. "No, no, no. He'd probably punch me if I told him."

"So, did you just like him? Or more?"

"Hard to say. Probably more."

"Did you have any idea about yourself back then?"

"Yes. I think so."

"But you dated this girl." Ronny shook his head. "That's not very nice."

Judson blushed. "Well, I wasn't sure. I mean, I didn't even know what gay was, you know. I knew I was supposed to like girls."

You did what you were told. Not something to speak aloud. Ronny sighed, sat back in his chair. There was a thought trying to come back to him, but he pushed it away. Noise, booming voices from the back of the bar near the pool table. They started talking about music and movies; Judson wasn't a big reader. He ordered a second pitcher. "You mind? I figure we might be here awhile."

"No, that's fine."

"I'm not trying to get you drunk or anything."

"Really?" Ronny giggled. "But I'm already drunk, sort of."

They leaned into the table, Ronny ate Judson's fries, Judson spoke in a nervous monotone, was from Pine Level, the son of a Church of God preacher, mother a cafeteria worker, he had been raised on Bible verses and school leftovers, having a gay son would be a disaster akin to demonic possession. Pray over him to snatch out the devil inside. Like that. He needed to talk, as if he had been stranded on a mountaintop and just returned to people. It made Ronny uneasy to like the guy. This was the thought he was having.

Then, walking past the next table loomed Tate, headed to the back of the bar; followed by Kathy, so pretty and bright; and behind her was Ben. Kathy was looking at Nina, the two of them talking, heads together. Ben walked like he had already been drinking. Shoulders hunched, looking down at the floor. The sight of them together, Kathy and Ben. Ronny shook his head. His heart picked up speed, ricocheted in his ribs. He had planned this? He had hoped for it? Maybe. But he panicked. Not sure what to do. Almost standing up, then quickly sitting down again.

Dizzy, lifting his beer. He felt so drunk all of a sudden. He asked the waiter for the check, but the pitcher was mostly full, and Judson was staring at him though he appeared very far away. Did I do something wrong? No, everything's fine, Ronny said. But we might as well pay while I can still count my money. In case I need to run, he thought. In case I can't stand it in here anymore. Ben at the back of the bar lifting a shot glass. Turned to face Tate and Kathy. Ronny leaned over the table. He and Judson were still chattering but he could hardly map what he was saying, that Judson was sweet, too, and cute, kind of—did he really say that?—and the music had gotten so loud all of a sudden, Pink Floyd, then Led Zeppelin, that shrill voice of Robert Plant, soaring, then the Rolling Stones, "Satisfaction," and Judson patting his back, hand light and warm. Tate saw them, Ronny and Judson, started toward the table, then stepped back. Ben at his side, staring at Ronny. Flushed. Drinking another shot. The waitress twisting in front of him, trying to flirt, a little apron, bow tied at her back. It would be too much, this compression of people and noise. Something bad would happen. Ben was grim, holding a beer can, crushing it in his fist, and the waitress went twisting away, and Ben took somebody else's shot glass—maybe it was Kathy's?—and slammed the liquid down, and the music changed again, "Without You," the Badfinger song, Nilsson's version, and someone nearby groaned and said, "Not this song, what a downer," and Ronny stood up. They had paid. He might be leaving. He felt the alcohol then—how many beers?—Judson was watching him, and started to get up too, and there was Ben looming over him. "You son of a bitch, so this is what you're doing?"

Poor Judson. Stepped back. Asked, "What?"

Ben was staggering a little. Looked at Ronny. "You heard me. Who's this piece of shit? Who is he?"

"Hey, dude, we're just having a drink—"

"Shut the fuck up. Nobody's talking to you."

Ronny was wavering now, holding the back of the chair. Ben grabbed him by the shoulder, shook him. People were watching, mostly in annoyance. Another drunk scene. Judson looked like he wanted to be somewhere else, mumbled something, and Ben rounded on him. He raised a hand, started to make a fist.

"Don't you call me that," Ronny said, and grabbed him by the shirt, pulling hard, almost ripping the fabric.

Ben blinked at him, lowered his fist. "Call you what? I didn't call you anything. I just asked you who this mother-fucker is."

"Come on, Judson," Ronny said. His head was clearing a little. "We better get out of here."

"You're not going anywhere, pussy."

Tate moving toward them, taking Ben by the shoulder. Judson backing away from the table, toward the door. The bartender had his eye on them. A bouncer was standing nearby.

"You're fucking drunk," Ben said. He had lowered his voice. "Go home with this piece of shit, then. Go ahead."

"What? I'm not drunk. Shit on you. You're back there with your girlfriend, aren't you? I can do what I want, too." Speaking at the same low volume. Ronny pulled away. Embarrassed already. He walked toward Judson at the door. They stumbled into the cold air, walked a few steps, toward Franklin Street. Muffled music coming from inside, draining to quiet, traffic passing on the street, someone shouting from a truck with its windows open. The cold stood him upright. He was suddenly sober now. Quick as that. So much adrenaline.

They were watching each other, Judson and he. Judson shaking his head. "What was that?"

"Nothing," Ronny said. "Don't ask."

"Are you all right?"

"I'm fine."

Puzzled, wondering what he ought to do, flipping hair out of his eyes. "I thought that guy was going to kill me. You knew him?"

"I used to."

They stood near each other. Judson was piecing it out. He turned, walked away a couple of steps. "Oh, shit."

"Yeah. Look, I had a good time. But I better go home."

"You sure? You want me to walk you?"

"You better not."

"Wow. Kind of crazy. Okay. I guess I'll see you around."

"Yeah."

They saw each other very starkly, and Judson no longer appeared soft or friendly. He walked away. Made it a few steps. Turned back and spread his hands, his body so lanky, angles of elbow and knees. *You set me up.* Did he say it or did Ronny just read it in his face? He had figured it out, shook his head, turned away. Ronny stood there a moment, until the guy crossed the street, passing in front of the Carolina

Theater. "Sorry," Ronny whispered. So you let the nice guy walk away. The preacher's kid who shoved his hands in his pockets, hunched his shoulders, pulled a wool hat over his head. Ronny stood in the wind, turned toward the road. Maybe stood there awhile, seeing Ben's face, that anger, the hand closing to a fist. He crossed the street, meaning to walk through the parking lot of University Square to the boardinghouse just on the other side. But a car roared into the parking lot ahead of him, slammed to a stop, and somebody got out. Ben stood at the driver's door. He was bellowing air, nostrils flared, face flushed. "Where's your little friend?"

Ronny froze where he was. Close enough to see that something was raging in Ben, that his face was purpled with anger; pushed to the edge of something, he was squared on his feet to fight it, whatever it was. Jealous. The thought flashed through Ronny, that Ben was the picture of what Ronny felt like inside. He said, "Judson went home."

Ben ground his jaw, pointed at Ronny. "Get in the car."

"What?"

"You heard me. Get in the car right now. Don't fuck with me."

Ronny wavered, tried to say something, and Ben shook his head. "Do what I tell you or I'll come over there and pick you up and put you in the car myself." He was breathing like he'd run a mile, panting with anger, with other feelings. He was Ben, he meant what he said. Ronny found he wanted to obey. So he stepped forward. Opened the door.

Ben slid beside him, put the car in gear, wheeled out of the parking lot. The only sound was their breathing. Navigating through the streets. Whole minutes went by. He had sobered, too. But he was still grinding his jaw. Yelling at Ronny in his head, probably. Then it came out. "What the fuck did you think you were doing. Parading your fucking boyfriend in front of me. Did you want me to kill the motherfucker? What the fuck? So this is what you've been doing all semester? Hanging out with that fucking skinny little weed? Jesus fucking Christ." He stopped to take a breath. They were at the edge of town by then, heading up the Pittsboro road.

Ronny said, "His name's Judson. I met him a couple of days ago at a meeting. We had a beer."

"Oh, bullshit."

"Ben, what the fuck is going on? What do you care?"

"You can't be bothered to go to the football game when I bring you a fucking ticket." His breath was chuffing now, he was upset. "But you can go out with some little dude and try to suck his dick."

"You need to pull over if we're going to talk."

"I'm fine."

"No, you're not. Look at you. You're about to tear the steering wheel off."

Ben wiped his eyes, jerked the car into the lot of a strip mall, took a deep breath. He calmed himself enough to park the car, and turned off the engine. Sat for a minute gripping the steering wheel, made a low sound of fury, pain. "What the fuck is wrong with you?"

"There's nothing wrong with me."

"What happened? Why didn't you come?"

Ronny took a deep breath. "Nina called this morning. She told me she was coming to get me. That was fine. Then she said we were taking Kathy, too."

"Kathy?"

Ronny shivered, started to blubber, wiped his eyes. "Yes."

"Shit." He pounded the wheel with his palms. "Shit, shit. You stupid fuck."

"I should have expected it, I guess. Kathy's a nice kid."

"Oh, shut up, you fucking dope. Kathy's engaged to Tate. You thought she was with me again?" He laughed, looking at Ronny for the first time. "Shit. I should have known. Tate just wanted Nina to give her a ride to the game. That's it. That's all."

Out of all that confusion, all the jealousy boiling inside him, it was the idea of Tate getting married that fixed itself on him, and he sat there amazed for a second and said, "Jesus Christ, Tate is engaged?"

Ben was staring, mouth half open, and suddenly burst out laughing; he wiped his eyes on his sleeve and let the sound come out. He was sitting with his back to the driver's window, facing Ronny across the seat. "Jesus, you should see your face right now."

"I can't believe it."

"You fucking shit, that's what you want to talk about?"

They sat there watching each other. Dawning on them both, that they were together in the car, that they had crossed the gulf of summer, that football season was nearly over, and they were sitting in Ben's Impala that smelled vaguely of cigarettes and beer. "Ben, this car doesn't smell so good."

"What? Shut the fuck up."

"I mean it, have you been living in here?"

Ben dove toward him, pulled their faces together, a warm flash, heat, right there in the parking lot, cars passing on the highway. A bolt of heat to his toes, his mouth wet, a feeling that they were both suddenly awake. They came apart, hung together, not wanting to move. Ben said, "You were jealous, you little shit."

"So were you."

289

He leaned back his head, closed his eyes. "I sure fucking was. I don't know who that guy is but you just about got him hurt real bad."

Still and quiet. Ben threw one leg out, across Ronny's. The weight of him like a drug. Ronny swallowed, wiped his eyes again. Ben said, "Maybe you better tell me about him again."

Ronny explained where they'd met, and Ben got upset at the mention of the gay association—"So he is a faggot, so you were going to sleep with the piece of shit"—and Ronny kept talking—"No, I already told you, I was lonesome, I only went to the meeting because I need to figure out this gay crap, and he's just a nice guy. That's all."

"Oh, bullshit. That guy liked you, you little bitch. You think I couldn't tell?"

Ronny sighed. "Well, so what?"

Ben tightened his leg over Ronny, as if he wanted to pull them both together again, looked at the traffic, the lights of the parking lot. "So you didn't do anything with him."

"No."

"You wreck the fuck out of me. I wanted you to see that game so bad. What the hell."

"I did see the game."

Ben wouldn't look up. Ronny touched the back of his hand. "Did you hear me?"

"I don't believe you."

"Fuck you then. I took the bus to Durham. I got a taxi to the stadium. I stood down on the fence and watched you for all four quarters. Such a dunce. Thinking the whole time you were with Kathy again."

"So stupid. What would I want with Kathy? She's a sweet girl. But that's all over." He fiddled with the keys in the ignition. "You were really there?"

"I told you. I haven't missed a game all season, I wasn't about to miss this one."

"How'd you get home?"

"*Tar Heel* photographer was there. She brought me back." Smiled a little. "I was pretty awesome today, huh?"

"Yes. You were. Especially deflecting that pass."

"I was fucking awesome."

Ronny laughed. "That's what you want to talk about right now."

"Nina told me she thought something was up with you. But she didn't know what."

"So she's not so pissed with you anymore."

"No. I guess she likes the fact I might have turned out to be a faggot." He was laughing, and shrugged. He stilled, his breath in Ronny's ear. "I know I said I would call. But it wouldn't have worked. I'd have melted. I'd never have gotten through this year." It was football he meant, this year of football. He had to do it, it was his last chance to play. Ronny felt a deep release in himself. What did it matter now, if the waiting was really over?

Their heads were together. Ronny kissed his forehead, easy and slow. But he was wary, and so was Ben, because here they were, out in the open. Nowhere safe. "That was some scene back there."

"In the bar?" Ben snorted. "You should see the shit that goes on in that place."

"Tate's not stupid, though. He's probably got this all figured out."

"Tate's had this figured out for a while. He hasn't said anything but I can tell. And Kathy's not stupid either. We don't have many secrets at this point, babe."

"Can you live with that? It won't be easy."

Ben leaned his forearm on the steering wheel. "It's so easy for you? Can we go somewhere? Back to your place? You still have the same room, don't you?"

"Yes."

Ben started the car. "This what you want to do? Stay with me tonight?"

"Well, technically you'll be staying with me."

He snorted, shaking his head. "Oh, horseshit. I had to get dicked up with a fucking lawyer." Pulling onto the road.

He took Ronny's hand, gripped it tight. Wiped at his eyes once, then held Ronny's hand again. All the way back to town.

The Brooch

ON CAMERON AVENUE RONNY SAW MISS Dee at the corner, standing in her nightgown, looking at the stones of the retaining wall near the Carolina Inn, the streetlight stark on her, tiny, fragile, and he said, "Oh my lord, stop the car. Please."

"What?"

"It's Miss Dee. I don't know what she's doing out here."

They were within sight of the boardinghouse. But the distance was vast in her terms. Ben pulled over to the curb and Ronny got out of the car. She was a shock, skin so loose, bones so tiny, her hair in disarray, feet pale, blue with the cold. She was looking for something, touching the stones with her fingertips, the thin nightgown fluttering, her body visible, a violation of her, to see her vulnerable like this, all lost. Ben was behind him now. Ronny said, "Miss Dee, sweetheart, what are you doing?"

She was shivering and watched him as though he might hurt her. "Who's that? Oh, lord, it's cold as the devil out here."

"It's Ronny, Miss Dee. I live in your house upstairs, you remember?"

"Yes, I do think I remember. And look here, it's your friend. Oh, my, it's Ben."

"Yes, ma'am, it is."

"So good to see you. Oh, boys, can you help me? I lost a brooch somewhere. But I don't know if it was here or not."

"Miss Dee, do you know where you are?"

She straightened. Ben was taking off his jacket. He hung it over her shoulders. "Lord, no. Oh, no, I don't know where I am. How did you find me?"

"Don't worry about it," Ben said, arm across her shoulders. "We'll get you home. Just get in my car right here."

"You've got a car?"

"Yes, ma'am."

"Well, I used to have one. Can't drive it no more. I'm so old. Is this it?"

"Yes, yes it is. Just sit right down in there." Ronny had opened the door. They were only a hundred yards or so from the house, but she was unsteady, barely moving, and so they put her in the backseat and drove her to the front door. Ronny sat beside her.

"Whose coat is this?"

"It's mine," said Ben. "Are you getting warm?"

"I think I am. Did you put it on me?"

"I did."

She patted Ronny's arm. "I'm glad you brought him back. I always liked him."

Ronny laughed, Ben laughed, they got out of the car. Nothing to do about the fact that she was barefoot. Ben nearly picked her up but decided it was better to let her walk. Her bones so fragile and thin. "This is my house, dear lord, now why did I ever come outside? It's too cold out here. I must have lost my shoes."

"I think they're in the house, Miss Dee."

"Is that Ronny? You're a little bit of a know-it-all, aren't you? Well, those shoes better be inside, young man, that's all I have to say." She marched to the house with a purpose. Now that she knew where she was, she had a firm step. "Lord, my feet are near about frozen."

Inside, Ronny found a pan and filled it with hot water. Ben took her into her bedroom, where she sat in a chair while he wrapped a blanket around her. She fumbled for her glasses and found them on the table beside her. Eyes so large now, through the lenses. A diminutive owl perched on the edge of her seat. Ronny put the pan of water on the floor and helped her feet into it. "What's this?" she asked, drawing back.

"Just hot water, Miss Dee. To warm up your feet."

"Oh, yes, that's a good idea, I believe." She shivered, lifting her feet into the water. "Now, you know you should never have took me outside in the first place, don't you?"

They looked at each other. After a moment Ben said, "It was a bad idea. We're so sorry."

"I forgive you. But I sure want to warm up. It must be January out there. Is it?"

"No, ma'am. It's November."

"Well. That's just as bad." She adjusted the glasses, stared down at her feet. There was a brooch on the carpet near her. She pointed, finger twined with blue veins. "There it is. I knew I would find it."

Ronny lifted it off the carpet, oval, lacquered, painted with flowers, all faded. He handed it to her. She tried to put it on her nightgown and fumbled, then set it on the table.

"My feet are getting nice and warm. You boys can go on, now."

"Well, let's wait a minute," Ronny said. "I don't want to leave that pan of water there."

"I'm through with it anyway," she said, and stood up, and walked to the bed, feet dripping. She dried them with a slip that had fallen on the floor. "That's better. Now you boys go on so I can turn out the light. You ought not to be in my bedroom anyway. I don't allow you boys to come in my bedroom."

Ben picked up the pan of water and waited. Ronny said, "We're so sorry. We just needed to get your feet warm."

"Oh, that's so nice," she said, pulling up the blanket and setting her glasses onto the bed. She reached over to click off the lamp. "My feet do feel so warm now. I hope I get warm all over." She lay into her pillows and closed her eyes. Ronny backed out the door, closed it quietly.

They waited and listened, Ben taking a deep breath, slumping against the doorsill, running a hand through his hair. He laid a heavy hand on Ronny's shoulder, the warmth and weight resonant with something beyond their coming together again, into some other feeling, Ben stoic, looking down at the worn floorboards. "Can we go upstairs?"

"I don't know," Ronny said. "I'm scared she'll start wandering again."

Ben nodded, rubbing his face, straightening from the door. "We can leave the door open. I'll come down to check on her." When Ronny failed to answer at once, Ben's expression darkened. "I won't hurt you. Jesus."

"That's not the problem."

"There ain't a problem," Ben said, and took Ronny by the elbow, guided him to the stairs. They watched each other, the moment searing, Ben shaken and Ronny heavy; here was Ben who had avoided him all semester, now wholly agitated, breathing like he had run a mile, nostrils wide, licking his lower lip.

But it wasn't sex. They came together in the dark with the door open, only to stand near, to breathe, to listen to the ticking windup clock. Almost but not quite touching along the fronts of their bodies, heartbeats shaking, not looking at each other, Ben's eyes closed most of the time, a deep pain lining his face, and then his arms reaching around Ronny, pulling bodies into fusion, and out of him this sigh, so long and quiet. Their heads together, Ben's curls on Ronny's ear. "You know what I'm thinking about?" Ben asked.

He did. It had occurred to him when they were helping Miss Dee to bed. "Your mom."

A low sound, like a sob turned into voice, extended, but so quiet and slow it almost pooled between them. "Miss Dee is so little," Ben said.

"I know. When I saw her out walking like that, in her nightgown. She would be so embarrassed."

"Does she have anybody to take care of her?"

"A niece. But she doesn't come around all that much. And she's pretty old, too."

In the dark and quiet there was a difference that Ronny could feel, that something had settled inside Ben, not only in this moment but altogether, a change in his body, in the spirit that coursed through him, an umbra of gravity, a feeling that he had aged. He was calm, even with the thought of his mother ringing around him. Ronny led him to the bed, sat him down, pulled the chair from the desk and moved it close, touched their fingertips together, felt Ben watching him. Ben edged the dark curls out of his eyes. "I just want to stay here, okay? I won't bother you."

"Bother me?"

"You know. I don't want to do stuff. I just want to be here."

Ronny said, "Okay."

"You don't mind?"

"I'm just glad you're here, Ben."

Talked about Miss Dee, then. How long had she been this bad? Well, it was hard to say. She had always been forgetful in small ways. And she was more feeble. Every month. One of the reasons Ronny had stayed in the house instead of going back to the dorm. Details. The morning he found Miss Dee at the back fence wondering where that big building, Granville Towers, had come from. Had it been there the day before? Because she remembered a house that way, her friend Naomi Winship, and it was gone, and had somebody tore it down overnight? Or the day she had dropped an egg and never noticed and stepped into it again and again, tracking raw yolk as far as her bedroom door. Walking laboriously to a shop on Franklin Street to buy a steam iron because her old one broke and then doing the same thing a day later and standing bewildered in the bedroom, two boxed irons on the bed, upset, tears coming to her eyes, because she had spent more money than she could afford. Or somebody had given her one of the irons, maybe? Was that how it had happened? She'd been too confused to think about it and sat in her chair for a long time. Ronny had taken back one of the boxes and gotten a refund for her, but it took some convincing, the store clerk skeptical, wary, thinking at first that Ronny was trying to cheat Miss Dee.

Ben had sobered up a long time ago, walked down to the kitchen for water, stirred around quietly, returned saying

Miss Dee's door was partly open, the way they had left it, and she was lying quiet under the blankets. Nearly three in the morning by then.

They fell asleep side by side on the bed, still in their clothes, the scratch of thick denim, Ben's heavy leg thrown over Ronny, his breath sour. It should have been the sweetest night. But Ronny woke up listening every hour or so and worried, out of tangled snippets of dreaming, Miss Dee in a strange hotel that was like a hospital, checking on her room over and over again, finding pictures of Ben's mother in the hallway under rubbish, images that succeeded one after another with no connection. Rushing through his rest.

In the morning Ben stayed. This was the fact that underlay the rest: going downstairs, telling Jamal and a couple of the other boarders what had happened. No one had the telephone number for Minette, her niece. Miss Dee had yet to get out of bed and the door was closed. It felt wrong to knock on the door—she might have forgotten about her walk, and she would surely be puzzled by their concern—and they were boys, all of them, and had no business in her room. So they whispered in the kitchen, with Ben looming at the back door, watching the morning; and later, turning to Ronny, raising a hand, and walking out.

So he was gone, and a moment of panic, yes. Was he really gone this time? Well, if he was, Ronny had things to do, and he could call later to find out what was what—a lowering, a disappointment in him, but they had made contact again, and it had felt good, his life felt good again, except for the worries. A few minutes later footsteps at the back door, Ben appeared with a newspaper, lifted it to show Ronny, who was on the phone talking to Sheila; he leapt up the stairs light-footed and Ronny watched his shadow disappear. The silliness of it all, that he could feel such a flood of warmth, and that such a feeling could lie alongside the worry he felt over Miss Dee. Sheila was saying, "Last time I was there I noticed how weak she was getting to be."

"I know. But last night was different. It was like she didn't really know where she was."

"Yeah. Leaving the house dressed like that. You want me to come over?"

"Do you have time? I feel like I can't go in there but I'm worried. I haven't heard anything from her this morning."

"You sure she's still in there?"

"Jesus. I didn't even think about that."

"I'll be over in a minute. Just keep Jamal away from me. Is he seeing anybody else?"

"Not that I've noticed."

She took a deep breath. "Okay. Well. I need to run a comb through my hair and then I'll be on my way. Maybe I'll change my skirt. I mean, put on a skirt. Crap." She was still talking as she hung up.

He was listening at Miss Dee's door, trying to decide; was she still there? The idea of it all was crushing; that she was so tiny and alone, that her mind was draining out of her, that she lived in a house with boys whose only idea of her was of a cute old landlady in faded dresses; her life had come to this, that she was in need of something, that she was falling, and no one would be here to catch her. This was the way it was, life, spinning and spinning until you lost control, until age caught up with you, until you were frail and tiny, lying in your bedroom, the only room left to you, and you lost a brooch and the fact of the brooch was one too many losses to take and so you searched for it everywhere, you lost yourself searching for something tiny and insignificant, the world slipping into darkness, and you were lying in a bed with your hair fanned out over your pillow, and no one knew whether you were breathing or thirsty or hungry or whether you were alive or dead, and none of it mattered to anyone even if they knew all the facts about you, because there was no one here with whom you had more than a slight connection, a tiny landlady renting rooms. A house in which you had lived once with a husband, and now with strangers. All this thinking in his head. He must have stood there for a while, because when he looked up—when a shadow fell over him—there was Ben, holding the newspaper, watching, frowning.

Ronny opened the door a little, as quiet as could be, and saw her there, still in the bed, drool coming out the corner of her mouth onto the pillow, lying on her back, her eyes closed. Still there, safe for the moment. He closed the door quietly. One of the guys upstairs brushed past, said hello. Ben nodded. Ronny followed him into the parlor. "I was scared she wasn't really in there."

"Yeah," Ben said.

"Sheila's coming over to check on her. I think you met her once. I don't remember."

"Maybe." Ben was looking out the window, sprawled on the old-fashioned sofa, the weight of him straining the springs. He watched Miss Dee's doorway, something blank and hard in his features. "What are you going to do?"

"When Sheila gets here?"

"Yeah, sure." He took a deep breath, a moment of agitation passing through him, followed by that calm again. "I mean, you can't stay here to take care of her all the time. You've got to figure something out."

301

"I know."

The sound of a television pooled in the room, echoing from upstairs, a Sunday morning talk show, something about football, the Washington Redskins, pregame, too early for the play to have started. Outside were birds calling, cars passing on the street, a Chevrolet Nova, sky blue, headed for one of the fraternities along the row. Autumn, an exhale of leaves downward, wind rustling, a possibility of rain, gray clouds. Ben had slumped, closed his eyes. "It hurts to watch somebody helpless like this."

He laid his hand on Ben's shoulder, firm and sturdy, and Ben responded by moving toward the touch, and they sat like that; when someone's footsteps sounded on the stairs and approached at the same moment Ronny tried to lift his hand and Ben said, "Leave it there. It's all right." Said it right away, and the flood of feeling back and forth between them, a wall of protection, so that when Jamal stood there looking at them, they barely acknowledged him, flowing together on the couch without moving, the thing that was joining them, the carelessness of a hand on the shoulder, and after a while Jamal said, "So, Sheila's coming?"

"Yes. I asked her to. How do you know?"

"She called me." Jamal shuffled his feet on the old carpet, sat in a chair nearby. He was watching them with only a little curiosity. "What's up that you want her here?"

"Somebody has to go in there and see if Miss Dee will wake up. I think if a guy does that it would scare her to death. And she knows Sheila. Maybe."

"Yeah."

"I'm sorry if it's awkward."

He buried his face in his hands. "This just freaks me out."

Still Ronny's hand was on Ben's shoulder, the hard round shape, softness of cotton tee shirt, Ben looking down, then across at Jamal—but anyway it was only a hand on a shoulder, buddies did that, friends. The feeling though, flowing in and out, was calmly inside them, as if they had never been separated. A couple of the other guys stopped to talk. They had heard there was a problem with Miss Dee. Really concerned for a moment or two, before heading out of the house.

Ben looked at him when the room was empty again, but for Jamal, and said, "I have to get back to Ehringhaus."

"Okay."

"Just for a while." They were watching each other. The moment felt so naked, as if anyone could read them. But Jamal was staring at his nails, looking out the front door.

"You're coming back?"

"Yeah. If that's okay."

Ronny slid his hand along the shoulder, broke the connection, and they sat quiet until Ben stood and stretched.

"I hear Sheila," said Jamal.

"I won't be long," said Ben, pitched for Ronny, as though there were no one else around. Like that moment, like whenever they watched each other, some stillness traveled along the contact, and they lingered in it. Ben was solemn when he spoke to Sheila on the porch. Midmorning light in the windows, dust motes blown about in the breezes. When he jogged away from her, lightly, on the balls of his feet, his grace struck Ronny to the core, the perfection of the moment. It made him ashamed, thinking of his happiness just then, while Sheila opened the door to Miss Dee's bedroom and slowly, slowly, edged her way inside.

Mrs. Delacy

SHE LAY HER HEAD ON THE pillow in the lightest way, mouth open, partly turned onto her side, and as he sometimes did, he tried to see what she had been when she was younger, as though her youth were buried inside her somewhere. What was fine and clear about her face had dimmed with sleep; her pale, lined skin had lost its elasticity and pooled and flattened against the pillow, her hair in wispy curls. Her pale, rheumy eyes moved under the veiny lids as she murmured and shook her head a little. She had been awake for few moments and spoken a name, then settled back against the pillow. Sheila leaned toward her, touching the edge of the bed. "I'm glad she went back to sleep."

"Me, too."

"Who do you think she thought I was? I didn't hear the name."

"It sounded like Mona or something. I don't know who that is."

"I was just thinking that maybe it was someone we could call," she said.

"Minette is her niece."

Sheila had sat lightly on the edge of the bed. "She must have written people's names and numbers somewhere but I don't want to start looking in her drawers."

"I wish I knew what to do."

"We could take her to the hospital."

"But what would we tell them?"

Sheila lowered her voice a tone, hand resting on the edge of the bed. "I don't know."

"Isn't this just what happens to old people?" As soon as Ronny asked the question, it sounded stonelike in the room, hard and cold. "I just mean, what can a hospital do for her?"

They were both sad as they watched her sleep, on a Sunday morning, with a church bell ringing the hour of worship somewhere nearby, a mournful pealing, Mrs. Delacy stirring on the bed as if she could hear, as if the bell were calling her. A rush of wind outside threw shadows of tree branches shivering over the carpet and bed, flurries of red and gold leaves rushing down beyond the panes, and the bright sunlight shaded over with cloud. She lay in the bed as though the weather were welcoming her or performing for her, head centered in the changing light, her breathing audible, a light snore.

"I don't even know her first name," said Sheila.

"I can't remember it either."

There was a bundle of mail on the dresser; her name was either Alberta Delacy, or Mrs. Lou Benning Delacy, or Louise Delancey; the last name was spelled in different ways even in the small stack of bills and advertisements resting on the lace runner. None of the letters looked personal. It did not occur to him that even this much was an invasion of privacy, the reason for the search being so clear, but once he set down the mail he took a deep breath. As though Miss Dee were watching him, but no, she was still asleep, breathing on a small, high-pitched note, fingertips trembling; in a dream she was reaching for something.

She grew more agitated, as though she were trying to wake, straining at a sound that would not become a word, and then he smelled something, dusky at first, and Sheila stood up; she opened her eyes with a cry, helpless; and the front door opened and closed with a particular emphasis, and there was Ben in the doorway, holding a bag, Miss Dee trying to sit up, looking at everyone, frightened, and saying, "I need to get up right now, please, I can't get up."

"All right, Miss Dee," Sheila said.

"Who are you? Are you Minnie?"

"I'm Sheila. You know me. Jamal's girlfriend."

By then they could all smell it, that she had soiled herself and the bed. She was fumbling with the bed linens, pulling at them. Her expression was horrified, exhausted. "Oh, I have to get up right now." But it appeared that she did not know exactly how to do that. She was reaching for her glasses, starting to shake and to weep, incoherent sounds. She was touching Sheila's wrist. Sheila was frozen. Ben stepped to the bedside. He had set down his bag in the hallway. He found her glasses, slid them carefully onto her nose, and she said, "Oh, thank you."

"We can help you out of bed if you want," Sheila said.

"I need to. But I can't, you know." She was not moving quite correctly. One of her hands appeared to be too heavy for her to lift it. The smell was stronger now.

"Take off the blankets," Ronny said. "Leave her covered up by the sheet."

Ben said, "I'm going to carry you into the bathroom, Miss Dee. Sheila will come with me."

"That's right."

She barely heard them. Tears streaming out of her eyes, along her cheeks, snot starting to pool in her nostrils. Ronny had stripped down the faded quilt and blankets beneath; Ben scooped her up then, ignoring the wet place at the front of her gown, the forlorn, runny turd that dropped out of it when he lifted her, the harsh smell.

It was the sight of Ben carrying Miss Dee, the tiny package of her, bones sharp and distinct inside her feathery flesh, arms and neck, ankles, the shape of her as he carried her, as though the slightest pressure would crumble her. As though she barely had a shape. Ronny's breath caught like a sob; but he shook his head, started to strip the sheets off the bed, frowning at the smell.

Sheila cleaned her as best she could while Ben held her, the sheet covering her, and she endured it, one arm around Ben's neck, huddled against him as though he were shelter. He was simply watching her, steady, as though it were nothing. Sheila said, "You're doing so good, Miss Dee."

"I don't even know why it's so cold in here," she answered, voice strangely slurred.

"You'll be all right when we get you in the bed again."

She rolled her head into Ben's shoulder. Ronny said, "We can't put her back in bed till the mattress dries."

"I guess she'll have to lay in the parlor," said Sheila.

"She won't like that."

Ben shrugged. "You'll be fine, won't you, Miss Dee?"

That time, though, she could barely reply.

"I think something's wrong," Ben said.

"She can't even talk," said Sheila.

When he carried her to the couch—after Ronny placed clean sheets over the cushions and back—she was so limp she might have been unconscious, and one side of her face had begun to droop. They saw this clearly when she laid her head into the pillow. Ronny said, "I'm calling an ambulance," and just at that moment an older woman walked into the room, Minette dressed as though she had come from church, with even a bit of a hat pinned to her hair, and Ronny recognized her, and she looked at them as though she had caught them at something alarming, and said, "What are you doing to my aunt?"

So: the call to the ambulance, the explanations after Minette, the niece (who most often saw her aunt at church on Sunday mornings, she said), walked into the bedroom to get a look at it; the emergency medical people asking what had happened; the story about finding her on the street the night before; but she's always been so clearheaded, said Minette; all this while they moved her onto a stretcher and into the waiting ambulance, methodical but urgent; it might be a stroke, they said; as Minette followed the stretcher and held Miss Dee's hand and sobbed, stood at the side of the bumper while the techs lifted the stretcher into the back, and then waited. "Do you want somebody to go with you?" Sheila asked.

She was stunned herself, the niece, not quite knowing what to do. "And you know, my mother hasn't been gone that long," she said, not exactly speaking to anyone. Drooping like a sapling in need of rain.

"I'd be happy to come with you."

"No. It's fine. I'll call my daughter." Minette stepped toward the ambulance, stepped back, stepped forward again, then stopped, lifting her purse, holding it with both hands, opening it to find a tissue. "I'll let you all know what happens."

Ben stood at the fence until the ambulance, lights still spinning, turned on its siren and maneuvered into the street. He was like a cauldron, radiating hurt, and Ronny remembered him from earlier, standing with Miss Dee bundled in his arms, looking down at her as though she were the most precious being; he turned to Ronny and let it all show, so openly, that he was aching, that he was thinking of his mother, that it was all about to rain onto him, the intensity of the loss, that he had watched his mother die, that Miss Dee, whom he liked, was on the same threshold, that this was a world of sickening and suffering and passing through. Something gathered them both, sent them inside again, into Ronny's room where Ben's satchel lay overturned on the floor, socks spilling out.

This was not the way anyone pictured two boys: one harboring another, collapsed and sobbing, Ronny cradling Ben, choking breaths that shook them both. He had waited a long time to do this. It would have been easy to state the obvious, to whisper comfort, but Ronny simply held him, head in his lap, shoulders rising up, like a little boy; they did talk, sporadically; I'm moving in with you, Ben said; Ronny said, Well, it's not a lot of room; Ben: We don't need a lot; Ronny leaning over to kiss Ben's ear, and Ben sighing. The house had grown quiet. Next door there was murmuring as Sheila and Jamal talked, too muffled to distinguish. The two boys—they felt like boys today, both of them—simply waited. A radio sports show talking about the Duke game. Mentioning Ben's name among the other seniors, talking about his pass deflection. In the afternoon they fell asleep, warm, tangled up with each other, still in their clothes. But still, in the end it was unfair, because they were not thinking only of Miss Dee, crying for Miss Dee, were they? There was so much more.

Minette

BY THE TIME SHE DIED THEY were to stand in a middle
ground between family and acquaintance, not only with
Miss Dee but with Minette and some of the people in the
boardinghouse. The ordeal drew them into a temporary
closeness. In the late afternoons the other tenants clustered
in the living room, awkward, wondering whether she would
come home: before the stroke one of them had seen Miss
Dee in the kitchen, bewildered, pulling all the pots and pans
out of cupboards and arranging them on the counter, sure
that something was missing; one of them had found her at
the back of the lot wandering in the overgrown shrubs; a
Frisbee had nearly hit her in the head while the boys were
gliding it to one another; she had been talking about her
steam iron in the hallway, it was spitting and hissing and she
was scared to use it. Ronny had never gotten to know them,
they were a kind of amorphous organism, all of them together,
standing and slouching and picking at their ears. Jamal and
Sheila slowly circled each other on the pretext of concern for

Miss Dee; maybe Ben did the same to Ronny, but on a deeper note, sounding the hollow cavern of the last few months.

Miss Dee came home in a few days. Minette took time off work, moved into the house and slept on a cot at the foot of the bed. She said she had a stroke, Miss Dee, and had to be watched, lying in the white light on the white sheets, marked out by her blemishes, by those limpid eyes, magnified by the lenses. Her face leaned into the light from the window, a liquid over her skin, a look of yearning in her eyes, as if she wanted to leave, to go up and out. There was something immensely precious in her that would be released. Wrapped up in sheets, trailing tubes. One visitor at a time. Ben made no fuss about going in, showed no special dread. This was after a night when he laid his head into Ronny's lap and shook and sobbed out his breath and let the whole shuddering arc of grief pass through him, most of it for his mother, the ghost haunting him, passed out of the world forever. He let himself feel it, in Ronny's lap in the dark. Every death echoed of every other. A deafening quiet in the house.

A life decays in movements of shadow and drops of water. Moments like the last day he saw her, when she had gone back to the hospital, when she had another stroke and fell out of her bed. In the hospital it was as though she had drifted into space where she was lying quietly, sensing nothing around her, a collection of cells on the mattress losing their cohesion and purpose, memory leaking out her, awareness, but slowly and in measures, so that when he left he felt it would be over for her soon. Ben was waiting in the room at the boardinghouse, and they walked out for dinner in the cold December, the town empty, leaves clattering everywhere, a wind like a sharpness, light fading behind the oaks and elms. He had been living with Ronny for over a week. No one had said anything yet but there was a feeling. It was their first time being seen as a couple, even if it was not overt. Jamal and Sheila were all right, still fighting, and Minnie spent her evenings on the back stoop, ignoring the cold, chain-smoking, sitting with her forehead on her palm, sometimes sullen and unfriendly, sometimes dabbing at her eyes and hungry to talk. The hospital would kill her, she said, would kill Miss Dee, sure as anything. Today they tried to give her somebody else's medicine. Could you believe it? And what was she, Minnie, going to do when Miss Dee got out of the hospital? She had to work, and Miss Dee would require care, somebody to look after her. You boys here, I don't know about the house. No telling what will happen. She would light another cigarette. She liked to talk to Ben—everybody did—they sat shoulder to shoulder on the steps in the cold. She would never let me smoke in the house, Minnie said. I still can't do it.

Minnie got a call from the hospital in the wee hours and phoned them later to give them the news. She was crying quietly, thanking them for all they had done. So it happened, Miss Dee passed away, a phrase that invokes some other direction than the ones we know, away into the after, and it was easy to tell she was gone, the whole house echoed of it.

One Sunset

LATE IN THE MORNING, A DAY after Miss Dee's funeral, Ben came to the door—he had driven off somewhere, maybe to practice for the bowl game the team was meant to play. He stood there toeing the wood with his sneaker and shrugged his shoulders under his varsity jacket. Ronny had never seen him in the jacket before. He preferred something from army surplus most of the time. "Let's go for a ride," Ben said. Ronny followed to the car.

Driving with the windows open, they let the cold rake along them, closing the windows and cranking up the heat, feeling the pulse of each other, a calm exchange now, less frenetic than before—they had hardly spoken a word—the streets decorated for Christmas, stores with fake snow sprayed on the windows. The campus receded behind the trees so calm and sedate, as though it were a religious place, as though one glimpsed another kind of world when staring into the poplars and elms on the quad, the weathered copper dome of the Morehead Planetarium behind the top of Dey Hall, brick walkways tracing connections under the canopy of bare branches. Down the road to Pittsboro a few miles outside of town, a narrow, paved road led across a deep ditch and into banks of trees, old wire fence sagging under the weight of heavy vines. Branching onto a dirt road, and then another, past weathered farmhouses, rusted trailers, and old barns, into a cove, over a tiny bridge that crossed a rocky creek. What looked to be a combination of mobile home and old shed stood in a tangle of blackberry that had been tamed away from the door and the stoop that fronted it. Were they visiting someone? No, there were no vehicles, and Ben had the key to the door.

There was the feeling that a cave had formed at the base of the forest, that the narrow creek cut through it, that branches and growth arched over them, that the darkness was less gloom than guardian. Ben held open the door and Ronny walked past. The room was shabby, bare except for a bit of furniture, clean, smelling of bleach and pine cleaner, on the paneled wall a calendar with a picture of Mitch Kupchak going for a layup, stained with something that looked like mustard. Ben loomed over everything in the room.

Ronny had begun to fathom what was happening. Dingy as the room was, there was something pleasant about it when Ben turned on a lamp. The kitchen had a Scrooge McDuck refrigerator magnet in the center of the door. There were chains of beads for curtains. "Hippies," Ronny said, running his hands along the beads.

"Probably."

Two bedrooms, one small, one tiny; two bathrooms, one crowded, one cramped. They walked from one room to another as though each of them had dropped his wallet somewhere, searching for it, studious and quiet, shoulders hunched. Ben waiting in the living room and after Ronny took one more look at the closets, he followed. Ben squared his shoulders. "We can rent this."

The words brought a slow hand of warmth to the pit of Ronny's gut, and he felt a change wave through his body, a quickening of blood, a sense of a moment happening, the look of Ben's black curls, the sharply defined shape of him. "Really?"

"I know the guy who had it before. Doesn't matter. We can rent it if we want to."

Cheap, too, as it turned out. So that could be the next thing, living in this bowl of shade at the edge of the woods, having a creek in the yard, taping Springsteen posters to the walls of this grungy trailer. Not bad. "You want to move out of Ehringhaus?"

"Fuck, yes." Ben snorted, jammed his fists into the pockets of the jacket. If God Is Not a Tar Heel. The jacket so blue and clean.

"You want me to do the same thing."

"Don't act like you don't know what I want."

There it was. Breathing in and out as though he had exerted himself, nostrils wide. Ronny felt as though waves were rushing through his body; Ben looked as if he wanted to shove his hands though the ceiling, reaching upward, stretching his shoulders.

"All right," Ronny said. "When?"

"Now. Whenever. It's ours. I already paid the deposit and shit."

So it happened, they stood there and drank it in. Ronny wandered through the rooms again and walked around the trailer outside, peering into the forest. A cardinal hopped on the ground, fluttering to the branch of a bare shrub, maybe forsythia, spring's yellow telegram. Ben walked up behind him. They stood, body to body, calm in desire, simply pressing each other. And Ben said, "I guess we might as well get it done today. There's no need to stay at the boardinghouse anymore."

"Minnie is closing it, right?"

"I don't know. She hasn't said. But you still need to move."

"Yeah. Might as well get it done."

Only a few months ago, he had packed to leave the dorm, carrying boxes along the balcony in air drunk with pollen, hearing the crack of a bat across the way from the baseball stadium; today, in the cramped boardinghouse room he slid around Ben, from the dresser to the makeshift closet, packing five boxes this time, and a stack of books. A dozen hangers, faded shirts. He called to have the phone turned off. Sheila came to the door, saw what they were doing. "Here we go. You heading home?"

"Yep," said Ben.

Jamal passed behind her, laid his hands on her shoulders. They had drifted together again without making much of it. Maybe it was Miss Dee, dying, who changed their minds. Who knew what would happen with them? They might stay together a month, or a lifetime. The four of them in proximity—the feeling had changed—they were older in a marked way, they spoke as if they had been friends for a long time, they had become entangled by the last few days, and now they were about to separate, but not without a difference. There was tacit agreement with what they saw in one another, two couples, even though they had preferred not to speak about it. Ben's staying in the room with Ronny through the last days had settled that side of the question. Maybe it would have been different without the finality of Miss Dee's dying, the closing of her boardinghouse, the end of the semester, the coming of the holiday. But they were parting, two from two, and so it was all right.

It had been the same at Miss Dee's graveside service. Two and two. Maybe two dozen people there, Minnie and her family, Miss Clara in her shaky lipstick and smeared mascara, a neighbor, the women's circle from Miss Dee's church. The four of them from the boardinghouse. Ben had refused to go at first but changed his mind; appeared to change his mind again during the service, while the casket, closed, hung on green cloth straps, waiting to be lowered into the grave. Maybe he wished he were somewhere else. Ronny stood alongside picturing his own mother, feeling the substance of death, the carpet of it, the next step toward oblivion, for himself, one day, and for everyone else. For Ben.

Everyone at the graveside sorry, but only mildly so, and embarrassed at the idea of her death, Miss Dee, lying in her box, safely out of sight.

Something about the coldness of this drew them near, Ben and Ronny. There was something true in the idea that a person could die so alone, something fearful about it, that people should stand around in slight embarrassment at a graveside to which they gathered more out of a sense of obligation than loss. It made Ronny and Ben want to stand closer, to sense each other. Kept Ben from fleeing the scene.

Later, Ronny had gone with Ben to Ehringhaus and visited Sheria while Ben was packing the stuff in his room. She was sitting on her bed again, wearing a black dashiki trimmed in bright colors around the neck, sleeves loose; she was reading a Toni Morrison novel and eating corn chips out of a plastic bowl. "Hello there, stranger," she said, and offered herself to be hugged. "We miss you down here. Where have you been?"

"Here and there. Busy semester. How about you, how are you?"

"I'm in a good mood today. But I go home tomorrow so the good mood won't last very long." She laughed, tossing back her head as if she were on stage. "I enjoy my sarcasm. Don't you?"

"I always have."

"What brings you to Ehringhaus? I haven't seen you in ages."

"I'm helping a friend move out. We're going to live together next semester."

"Nice. I have a boyfriend now, you should meet him sometime."

"Yes?"

"Oh, yes. My mother is having to eat her words." She gave out that throaty laugh again. "It's kind of wonderful. I'm taking him home to meet the family for Christmas."

"Well, don't let that ruin the romance."

"It's out of my hands," she said, offering her palms in a gesture of helplessness.

He took one of her hands, studied the lines there, the clear strong head line, the heart line all feathery loops and ovals, the life line short and abrupt. She pulled her hands back and slapped his wrist softly. "Don't try that mess on me. You know I don't believe it."

"It was just an excuse to hold your hand for a minute," he said.

"Isn't that sweet."

They watched each other. She was lighter, some of her pain was gone, and he understood the difference. She had met somebody who cared.

When he went back to the car there was Ben with his suitcase and boxes. He arranged everything in the backseat; he had already filled the trunk, he said.

"Should I go say goodbye to Tate?"

"He's not there," Ben said. "Out with Kathy, probably. You'll see him sometime."

They watched each other, then slid into the car without a word, and drove away from the dorm, the pines, the baseball stadium, the lawn. Shadows slid across the windshield.

So, here they were, setting up house in the forlorn steel box, overwhelmed by the greenwood at the edge of which they hovered, a sense of peace and privacy that pervaded everything. Ben found Christmas lights in the closet and hung them at the window. An old string, paint chipping off the glass. They sat in the room in the ghostly colors. Ben had brought a small television from the dorm room. They plugged it into the living room wall and watched a football game, Dallas playing the Forty-Niners. Ben pounded the arms of the couch and hollered at the screen, grinned at Ronny, relaxed, threw an arm across Ronny's shoulders, drank beer, ate cold pizza, and they felt a sense of ease.

Late in the evening, Ben said, when they were settled against each other, listening to the owls outside, "Thank God you came to the dorm that night."

"When it rained?"

"Yeah." Breathing out a puff of air, a sigh, a sound that was a touch of music.

"You think you would ever have called me?"

"Yeah. When the season was done. I couldn't mix you and football, babe. I just couldn't do it. You believe me?"

"I think so."

"Nina would have made me call you sooner or later." Again, that small breath. "I'm sorry."

"It's okay."

That was enough. Ronny had been quick to forget it all, maybe too quick, but this was as much explanation as he needed, and it came without his asking. After all they had been through with Miss Dee, it mattered less anyway.

Once the phone was installed, Ronny called his mother. Two hours earlier in Nevada. Her voice was one long rasp. She said, "Oh, hey, honey, it's so good to hear from you. I been thinking about you. You know how I am. I told Rayford this morning you would probably call."

It was a comfort to hear her voice. She sounded strong. It made a difference. He understood how lucky he was. So many small thoughts sparking one another, while Mom prattled on and on, about shopping for a house in Reno, and Ray's sports store, you know, where they sell sports stuff, a lot of camping and fishing in Nevada, you would be surprised, it's all rednecks wall to wall. He never told her about Miss Dee. It wouldn't have made sense to her. She wasn't a mom for understanding. She told him about her backyard, where she was planting desert stuff, she said. Succulents. "You know how I love to grow them. Don't need too much trouble, just a little water now and then. Like you," she said, and laughed. "Oh, come on, you laugh, too. It's funny."

"Haha."

"There you go, that didn't kill you."

"You sound happy, Ma."

She sighed. He could hear the striking of a match, another cigarette. "I am. Don't you worry about me."

"I'm sorry I can't get there Christmas."

"That's fine. We don't hardly have anywhere for you to sleep till we get a bigger place. Which we will by next year. Okay?"

They hung up and he stood there listening to sounds in the bedroom, the one they shared, he and Ben; Ben shuffled out and watched him and asked, and Ronny answered, he had called his mom, she was fine, everything was all right, and they stood together in the ruby and gold shadings of the Christmas lights.

You had to have this to live, everyone said so. It struck him fearful to need anything. But he might as well take a chance on something he wanted. Anyway, the choice was already made, here he was, alone in Ben's trailer, the two of them to live together for their last semester of college. The only way to endure the feeling was to understand its fragile nature. He stayed in the house alone while Ben went off to play in the Liberty Bowl, his last football game. Ronny kept himself sane the same as always, books and his typewriter, stocking the kitchen, working at the newspaper, cleaning the trailer top to bottom. Driving to town a couple of times in the decrepit car he had bought. Dinner with Lily. The last day of solitude he walked up the gravel road to see where the barking dogs lived, then walked back to his island. The next day Ben came home.

Years later, when everything was done, he would look back at that moment. A fear had been tickling him that Ben would leave him stranded, no matter his previous tenderness. He would simply never show up at the door again. Nothing like this could last very long. The dread became more and more. So he walked in the yard while the sun dropped behind the trees; suddenly the shade under the branches grew to gloom, the watery light ebbed out of the cove, a yard light flickered on, the dogs began to bark. He would be here for-ever, alone, or somewhere like this, alone: but before the fear could solidify there it was, the old Impala, headlights yel-lowed, horn blaring, turning into the driveway. There was Ben stepping out of the car, and Ronny slowly ambled in his direction while the shadows pooled and the owls sang.

AUTHOR'S NOTE

There was a boardinghouse that I knew and lived in, and a landlady who lived there too, and other similar circumstances, enough to make it necessary to note that this book is set in a fictional place, a 1976–77 of my imagining. The Chapel Hill depicted here is very like the one I knew in those days. But there are gaps in the portraits and places that I have filled in with my own details. Much of the campus has changed, and I might have erred here and there in peeling back the years. The schedule of games for the football season is from the real year but there is no congruence between the inhabitants of the Ehringhaus of my book and the people I knew or encountered. I do not think the Carolina Gay Association had its meetings in the student union but that change of venue is a very minor invention. The movie *That Obscure Object of Desire* was not released until later in the year than I depict, but the title of the movie suited my purposes too well to lose. In fact the whole of the book should be taken to exist in a parallel world in which everything was exactly as I say it was. I have not attempted to discover the real dates of the academic calendar for 1976–77. Other departures from reality are likely but not of much consequence to the story.

ACKNOWLEDGMENTS

My thanks to the late Lynna Williams, who was my first reader for the manuscript; further thanks to Frances Foster, Elisabeth Lewis Corley, Madeleine St. Romaine, Peter Hagan, Elisabeth Scharlatt, Ina Stern, Craig Popelars, and to my former colleagues at Emory University, including Jericho Brown, Tayari Jones, Natasha Trethewey, Joseph Skibell, Hank Klibanoff, Ben Reiss, Sheila Cavanagh, Laura Otis, Michael Elliott, Carla Freeman, many others. I retired from Emory just as the pandemic took over the world. I am grateful to Melanie Jackson for her guidance; to Arthur Levine for his careful shaping of the manuscript; to Meghan Maria McCullough, Antonio Gonzalez Cerna, Alex Hernandez, and the people of Levine Querido for making this book; to Trent Duffy for relentless copy-editing; to Jonathan Yamakami for a moving design. I am grateful to my family, as always.

SOME NOTES ON THIS BOOK'S PRODUCTION

The photo on the cover, entitled "Deltoid," is by Matthew Finley. Jonathan Yamakami created the pattern overlaid on this photo using brush and ink on paper, which he then digitally manipulated using Photoshop. The text was set, by Westchester Publishing Services in Danbury, CT, in Miller Text, designed by Matthew Carter and released through Font Bureau in 1997, famous for its use in U.S. newspapers. The display text was set in Columbia Sans, a sans-serif typeface designed in 2017 by Jean-Baptiste Levée of the French foundry Production Type, and was originally conceived as a sans-serif version of Times New Roman. The book was printed on FSC™-certified 98gsm Yunshidai Ivory paper and bound in China.

Production was supervised by Leslie Cohen
and Freesia Blizard
Book design by Jonathan Yamakami
Edited by Arthur A. Levine

LEVINE QUERIDO